The Murder of Twelve

A *Murder, She Wrote* Mystery

OTHER BOOKS IN THE *Murder, She Wrote* SERIES

Manhattans & Murder

Rum & Razors

Brandy & Bullets

Martinis & Mayhem

A Deadly Judgment

A Palette for Murder

The Highland Fling Murders

Murder on the QE2

Murder in Moscow

A Little Yuletide Murder

Murder at the Powderhorn Ranch

Knock 'Em Dead

Gin & Daggers

Trick or Treachery

Blood on the Vine

Murder in a Minor Key

Provence—To Die For

You Bet Your Life

Majoring in Murder

Destination Murder

Dying to Retire

A Vote for Murder

The Maine Mutiny

Margaritas & Murder

A Question of Murder

Coffee, Tea, or Murder?

Three Strikes and You're Dead

Panning for Murder

Murder on Parade

A Slaying in Savannah

Madison Avenue Shoot

A Fatal Feast

Nashville Noir

The Queen's Jewels

Skating on Thin Ice

The Fine Art of Murder

Trouble at High Tide

Domestic Malice

Prescription for Murder

Close-up on Murder

Aloha Betrayed

Death of a Blue Blood

Killer in the Kitchen

The Ghost and Mrs. Fletcher

Design for Murder

Hook, Line, and Murder

A Date with Murder

Manuscript for Murder

Murder in Red

A Time for Murder

For Angela Lansbury,
who brought Jessica Fletcher to life

The Murder of Twelve

A *Murder, She Wrote* Mystery

A NOVEL BY JESSICA FLETCHER & JON LAND

Based on the Universal television series created by
Peter S. Fischer, Richard Levinson & William Link

BERKLEY PRIME CRIME
New York

BERKLEY PRIME CRIME
Published by Berkley
An imprint of Penguin Random House LLC
penguinrandomhouse.com

Library of Congress Cataloging-in-Publication Data

Names: Fletcher, Jessica, author. | Land, Jon, author. | Fischer, Peter S.,
creator. | Levinson, Richard, creator. | Link, William, creator.
Title: The murder of twelve : a novel / by Jessica Fletcher, Jon Land.
Other titles: Murder, she wrote (Television program)
Description: First edition. | New York : Berkley Prime Crime, 2020. |
Series: A Murder, She Wrote mystery | "Based on the Universal television
series created by Peter S. Fischer, Richard Levinson & William Link."
Identifiers: LCCN 2019044673 (print) | LCCN 2019044674 (ebook) |
ISBN 9781984804334 (hardcover) | ISBN 9781984804358 (ebook)
Subjects: LCSH: Fletcher, Jessica--Fiction. | Women novelists--Fiction. |
GSAFD: Mystery fiction
Classification: LCC PS3552.A376 M87 2020 (print) |
LCC PS3552.A376 (ebook) | DDC 813/.54--dc23
LC record available at https://lccn.loc.gov/2019044673
LC ebook record available at https://lccn.loc.gov/2019044674

First Edition: May 2020

Printed in the United States of America
1   3   5   7   9   10   8   6   4   2

Jacket image of building by Michael Overbeck / Stocksy
Jacket design by Ally Andryshak

Cast of Characters

THE WEDDING PARTY

CONSTANCE MULROY—mother of the groom

MARK MULROY—fraternal twin of the groom

LOIS MULROY-DODGE—niece of Constance Mulroy

BEATRICE AND OLIVIA SPRAGUE—elderly twin cousins of Constance Mulroy

DOYLE CASTAVETTE—father of the bride

TYLER CASTAVETTE—brother of the bride, and Doyle's son

VIRGINIA DA SALLE—actress, and Doyle Castavette's date

HENLEY LAVARNAY—mother of the bride, and Doyle Castavette's ex-wife

HARRISON BAK—esteemed lawyer, and Henley Lavarnay's companion

IAN AND FAYE—good friends of the bride- and groom-to-be, the best man and maid of honor, respectively

THE MISSING

HEATH MULROY—husband of Constance, believed to have committed suicide

DANIEL MULROY—the groom

ALLISON CASTAVETTE—the bride

HOTEL STAFF

SEAMUS McGILRAY—manager and part owner of Hill House

JANEY RYLAND—front desk clerk

EUGENE—recently hired temp kitchen worker

Very few of us are what we seem to be.

—AGATHA CHRISTIE,
FROM "THE MAN IN THE MIST"

The Murder of Twelve

A *Murder, She Wrote* Mystery

Chapter One

G onna be a killer for sure, Jessica."
Seth Hazlitt looked at me across the table at Mara's
Luncheonette. I couldn't tell whether he was sniffing
the air for a hint of the coming snowstorm or soaking up the
aroma of his hot-out-of-the-oven morning blueberry muffin.

"This'll be one we'll be battening down the hatches for, *ayuh.*"

Sheriff Mort Metzger peeked out from behind his copy of
the *Cabot Cove Gazette.* "You say that at least once every year."

"And every year it turns out to be true," Seth countered.

"Tell me again how it is Cabot Cove suffers a once-in-a-
century storm every winter."

"Just lucky, I guess," I said, noticing the headline splashed
across the top of the paper's front page read simply BLIZZARD!

Local forecasters were predicting upwards of two feet,
while the Weather Channel had the amount closer to three.
But Dr. Seth Hazlitt, our resident family doctor and certified

curmudgeon, shook his head furiously when I voiced those estimates.

"Nope. We're looking at four, maybe five, feet for sure. I can tell. It's all in the nose," he said, and pinched his nostrils.

Mort looked less than convinced. "And how's that, exactly?"

"I can smell it on the air. Smelled it back in 2013 for Nemo, when we got thirty-two inches in these parts, and two feet in 1979, before they started giving storms names."

"How about 1952?" Mort quipped. "Or the storm back in 1935?"

"Who's asking, since Maine was just a speck on the map for you until you up and retired here?"

"Both of those dumped around two feet all the same, Doc."

"Nothing compared to what we're going to see this time," Seth assured us both.

"Have they given a name to this storm yet?" I wondered aloud.

"No idea," Mort said.

"Think they're up to the letter *J* or maybe *K*," Seth suggested.

I turned my gaze out Mara's front window in anticipation of the first fall of flakes. It had been a habit of mine since I was a little girl when a storm was in the forecast. There's something uniquely serene about being somewhere safe and sound as the snow begins to mount, about being home while the world beyond stands still amid a growing blanket of white. Of course, home for me for some months now had been Cabot Cove's Hill House hotel. Construction problems and challenges had repeatedly delayed returning to my beloved home at 698 Candlewood Drive. So I would be watching the snow pile up through the window of my suite instead.

A week ago, the forecasters predicted a bad storm in the eight-to-twelve-inch range. That had given way to warnings of a blizzard, and as of this morning, something in the potentially monstrous range, a record setter by all accounts. A winter storm warning encompassed all of New England, and the storm steaming northward had begun to intensify over Boston. If the forecast held, we'd see the first flakes in early afternoon, with measurable snow within an hour or two. After that, it was anyone's guess. The Cabot Cove Public Works Department maintained only two dedicated plows but usually contracted a half dozen local vendors, many of them fishermen and landscapers looking to boost their winter income. For this storm, though, Mort had mentioned that twice that number, an even dozen, had been retained. The main roads that ran into, out of, and around our town were the responsibility of the state, fortunately. And, in my mind, anyway, the lack of traffic that accompanied the foreboding forecast proved a welcome relief from the ever-growing number of seasonal visitors who besieged Cabot Cove during the summer months.

"Why stare out the window, Jess," Seth Hazlitt said to me, "when I told you the snow wasn't going to start until one-ish?"

"What time is that, exactly?" Mort asked him.

"What time is what, exactly?"

"One-ish."

"Sometime between one and two o'clock, but not after one thirty, because that would be two-ish."

"Oh," Mort noted, as if that were some kind of revelation. "Well, there's one good thing about a blizzard, Mrs. F.," he added, turning toward me.

"No crime?"

"Murders, specifically, with everybody pretty much stranded."

"I wouldn't be too sure about that, Sheriff," Seth groused. "During the blizzard of 'seventy-nine, Agnes Menfredi took a frying pan to her husband, George's, head when he wouldn't shovel their walk. Ended up with a concussion that stole a whole bunch of his memory for a time, not a bad thing, given that Agnes was the kind of woman you wanted to forget. I'd opened my practice the year before, and I remember trudging my way over to the Menfredi home because the rescue squad got stuck in a snowdrift."

Mort Metzger was nodding. "Don't tell me, Doc. Uphill all the way."

"As a matter of fact . . ."

Seth's voice had already faded when I heard a Cabot Cove Sheriff's Department dispatcher's voice through Mort's shoulder-mounted microphone.

"You read me, Sheriff?"

"Loud and clear."

"You're needed at the old textile mill off Route One. Abandoned vehicle. Deputy Jenks just called it in."

"Why's he need backup for an abandoned vehicle?"

"Because he found a dead body inside."

There's a part of Cabot Cove located on the town's outskirts that nobody talks about much anymore. It's part of our legacy and our past dating back long before the world discovered our village, which had remained quaint and isolated for so long.

I'm talking about an area devoted to industry, primarily textile mills that had been set up during the Industrial Revolution. The largest of these was the long-shuttered and crumbling Cabot Manufacturing Company. It had been saved from being razed only by our local historical society's designation of it as a landmark, marked as such by a plaque that had to be glued in place over the entrance since it was feared nailing the plaque might lead the rotting façade to collapse.

In a gravel parking lot we found a plain dark sedan, centered in the shadow of a still-massive structure that seemed to shed fresh parts of itself with every stiff wind.

"Thanks for coming along for the ride, Mrs. F.," Mort said, parking his department-issue SUV near the patrol car that had come upon the vehicle during a routine sweep of the area, "even though this one's not up your alley."

"We'll see about that, *ayuh*," Seth Hazlitt said from the cruiser's backseat. "Since when did you know a death in Cabot Cove that wasn't murder?"

"There was Gladys McCrady just last week," Mort answered, throwing open his door.

"She was a hundred and one," Seth reminded him. "Used to tell me at her checkups she enjoyed a spot of gin every day since she was fifty and said it was the reason she'd lived so long."

Mort turned to flash me a look before climbing out of the SUV. "I could see how this town could be enough to drive anyone to drink, and I don't mean for medicinal purposes either."

I started to exit from the passenger side and accepted Seth's help in getting out. He'd accompanied us because, in the absence of a full-time medical examiner, Seth had long maintained the role of de facto coroner, something he'd gained considerable experience in over the years through both Amos Tupper's tenure as sheriff and then Mort Metzger's after Amos had retired to live with his sister in the Midwest.

At first glance, especially under gloomy skies, the remains of the Cabot Manufacturing Company looked like something out of a Stephen King novel. The weather-beaten wood-frame structure had been expanded so many times it was hard to tell where the building's original footprint ended. The building stretched three stories high in some areas and four in others to account for the sprawling, high-ceilinged factory floor where hundreds of workers had operated the presses, lathes, and cutting stations that produced tons of tailored cloth on an annual basis. Three shifts over twenty-four hours a day was the standard practice during the boom times of war years, when the need for uniforms drastically increased the factory mill's overall output. Some of the wings farthest out and the older, single-story storage sections that had been damaged by fire either had collapsed or looked like they were about to at any minute.

The central part of the building, and likely the oldest, stood reasonably strong, though, in spite of the fact that the wood had turned so dark with rot and age that the frame looked charred. Listen hard enough, the tour guides from the Cabot Cove Historical Society used to say when the building had been open for viewing, and you might hear the sounds of the lathes fashioning material. Look hard enough and you might be able to glimpse smoke wafting out of the crumbling brick chimneys. Where the original building's façade didn't look charred, it had been ravaged by our harsh winters and summer sun. In short, the Cabot Manufacturing Company had the look of a building Seth Hazlitt would have already pronounced dead, had that been part of his role as de facto town coroner.

He had his trusty old leather doctor's bag in hand as he trudged alongside Mort across the weed-speckled parking lot. I followed, feeling the hard gravel crunching beneath my heavy winter shoes. Strange how Seth always lugged that bag along with him on trips like this, even though inside were tools for checking or maintaining people's health as opposed to passing judgments on their deaths. Come to think of it, I'd glimpsed Seth actually extract something on only a few such occasions, and then just a stethoscope, really, to confirm the deceased person's heart had indeed stopped beating.

Seth seemed to be sniffing the air as he walked. "Gonna be a bad one, all right," he noted, even though the flakes hadn't started falling yet. "Worst we've ever seen, by the look of things."

"You mean *smelled*," Mort said. "That's what you were doing—smelling the air."

"I know what I was doing and I was looking at it too. Very first flakes are there to see if you look hard enough."

I'd drawn even with them on Mort's side by then and he shot me a glance.

"He's got a point, Mort. I think I can see them too."

Mort took off his Cabot Cove Sheriff's hat and scratched at his scalp through his still-thick salt-and-pepper hair. "Is it too late to unretire from my last job?"

"Think the NYPD would have you back after all these years?"

"With bells on, thanks to all the experience I've gained in Cabot Cove."

Rosy-cheeked, freckle-faced Deputy Andy approached when we neared the sedan he'd posted himself near.

"Morning, Sheriff." He moved his eyes to Seth and me, adding, "Doc, Mrs. Fletcher."

At that point I could see a man behind the wheel who was slumped backward in the seat as if he were taking a nap. His mouth had locked open in a crooked fashion and his gaze was utterly empty. I also noted the discolored patch of gravel directly in line with the vehicle's tailpipe and figured that for a clear indicator that he'd died of carbon monoxide poisoning. Either suicide, which seemed unlikely, or a tragic accident after he'd drifted off to sleep with the engine still running and windows all closed up tight.

Force of habit led me to touch the tailpipe, only to find it cold and dry even at the end. While Mort crouched with his hands on his knees to peer inside the cab, I moved to the hood and found it similarly cool to the touch, indicating the victim behind the wheel had likely been dead for some time. The road off which the factory mill was located was hardly ever traversed, and even the nearest main road, Route 1, saw little traffic these days. This dying, or already dead, part of Cabot Cove stood in stark contrast to the parts of our village that were thriving closer to the coast and the center of town. I imagined there were stretches when you could count on your fingers the number of vehicles that passed down this road for days at a time, which explained why the Sheriff's Department didn't know of the car's presence, or of the dead man inside, until Deputy Andy spotted it during his rounds. The corpse of the man slumped behind the wheel looked lonely more than anything else amid the otherwise empty gravel parking lot. And, come to think of it, "lonely" was as good a way as any to describe the Cabot Manufacturing Company itself in its current state.

Mort pulled on his evidence gloves, which looked identical to the pair Seth squeezed over both hands in order to examine the deceased. Mort found the Ford Five Hundred's driver-side door in pristine condition and unlocked. When he eased it open, the dead body rocked and nearly spilled out.

"Yup," Seth said after a brief examination of the corpse, "it was carbon monoxide poisoning all right, almost for sure." He ran a small penlight about the man's face to better regard the skin's texture and tone. "You can tell by the cherry pink coloring of the skin. Yup, plain as day in my mind."

"Accident or suicide, Doc?" Mort asked him.

"Hard to say at this point. Suicides normally snake a tube inside the car from the tailpipe to quicken the procedure, but there's no indication of that here, obviously, which leads me to believe the victim parked, left his engine on to stay warm, then drifted off to sleep . . . and death."

"Can you get his wallet for me, Doc?"

I watched Seth maneuver the body, and his gloved hands, to fish the wallet from the man's back pocket. He handed it over to Mort, who eased it open as I looked on. We saw the distinctive ID at the same time, above a chintzy-looking badge.

"Loomis Winslow, private eye out of Boston," Mort noted, flapping the wallet, more an ID case, in the air. "Must not have noticed the 'Welcome to Cabot Cove' sign. Anybody in their right mind sees that and turns around."

"Tell that to the summer people, Sheriff," Seth said, continuing his preliminary examination of the body.

"After you tell me how long he's been dead."

"Since late last night or very early this morning, based on the settling of the blood and level of rigor mortis. Say as much as twelve hours, as few as six."

Mort turned toward me. "Here's how I see it, Mrs. F. Man pulls into an abandoned parking lot to make a phone call or something and falls asleep with the engine on to keep warm. Must've had the misfortune to have enough gas left in the tank to make sure he never woke up again. Case solved."

"It doesn't bother you that he happened to be a private investigator?"

"Why should it?"

"Because somebody must have hired him," I said. "And whatever he was hired for must've been important enough for him to head north with a blizzard in the forecast."

Seth cocked his gaze our way. "She's got a point, Sheriff."

Mort took his cap off and scratched at his head again. "Have you ever seen a dead body you didn't think was murdered, Mrs. F.?"

My gaze drifted to the body in the driver's seat. "He unclasped his seat belt."

"So?"

"If he pulled in just to make a call, maybe check his directions or just get his bearings, he wouldn't have done that—at least most people wouldn't."

Mort rolled his eyes. "Here we go."

I could feel the wind picking up, blowing in that dreaded

direction indicating a classic nor'easter was coming. "Think about it," I told him.

"Do I have to?" Mort turned back toward the car, maybe trying to pretend I wasn't there at all. "Any signs of trauma, Doc? Like maybe somebody conked him on the head and left the guy with the engine on to kill him?"

"No, sirree, Sheriff, least nothing I can find. Near as I can tell, Mr. Winslow here slipped off to sleep and died while he was dreaming."

"Any objections, Mrs. F.?" Mort asked me.

I had my eyes still fixed inside the Ford Five Hundred. "Well . . ."

"Uh-oh."

"Can I borrow your penlight?" I asked Seth.

He handed it over and moved aside so I could replace him leaning over the front seat. But my attention, and the penlight's beam, were focused on the leather seat upholstery on either side of where Loomis Winslow rested. I thought I'd spotted something there when the body shifted to the left once Mort jerked the door open.

Turned out I was right.

Chapter Two

Notice that?" I asked Mort, who was leaning close enough to my shoulder to make it seem like I was sporting a second head.

"Notice what?"

"Parts of the upholstery are discolored on both sides of the body."

"Come again, Mrs. F.?"

"Loomis Winslow went to great pains to keep his car looking showroom bright, including wiping a lubricant like Armor All on the seats. But these less shiny patches indicate to the naked eye something removed the lubricant on both sides of the body, equidistant on either side."

"Something," Mort repeated.

I turned and eased myself from the car's cabin. I didn't dare touch anything without evidence gloves and figured doing so was a task better left to Mort anyway. "See if you feel anything when you touch the discolored spots."

"Like what?"

"If I'm right, you'll know immediately."

Mort leaned in to take over the space I'd just occupied. "Where are these spots, again?"

I realized I was still holding the penlight and shone its beam on the spot closest to Mort's reach. Then I watched him touch it with the tip of his right index finger.

"Sticky," he noted, and proceeded to touch his gloved fingers to the man's clothes. "Here, too."

I nodded. "Residue from some kind of tape."

"Hold on, Jess," Seth interjected. "Are you saying somebody taped this poor man to the seat and left him to die with the engine running?"

"That seems to be what happened here, yes."

"In which case," Mort started, "he stuck around long enough for the deed to be done. A couple of hours, at least, to remove the tape and make it look like an accident."

Seth took the penlight back and did a fresh inspection of Loomis Winslow's face. "No tape residue here. Means this man could've been screaming up a storm, at least until he passed out."

"With no one around to hear him in these parts, Doc," Mort noted. "If the good lady here is right, we've got death by duct tape. Feel free to use that as a book title, Mrs. F.," Mort added, turning toward me. "No charge."

"Why not just cover his mouth, too?" Seth wondered aloud, getting back to the subject at hand.

"How long would it have taken you to spot signs of that on the skin of the victim's face?"

"Five seconds, maybe."

I left things there.

"I'm thinking I should have left you at Mara's," Mort sighed.

"Crime scene technicians would have spotted the same thing I did."

"Sure, but that would've been tomorrow. Last thing I need *today* with a killer storm bearing down is a murder investigation." Mort stopped and stared as much through me as at me. "You've got that look, Mrs. F."

"What look is that?'

"The one that says you've got something else to tell me."

"I do, Sheriff, and it's not going to wait until tomorrow either."

I took the penlight back from Mort and shone it down into the well beneath the dashboard where the dead man's legs and feet rested atop one of those fancy floor mats I couldn't recall the name of, since I don't own a car and never even got my driver's license.

"What do you see, Sheriff?"

"Dirt."

"Gravel," I corrected.

"That's what I said."

"Gravel that at first glance seems to match the surface of this parking lot."

Mort looked toward Seth. "This just keeps getting better, doesn't it?"

"You're the one who asked her if she wanted to come along."

"Excuse me," I broke in, "but I'm standing right here."

"Okay," Mort said, nodding reluctantly, "so Loomis Winslow stepped out of the car. At least that might explain why he took off his seat belt."

"Check his shoes, Mort."

"For what?"

"More gravel. The tread. If he did more than stand outside the car, you'll find evidence of it there."

Mort worked his way into the cab on an angle that allowed him to inspect the soles of Loomis Winslow's shoes. "Smeared with gravel dust and grit on both sides, left and right," he reported.

"How deep into the tread?"

Mort checked the shoes again. "Deep enough. You thinking the guy took a walk?"

"I am."

"Where, exactly?"

I pointed over the Ford Five Hundred toward the crumbling remains of the Cabot Manufacturing Company. "I'm guessing inside there."

The inside of the Cabot Manufacturing Company was a warren of collapsed timbers, cobwebs, and decaying flat wooden tables that had once held the lathes and other machines that had made this the largest textile factory in New England for a time. The debris-riddled plank floor formed an obstacle course that left us dancing between objects both big and small. Every time the increasingly stiff wind blew, the building shook and creaked, leaving me glancing upward in fear the roof might be about to shed fresh pieces of itself. It smelled of age and decay, the kind of place you wouldn't want to hold in your memory once you left it behind. Dust swirled about the air, and I couldn't help but picture the snow that was to come, leaving a fresh coat of white everywhere the holes in that roof allowed it to enter.

"What are we looking for, exactly?" Mort asked, kicking at some clumps of rotten wood as if to see what lay beneath it.

"I'll tell you when I find it," I told him, hoping I found it fast so we could be gone from this place.

Some say buildings have souls, the collected experiences of the many who'd gathered held between the walls that had survived so many years, however poorly. If that were the case, I had the distinct sense that the soul of the Cabot Manufacturing Company had rotted away as much as the wood framing had, leaving behind a residue of hopelessness and pain. I'd heard more than my share of horror stories about the working conditions back in those days long before unions and workers' rights. I even found myself wondering if the darker patches staining a number of the heavy tables with Rorschach test–like blotches were bloodstains instead of mere signs of disuse and decay.

I could feel both Mort and Seth growing as antsy as I was at being inside a structure that felt like it might collapse at any moment. We hadn't spotted a convenient trail of footprints leading from Loomis Winslow's Ford Five Hundred to the rickety, double-door entrance to the factory. But pinned under a rock just short of the stairs we did find a gum wrapper that matched a pack Mort had spotted on the car's passenger seat.

That made for a clear indication that Winslow had, in fact, entered the building after parking his car.

"You're thinking this detective came here to meet someone, Mrs. F.," Mort said, his voice echoing in tinny fashion through the cavernous confines.

"Why do you always tell me what I'm thinking?"

"Because you wouldn't tell me otherwise."

"Well, right now I'm thinking whoever he came here to meet last night ended up duct-taping him to the driver's seat with the engine running."

"And then stuck around to remove it once the deed was done," Mort picked up, drawing close to me with Seth on his heels. "That's a long time to wait in the cold or even in whatever car the killer used to get here."

Sometimes in times like this, the lines between fiction and reality blur. I start thinking more like a writer and less like an investigator, how I might *write* the crime in question instead of solving it. It was Sherlock Holmes himself who once said, "We balance probabilities and choose the most likely. It is the scientific use of the imagination." The imagination, I suppose, serves me as well when I'm investigating a real case as when I'm inventing a fictional one. But I feared in this particular instance I was veering more toward the latter, keeping in line with another famous Holmes quote, "Where there is no imagination there is no horror."

Because I saw horror in what had transpired in the hours it took Loomis Winslow to die and felt the presence within these dark, decrepit walls of a killer I truly hoped was long gone from Cabot Cove.

Mort was busying himself with the floor, searching for some indication of where Winslow had met his killer. He kicked at the debris with his heavy shoes and smoothed parts of it aside when it seemed he might have happened upon something.

For his part, Seth Hazlitt paced and fidgeted, wanting very much to be out of this place and back within the warm safety of Mort's SUV.

"Think I've got something, Mrs. F.," Mort called out suddenly. "Come have a look."

He'd called me "Mrs. F." for years after taking over for Amos Tupper as sheriff of Cabot Cove, before I finally broke him of the habit and got him to call me "Jessica" instead. I mean, when you've solved as many murders side by side as we have, the least you can expect is to be on a first-name basis. Only in recent months had he gone back to using "Mrs. F." again, as much to annoy me, I thought, as anything else. Old habits not only die hard; sometimes they come back.

I'd just started toward Mort when Seth Hazlitt banged into a ladder standing in the shadows not far from where Mort had crouched over a dusty patch of plank flooring. The ladder rattled, saved from toppling over only when Seth braced himself against it.

"Easy there, Doc," Mort said up to him. "Don't want to end up needing to treat yourself."

Seth finally got the ladder steadied. "Place should have been condemned and leveled back when my mother was still alive."

I crouched alongside Mort, noting what he'd uncovered. "A

footprint," I said, making out the thinnest of shapes clinging to the contours formed by the dust caking.

"And, wouldn't you know, it matches our victim's shoes."

I nodded, impressed. "You can tell?"

"Well, I am a trained investigator, after all." Mort started drawing patterns in the air over the footprint's outline. "Same general tread, something between a sneaker and a shoe, exactly what he's wearing. Same size, I'm guessing, too."

"Strange," I heard myself say.

"What?"

"Tell me what you don't see, Mr. Trained Investigator."

Mort rubbed his chin dramatically. "Hmm, another footprint? It would seem our poor Mr. Winslow came inside to meet someone who never showed."

"Why leave the comfort of his warm car at all, until whoever he was supposed to meet arrived? If Winslow did come here to meet someone, he must've had reason to believe they were already here."

"Like another vehicle in the lot outside?"

"You read my mind, Mort."

"Makes up for the fact that he doesn't read your books, Jess," Seth couldn't help but interject.

"Anyway," Mort said, pushing himself up to his feet, both knees cracking, "since there's no other footprint in the general area, whoever was driving the second vehicle never met Loomis inside—at least not here, unless you can tell me what kind of man doesn't leave any footprints."

"How about a ghost?"

"A ghost only *used to be* a man. And they don't leave footprints because they float around."

"That a scientific opinion, Mort?"

"Close enough."

"Well, here's another," I said, steering my gaze along a strangely cleared path of plank flooring that seemed to extend all the way to the entrance. "I think somebody dragged his body from here back outside to his car."

Mort followed my gaze. "Sounds more like supposition to me, Mrs. F."

"Sometimes science and supposition are the same thing."

Still, something about that scenario didn't sit right with me. Sherlock Holmes also once said, "There is nothing more deceptive than an obvious fact." And I had a feeling that I was missing something here.

"What's wrong, Mrs. F.?"

"Nothing."

"That's not your 'nothing' face."

I looked toward the ladder Seth had nearly toppled over. "What's that ladder doing here?"

"Way I see it, for somebody who once worked here to climb up on," Mort replied, holding back a grin.

"Then look again. That ladder has a slew of warning labels attached to it. When did this place close, Seth?"

"Oh, sometime after World War II."

"I don't think ladders were required to carry warning labels back then, Sheriff."

Mort's expression flattened. "What's your point?"

"I don't have one beyond that." My gaze returned to the ladder that rose maybe a yard from the spot where I believed Loomis Winslow had been attacked. "Not yet, anyway."

With the storm drawing ever closer, Mort dropped Seth off at the same house he'd lived in since he came back to Cabot Cove fresh out of medical school.

"Next stop, Hill House, Mrs. F.," he said after I climbed into the front seat.

"I was thinking the sheriff's station."

"*My* sheriff's station?"

"Is there another in town? I figure you're going to do some digging into Loomis Winslow and I want to be there."

"Digging and finding are two entirely different things."

"Exactly. So once we get to the station, you grab your shovel and I'll grab mine."

I was in no particular rush to get back to Hill House, truth be told. Not since I figured it would be a few days before I'd be able to venture out again, if forecasts of the looming storm's severity proved accurate. Beyond that, the hotel's entire second floor had been rented out to a wedding party. Bad enough to be cooped up for an extended period of time. But cooped up with strangers anxious over whether their entire planning was about to be waylaid? That I could do without and I suppose I was putting it off for as long as possible. I have no idea who schedules a wedding in the depths of winter, in Maine no less, and didn't particularly want to find out. Kind of like sitting next to someone on a flight whose mouth moves as fast as the plane. At least at Hill House I'd be able to retreat to the confines of my suite, while a plane offered no such respite.

The coming storm had Mort's deputies out and about to deal with any traffic issues and try to cajole a few of our least mobile residents to accept a move to a shelter that had been set up at the high school. So it was just him, me, and the dispatcher present in the quaint open office that featured a single cell in the basement. I took one of the deputies' desks on the floor, while Mort adjourned to his office. He started to close the door, looked at me with his usual snicker, then left it open instead.

"I'm going to see what I can learn from Loomis Winslow's office down in Boston, maybe get a notion as to what he was doing up in these parts."

"Not to mention who he was working for."

"It's never that easy, though, is it, Mrs. F.?"

"That's the fun part when I'm writing."

"But you're not writing now."

"No," I said, flashing my iPhone, "I'm calling."

I wondered how many times exactly I dialed or pressed the New York exchange that was ringing now.

"Harry McGraw. State your piece."

"Is that your new greeting?" I asked the best detective, private or otherwise, I'd ever known.

"I'm trying it out. How's the storm treating you up there, little lady?"

"Hasn't started yet. I'm still hoping it'll miss us."

"Right, tough weather to bike in for sure."

"Alas, my trusty new Pashley is put away for the winter."

"So how do you get around, snowplow?"

"Without a driver's license?"

"That's for a car," Harry said. "I figured maybe you got your commercial license without any of us knowing."

"Jessica Fletcher driving a snowplow?"

"I was thinking more along the lines of one of those monster trucks. Love to see you behind the wheel of that."

"I doubt you'd be able to see me behind the wheel of that, Harry."

"So, what do you need, dear lady? I'm at your service, unless you want me to shovel your walk."

"You're sounding awfully accommodating these days," I told him.

"Part of my fifteen-step program to become a better person. That's number six: Be helpful."

"I thought it was twelve steps."

"No, that's Alcoholics Anonymous, and I already tried that. Worked for a while."

"What happened?"

"You kept calling me."

I could picture Harry grinning on the other end of the line.

"Anyway," he continued, "I'm supposed to give up my seat on the subway to an elderly person, or something like that, every day."

"How's that working for you?"

"It isn't, because I don't ride the subway. Another option is carrying a neighbor's groceries in for them."

"Sounds like a better choice," I told him.

"Except I live in a six-story walk-up, so I've limited myself to helping only those who live on the first floor. I'm also supposed to practice forgiveness. That's number four."

"And?"

"I forgive you, Jessica."

"For what?"

"Do I really need to make you a list?"

"Mind if I add to it, Harry?"

I heard him force a sigh. "Why ask me if you're going to anyway?"

"Ever heard of a private detective named Loomis Winslow?"

"What, you think we all know each other or something? Like we all attend the same annual convention, like circus clowns?"

"I didn't know clowns held an annual convention."

"Figure of speech. And the answer is, no, I've never heard of a private detective named Loomis Winslow. Are you thinking of hiring him?"

"Why would I when I've got you?"

"Who is he, Jess?"

"You mean, who *was* he."

"Don't tell me. . . . Murdered?"

"You told me not to tell you."

"The phone rings, my first thought is, who died in Cabot Cove? I'm giving serious thought to changing my number. There'd still be bodies, but I wouldn't have to hear about them."

As always, Harry sounded gruff and flippant. I'd long grown used to his quirks along with his quips, and I was continually amazed at his ability to turn up dirt under stones others would have been hard-pressed to find in the first place.

"You need to hear about this one, Harry."

"Why?"

"Because he was a PI. Like you."

"Like me? You mean you stiffed him on his bills, too?"

"Maybe you should start sending them to me."

"Don't worry, Jessica. I've let go of my anger for you stiffing me, because that's number three. Number five is to be honest and direct. So, what were we talking about, again?"

We'd finally gotten back to the point. "Loomis Winslow."

"Sounds like the name of a character from one of your books."

"Can you look into him, Harry?"

"In search of what, exactly?"

"Who might have had reason to kill him and what might have brought him to Cabot Cove."

"Step number thirteen is 'don't show up empty-handed,' so let me see what I can find out."

"He's based in Boston. I've got his e-mail and phone number from a card in his wallet, if you need it."

"Don't bother, little lady—I'll look it up. Us private eyes are expert at investigating each other. And I want to surprise you. That's number fourteen on the list."

"Since you never let me down, it won't be much of a surprise, Harry."

"*Shh,*" he hissed out. "Don't tell anyone, because I want to have another box I can check off. I never realized how easy it was to become a better person. I would've tried it years ago if I'd known."

"What's number fifteen on your self-improvement list?"

"Compliment yourself. I'm having trouble with that one."

As I ended the call, I saw Mort burst from his office fastening his sheriff's cap in place.

"Let's go, Mrs. F."

"Where to?"

"To watch history being made."

Chapter Three

We headed over to pick up Seth Hazlitt on our way to the town hall, where an emergency meeting had been called by Cabot Cove's mayor. Apparently, the blizzard had gone from big to historic, the forecast upped to three feet even in these parts close to the Maine coastline. The governor had already declared a state of emergency and urged all municipalities to man their respective barricades as well, calling in public service reinforcements in the form of first responders and snowplow drivers, along with mechanics at the municipal depot to keep those plows on the road through what promised to be treacherous conditions.

In 1978, a similar blizzard had struck with such ferocity, piling up over four feet in many areas of New England, that all of Rhode Island was shut down for a week. A few winters back, when Boston's total snowfall exceeded ten feet, narrowed streets were switched to one-way once hours-long traffic jams resulted in nobody getting anywhere. I remember reading about a shooting that occurred when a man snatched an on-street parking space from a neighbor who'd spent all of eight hours clearing it.

So it was no wonder our mayor had called this emergency meeting upon learning the forecast had been increased to dangerous, even life-threatening proportions. Normally, Mainers shrug off snowstorms with the ease of swatting a mosquito. Every once in a while, though, a storm comes along we can't shrug off, and this one had the makings of a true storm of the century. On the way over to Seth's, Mort was droning on about three weather systems currently on a collision course and destined to explode in what was being called a meteorological bomb. The first flakes had just begun to fall, leaving on the road a soft coating that deepened seemingly between blinks of the eye. Mort switched his SUV into all-wheel drive and we passed a number of vehicles already having trouble negotiating the slick roads.

"You haven't told me what you managed to learn about Loomis Winslow, Mort."

"That's because there isn't much to tell—nothing, in fact. My call to his office number went to voice mail, and I haven't been able to find anyone else capable of telling me anything about his background. Nobody's answering their phones or e-mails because everything down there is pretty much closed. Boston's getting hammered as we speak."

"You try Google?" I asked Cabot Cove's esteemed sheriff. "The site doesn't close when it snows."

"Now, why didn't I think of that?" Mort shot me a quick look, not wanting to take his eyes off the road. "Of course I googled him. But all I got was his office address and phone number. Since Loomis Winslow is such a unique name, I was hoping for more."

"Maybe Harry McGraw will have more luck. Anything else I should tell him that might help?"

"Winslow's not in the system, either DNA or fingerprints. I dug as deep as the federal no-fly and terrorist watch lists. Not surprisingly, he's not on either. So he's never been arrested, I can find no evidence of him ever getting married, and his credit score is in the low seven hundreds. That enough for you?"

"I didn't ask about his credit score, Mort."

"You should have. It's the new gold standard when it comes to even the simplest background checks and affects pretty much every facet of your entire life, from buying a house or car to applying for insurance. Anyway, I was starting to do an even deeper dive, into his charge cards and such, when I got the call about the emergency meeting."

"You haven't mentioned anything about Winslow's cell phone."

"That's because he didn't have one on him or anywhere in the car."

"Maybe the killer took it with him," I surmised, "to hide the fact that his, or her, phone number was on the call log."

"Speaking of which, Loomis's cell phone number was on the business card we found in his wallet, and I've already requested a call and text message dump from his cellular provider."

"How long do you expect the call dump to take?"

"A couple days, anyway. That's business days, which means we're looking at early next week. Could be even longer if the office holding those records is in the path of the storm."

"I'll bet Harry comes up with something before that."

"Because he's a better investigator than me?"

"Because he hasn't got a town to protect during a blizzard."

We pulled up in front of Seth Hazlitt's picket fence to find him waiting for us, all bundled up with his ever-present cap in place.

"Don't know what they need me for," he groused, climbing into the backseat of the SUV and pulling off his gloves.

Mort flipped the windshield wipers to the next interval level. "It's a meeting of principal chief responders, and you're a principal first responder."

"And me thinking I was just a country doctor . . ."

"A country doctor who agreed to serve on our ad hoc nine-one-one team."

"When did I agree to that?"

"Around the time I took over as sheriff, Doc."

"And I'm supposed to remember that?"

"No, you have me for that."

Seth leaned forward to give himself a better view of the rapidly intensifying storm through the windshield. "I told you she was going to be a bad one, didn't I? Could feel it in the air—smell it, too. *Ayuh*, this is going to be one for the ages."

"Anybody lose their life in those historic storms that preceded this one?" Mort asked him.

"Well, if memory serves, Whitney Londine lost her dog in the 'seventy-nine storm."

"I'm talking about lost *human* lives, Doc."

"We're a hardy bunch, Sheriff. You've lived here so long, I figured you'd know that by now. Nope, no deaths." Seth turned his gaze on me. "You talk to Harry McGraw?"

"What makes you ask that?"

"Because our murder victim's in the same line of work, and I know how you think."

"Harry doesn't know Loomis Winslow, or has ever even heard of him," I told Seth. "It's not like private investigators all belong to the same fraternity."

Mort glanced at me again, even quicker. "You were president of your sorority in college, weren't you, Mrs. F.?"

"Community service chair."

"Organize anything big?"

"The school was in New Hampshire, so we always made sure to shovel out our elderly neighbors."

"Where do I sign up?" Seth asked me.

Sam Booth had been mayor of Cabot Cove for longer than most residents could remember. The slogan for his last reelection campaign had been "The Do-Nothing Mayor," which pretty much summed up the rigors of the mostly ceremonial job. And since he'd run unopposed in the last six elections, the voters were clearly expecting no more than what he'd promised.

But sometimes the position of mayor becomes a *real* job,

and this was one of those times. Mayor Sam, as he was affectionately known, sat in the center of the raised table where town officials conducted the official business of Cabot Cove. Approximately sixty folding chairs were set up neatly on the chamber floor. Besides rare occasions like this, normally the only times all of them were filled (and then some) were during zoning board meetings, when the most contentious battles of the day were fought, with various sides often shouting at one another, and even coming close to blows from time to time.

I grabbed a chair near the front, on the aisle, while Mort and Seth took their respective seats on the dais flanking Mayor Sam, along with our fire chief, Dick Mann, and Cabot Cove's chief town elder, Ethan Cragg, a local fisherman and longtime friend of mine. Mayor Sam seemed to be searching the long table for a gavel with which to convene the meeting but couldn't find it. He had worn a shirt and tie for the occasion, though the media turnout in the form of the local papers, radio stations, and television outlets was pretty thin. I did spot Evelyn Simpson, editor of the *Cabot Cove Gazette*, who was likely more interested in who was in the audience than with what anyone had to say.

"Okay," Sam Booth started, "as mayor of Cabot Cove, I call this unofficial meeting officially to order. As you all know, the weather folks are now referring to this storm as a meteorological time bomb. I don't know what a meteorological time bomb is, but I know it can't be good. So we all thought it might be a good idea to convene Cabot Cove's department heads associated with public safety, so each can update you on the storm from their viewpoint. Chief Mann, why don't we start with you?"

Dick Mann cleared his throat. "I've called as much of our volunteer force as I could to the station to wait out the storm, in addition to keeping all four of our full-time firefighters and all three paramedics on shift for the duration. We'll be focused on responding to emergency calls so long as the plows keep the roads reasonably clear. Our big trucks can operate in up to eighteen inches of snow in the event of a fire. We're also prioritizing evacuations of those who find themselves stranded with no power, which is another eventuality we're considering. In my experience, with a storm of this magnitude there are also going to be power outages. And with the wind speeds being upped in the latest forecast, those are virtually inevitable."

Evelyn Simpson raised her hand. "Mayor Sam, based on what Chief Mann just said, have you arranged for outside electrical crews to be on standby in order to restore power as quickly as possible?"

Booth leaned forward, stretching himself toward a microphone that wasn't there. "To tell you the truth, Evelyn, the first I heard of the likelihood of power outages was just now, just like everybody else. But I'll get right on it," he said, the look on his face telling me he had no idea who to call to make such arrangements.

Evelyn wasn't finished yet. "And what happens with evacuations if the plows can't keep up with the snow enough for the emergency vehicles to be able to traverse the roads? The latest forecast, as you know, Mayor Sam, is predicting snowfall rates of up to four, even five, inches per hour overnight."

It was clear from Booth's expression that he hadn't known

that either until Evelyn informed him. Fortunately, Mort was there to save the day.

"Chief Mann and I are coordinating to have a fleet of snowmobiles, driven by our personnel and local volunteers, available if they become needed for reaching anyone in need or distress."

"So long as you've got the floor, Sheriff Metzger, why don't you keep it?" Mayor Sam suggested, eager to relinquish that floor as much as possible.

"Not a lot to say from the Sheriff's Department's perspective. We'll be coordinating all rescue and service efforts with Chief Mann's people, along with the snow removal teams. We're going to set up a kind of central command in our squad room, where the town's emergency command-and-control machines are located, to monitor weather, traffic, and a grid map detailing the state of every street in Cabot Cove. My deputies are setting it up right now, and we're also making sure the town's six propane-fueled emergency generators are ready to go."

Mayor Sam nodded again, starting to look overly pleased with himself. "Another perfect transition to Ethan," he said, turning toward my fisherman friend. "What says the head of the snowplow force?"

Ethan rose from his chair before answering. He knew this town better than anyone else and loathed the change forced upon us by the outside world, especially in summer months. He personally hadn't changed much in all the years we'd known each other. Sure, his thick hair had gradually gone from black to gray, and he was showing more lines and furrows dug out of his face from all those years at sea. But he had the same rugged build and the strongest hands of any man I'd ever known, scarred and calloused thanks to hoisting fishing nets from the water for so long.

"I've been coordinating with Public Works," Ethan started, after clearing his throat, "both local and state, to assure we don't overlap plowing territory. And I've brought on twelve additional plow trucks to supplement the two the town owns, which is eight more than usual," he said, looking toward Mayor Sam. "I'm as confident as it gets that we're ready for anything."

Mayor Sam flashed his trademark nod, which looked like that of a marionette controlled by someone pulling its strings. "Which brings us to Seth Hazlitt. What have you got for us, Doc?"

"I don't even know what I'm doing here, tell you the truth," Seth said, pushing his chair under the table with an annoying squeal. "But I have checked in with the hospital and can reassure folks that they're fully staffed and will remain so through the duration of the storm. I wasn't there when they tested their backup generator system, but I was assured everything checked out just fine and dandy." A scowl spread over Seth's face that reminded me of what he looked like when he bit into a boysenberry pie he'd been served in accidental place of his customary strawberry rhubarb. "I'll be waiting out the storm in the confines of my trusty home, where anyone with a phone can reach me. Pretty much everybody already has my number, but I added it to the listings on that Emergency Response page that pops up when you click on the town's website. I've also put myself in charge of making sure all emergency responders are properly fed and am pleased to report that Mara is cooking up a storm of sandwiches, salads, and those famous cookies as we speak. I've also arranged to have a bunch of those cardboard boxes filled with coffee on hand at all gathering sites, and you'll be pleased to hear that this time I remembered the cream and sugar, *ayuh*."

A fresh chuckle lifted through the crowd. Seth was referring to a similar emergency situation a few years back, when a late-season hurricane came barreling up the Maine coast. People didn't have a lot to complain about in terms of preparation for that, so they harped on the fact that first responders and those seeking shelter had to drink their coffee black.

"But as a doctor who's practiced in Cabot Cove for going on thirty-five years now, I've got some advice for those of you over fifty." Seth pushed his chair back and rose to stretch himself across the table, closer to the audience. "Throw out your snow shovel. At least chain it to a wall with a lock you don't have the combination for. Fact is, research shows a sharp spike of hospital admissions for heart problems two days after storms far less severe than the one about to bear down on us. Why two days, you ask? Because the afflicted can't get to the hospital the day of the storm. Any questions?"

When no one raised their hands, Seth sat back down and crossed his arms. He met my gaze and winked. I nodded, not bothering to hide how impressed I was. Once Seth had finished, Dick Mann looked up from checking his phone and whispered something into Mayor Sam's ear.

"The chief tells me," he started, "that we're now looking at three feet for starters, and any hope of the storm going out to sea is out the window. We're going to stay here for a time to take any questions you may want to pose individually. But the most important thing right now is for everyone to go home, check your emergency procedures, and batten down the hatches. Once this thing intensifies, nobody's going to be able to get anywhere for a while, but rest assured, in an emergency we will be prepared to come to you."

Now it was Mort checking his phone, shaking his head with a look that told me something else had just come up. At first, I figured it must have something to do with the murder of Private Detective Loomis Winslow out of Boston. As he stepped down off the dais and approached me, though, I could tell it was something else.

"I'm needed somewhere, Mrs. F. I can drop you off at Hill House on the way."

I had risen to my feet, but I made no move to accompany him down the aisle. "And what does this 'somewhere' entail?"

"Nothing that concerns you." He glanced out the row of windows that dominated an entire wall. "Storm's picking up. We'd better get you settled so I can check on Adele before I hunker down at the station, maybe set up a hooch just like I did in Vietnam."

"You can drop me off after you check on Adele," I said, referring to Mort's wife. "Be nice to say hello to her anyway. And I could keep you company."

"Where?"

"Wherever you're going."

"No murder this time, Mrs. F."

"I could tell that from the look on your face, just as I could tell it's still something that could use my attention. Care to give me a hint?"

"How about something else that makes no sense?"

Chapter Four

"A nything more on Loomis Winslow?" I asked Mort, as we trudged through the biting winds and the initial fall of snow toward his Sheriff's Department SUV.

"Not a peep. Nobody in law enforcement down in Boston is focusing on anything but the storm hammering them. Forecast there just got upped to eighteen to twenty-four inches."

"We'll be lucky if that ends up the case here, Mort."

There were two inches on the ground already and the snow was piling up fast. Looking up at the sky was like staring into a dark abyss. And this, we'd been warned, was just the beginning. The dueling fronts predicted to form a meteorological bomb hadn't even joined up yet. Call this the preliminary match before the Maine event.

The snow had actually slowed to a mere flurry as we set out through town toward where Route 38 dumped cars onto an access road just short of the WELCOME TO CABOT COVE sign.

That sign appeared in distant view down the long straightaway as we came upon a fancy SUV parked on the shoulder but on an angle that left its tail end in the roadway, both its front doors open. A Cabot Cove deputy's vehicle parked behind the abandoned SUV had its lights flashing to warn drivers coming in either direction.

"Passing motorist called it in, Sheriff," the deputy, whose name I couldn't recall, told Mort after we'd hopped out of his SUV.

I used to know all the Cabot Cove deputies by name, but now Mort kept a complement of fifteen on even during the winter months to avoid having to staff up with too many part-timers during the summer. Officers looking for a summer gig like that were usually available because they were either re-tired or lacking in experience, both a bad fit for overseeing the hustle and bustle of what had become a typical Cabot Cove summer.

"You got a time for me, Jack?" Mort asked him.

"I got the call at one seventeen sharp, so I'm guessing a couple minutes before that."

Mort approached the abandoned Lexus and peered at its front seat through the open passenger-side door. "In other words, this couldn't have happened all that long ago."

As he said that, my gaze instinctively went in search of footprints in the freshly fallen snow, but there was nothing. I held the hood of my parka up over my face against the deter-mined attempts of the wind to blow it off and eased closer to the shoulder to see if I could detect any tracks there.

"Careful, Mrs. F.," Mort warned. "You don't want to become this storm's first casualty."

I backed off, having seen enough to know there were no footprints there either.

"Thirty minutes," I said, drawing even with Mort and his deputy.

Fighting the wind for even that brief distance left me huffing for breath and picturing those rope lines people use to guide their way outside in the worst wintry places. Plenty had perished when their gloves slipped off that line and they couldn't locate it again. The old cliché that you couldn't see the hand in front of your face applied perfectly in this case.

"Thirty minutes *what*, Mrs. F.?"

"The skies opened up for a time then, while we were still at the meeting. Dumped those couple inches we drove through to get here, enough to cover any tracks that may have been there before."

Mort's gaze moved to the shoulder where I'd been standing, looking down at the drop that leveled off into the woods that rimmed the access road. "Long time for a vehicle abandoned like this to go unreported."

"Up until a few minutes ago, the snow was coming down too hard for drivers to pay attention to much else besides the road before them. Maybe twenty-five minutes instead of thirty—twenty even."

Mort stepped aside and gestured dramatically for me to take his place peering into the vehicle. "Then, by all means, tell me if you can see something I'm missing."

There was nothing. The interior of the SUV smelled fresh and new, and the black leather seats were so shiny I thought I might be able to spot my reflection in them. Having never driven, I'm not good at judging the relative merits of vehicles, but one thing I'm pretty sure of is that all these newfangled extras, confusing controls, and touch screens would drive me crazy. I could picture my late husband, Frank, saying we got along just fine without any of that, and in my mind, the more a car could do for its driver, the less its driver paid attention to what they should be doing themselves.

The Lexus had been outfitted with tailored winter floor mats embossed with the luxury brand's logo. I stretched my hand inside the passenger side, removing my glove to touch the mat there with a fingertip. It came away damp, and on closer inspection I could see darkened wet patches where snow carried in by the shoe tread of whoever had been in the passenger seat had left its mark.

I was about to stop my inspection there when, on a whim, I moved to the rear passenger-side door and asked Mort to open it since he was wearing evidence gloves and I wasn't. The wind caught the door and blew it the rest of the way, taking every bit the hinges would give and nearly knocking Mort off his feet.

"You plan that gust, Jessica?"

"So I'm 'Jessica' now?"

"Yup, because Mrs. F. would never do such a thing."

"In that case, Mrs. F. thinks you should have a look inside here."

Mort drew even with me and squinted, whistling when he saw the same thing I had.

"If I didn't know better, I'd say you planted it there to get a rise out of me," he said, peering backward my way.

"That's right. I snuck a handful of gravel from the parking lot of that old mill and dumped it on that backseat floor mat when you weren't looking."

And now we were both looking at a splatter of gravel, present only on the passenger side of the backseat, that seemed identical to what had been caked in the tread of Loomis Winslow's shoes. Something also occurred to me about how the positioning of the seat itself hid a portion of the floor mat from view, but I couldn't quite grasp the thought and I let it go.

"I need to tell you what this means, Mort?"

"Why don't you, while I'm still trying to clear my head from you whacking me with a car door?"

"It barely grazed you."

"You were saying, Mrs. F. . . ."

"Someone who'd been at the old Cabot Manufacturing Company was riding in the backseat. Since there's no trace of the same gravel on the mats in the front seat, it's a safe bet the driver and passenger weren't there with them. And, since there's no gravel or melted snow on the backseat driver's side, we're looking at the driver and two passengers currently missing from the scene."

"Since you're on such a roll, how about telling me what happened to those three, at least the two who were riding up front?"

I looked about through the storm, which had begun to intensify again. "I have no idea, but the next question is obvious."

"What made two people flee their vehicle into a snowstorm and not even bother to close the doors behind them?"

"Must've been in a hurry, Sheriff," the deputy Mort had called Jack put forth. "Maybe they were being chased."

"Or following instructions, orders," I said as the thought occurred to me.

"By whoever was in the backseat." Mort nodded.

"Something to consider."

"Except that gravel could have been left in the backseat yesterday, the day before, or even last week."

"Pennsylvania plates, Mort," I noted. "That would seem to eliminate anything but today or, maybe, yesterday. And the darkened wet patches of rubber around the gravel makes it clear whoever was in the backseat was in it today, and recently, to boot."

Making up a clue like this in one of my books and discerning one in the real world were really the same thing . . . only different. Different because I try to stay one step ahead of my readers, while in moments like this I always feel a step behind. The same because such clues help me get a sense of a bigger picture, first blurry and then crystal clear. And what was starting to clarify in my mind here, what I was starting to picture, was whoever had been in the front seat fleeing whoever had been in the back. That would explain their doors being left open. Had the occupant of the backseat followed them into the woods, across the road, or down it? That part of the picture was still blurry.

"Any chance we can search the woods, Mort?" I posed.

"Asks the lady who must've forgot we're about to be hit by the biggest blizzard in the state's history. 'So, how am I supposed to round up the manpower?' asks the beleaguered sheriff who retired in the murder capital of America."

"Have you ever thought of becoming a writer, Sheriff?"

Mort winked at Deputy Jack and suppressed a smile when he looked back my way. "No. Have you?"

I felt my phone vibrating in the pocket of my parka, the ring muffled by all that insulation. Smartphones have gotten too big to maneuver easily even without gloves on, so I retreated to Mort's SUV in the hope it was Harry McGraw calling with something to tell me, hopefully about Loomis Winslow.

"How's the storm treating you, little lady?" he greeted, as soon as I answered.

I got the door closed and the hood of my parka yanked down in order to continue the conversation. The light coating of snow that had speckled my coat had already melted, freckling it down the front. I unzipped the jacket and settled into the passenger seat as comfortably as I could, while Mort continued his inspection of the abandoned vehicle.

"Worse is coming fast, Harry," I told him.

"You sound out of breath. Please tell me you're not with Mort at another crime scene."

"I'm not with Mort at another crime scene."

"You're lying, Jess."

"You told me to tell you I'm not."

He uttered a sound like a growl. "Well, I've got some things to tell you about the late private investigator you found. I did some checking, asked around a bit, even studied the man's website, which makes mine look good."

"You don't have a website."

"Precisely my point. Okay, so I can't tell you what case brought Winslow to Cabot Cove, but I can provide a notion as to where his particular areas of investigative expertise lay."

I realized how cold it was in the SUV without the heater running. Nothing I could do about that, since Mort had taken the keys with him.

"I'm listening, Harry."

"Loomis Winslow, by all indications, was more of a behind-the-scenes guy. You know, forensic-type stuff."

"Assume that I don't know."

"Private investigative work tends to run the gamut from divorces, detailed background checks, active crime investigation, to more wet-oriented work, as in personal protection or bodyguard services. Loomis Winslow's specialty was none of these. He was the kind of PI you hire when you have reason to suspect financial malfeasance, either business or personal. Somebody close to you stealing from you. You can't believe it's happening, and you don't want to report a friend or family member to the police, so you hire someone like Winslow to dig around and find out if your suspicions are well founded or not. It sounds easy, but this kind of financial scheme or scam tends to be quite complicated with all kinds of layers. I ever tell you I represented a few of those bilked by none other than Bernie Madoff?"

"No."

"Of course, because you probably figure you're my only client. Since you don't pay your bills, I have to make a living somewhere."

"Harry—"

"Anyway, my clients actually came before the bust that set the finance world on fire. They all suspected Bernie the bastard was up to something, but they had nothing to go on."

I measured my thoughts on what Harry had just told me. "Since when is that kind of forensic investigation your specialty?"

"I've got a lot of specialties, little lady. When somebody's about to ask me if I can handle something, my pat response is, 'The answer's yes. What's the question?' If I'm not an expert on something, I can learn fast."

Having seen him in action enough times, I knew there was no disputing that. I'd learned long ago Harry could handle pretty much anything, and nobody could educate himself on a particular area of interest quicker than he. It was as if he could scroll through an entire voluminous document and seize upon only the information with which he needed to acquaint himself. It was almost like his eyes and brain were connected on some kind of intuitive level.

"So, what'd you learn about Loomis Winslow?" I asked him.

"I'm getting to that. First, back to Madoff. I was able to gain access to that famous floor in the building even his sons couldn't get onto."

"You impersonate someone from the SEC or something?"

"Close. Try the New York City Health Department."

"Come again, Harry?"

"You heard me. I knew the figurative front door would be

locked, but you'd be surprised at how responsive people are when you show up at a side door telling them there are ditzem bugs running rampant through the walls, breeding up a storm and ready to break free."

"What's a ditzem bug?"

"Nothing. Doesn't exist. I made it up. But I came complete with pictures of a particularly nasty bug species native to South America that looked like something out of a fifties horror movie. I was dressed for the part, with ID badge, hazmat suit, and sprayer. You've never seen people run out of an office so fast, all three of them at the same time, so fast one of them left their computer on."

"Bingo."

"Well, not exactly, but close. The contents of the computer I cloned onto a thumb drive was enough to reveal plenty of shady doings, but nothing directly related to my clients. Before I could dive any deeper, the feds stormed in and the whole thing blew up."

"Is that how a detective like Loomis Winslow would have handled things?"

"A guy like Loomis works paper to find where the bodies are buried. From what I can tell, he was pretty much a one-man shop. Deliberate and thorough. The kind of guy you hear about through word of mouth, not the yellow pages."

"I'm not sure the yellow pages even exist anymore, Harry."

"Then why do I keep re-upping my ad? No wonder business is down. Good thing you're there, Jess. I wouldn't be able to pay the bills without you. Speaking of which, I'm caught up on almost everything—only three months behind now."

"Get back to Loomis Winslow. I assume you have no idea of what brought him to Cabot Cove."

"No, but it's a safe bet money had everything to do with it. Somebody stealing, hiding, embezzling, extorting, or cheating somebody out of what they believed was rightfully theirs. All done under the radar to keep things in the family—that's literally, in many cases. You go where the trail takes you."

"That's it?"

"It's only been a couple hours, Jess."

"I've come to expect miracles from you, Harry."

"Miracles cost more. I'll get back to you when I find one."

The snow was really picking up again by the time I rejoined Mort by the Lexus SUV. In the half hour or so we'd been there, only a single car had gone by, indicating that people were heeding the warnings not to venture out unless there was an emergency.

"Glove compartment's empty, Mrs. F.," he reported. "Somebody didn't want to make it easy for us to figure out who owns the car." He rotated his gaze about, as if sniffing the air. "Challenge being, how exactly am I supposed to process the vehicle in this, going on the assumption it's a potential crime scene? I'm not going to be able to get a State Police crime scene unit out here with this storm bearing down on us."

"Closing the doors and having the car hauled away will still leave any prints on the steering wheel, seats, insides of the doors, and dashboard intact, won't it?"

"A good lawyer might be able to argue about a contaminated chain of evidence, but we're a long way from that right now. I'll go for a wrecker right now and we can follow it to the impound lot to secure the scene."

I smiled, trying to picture Mort's predecessor Amos Tupper saying something like that. The temperature was dropping as the storm drew closer, and the bite of the wind felt like sheets of frigid water slamming against my face.

"Why don't you wait in the car, Mrs. F.?" Mort offered, dangling the keys this time so I could switch on the engine to warm up.

Mort joined me in the sheriff's SUV a few minutes later to wait for the wrecker, activating the laptop computer attached to his dashboard to run the plates of the Lexus SUV. It booted right up, but Mort got nowhere when he tried to log on to a site that would normally have allowed him to identify the owner of the Lexus.

Mort tapped the machine a few times, as if that might help jar the site to life, before finally giving up and leaning back in his seat with a sigh.

"Must be the storm," I noted. "Too many people inside their homes overloading the Internet."

"You can overload the Internet?"

I nodded. "When too many try to log on at once, often in a time of crisis, absolutely."

"Well, whoever they are, we've got two people, maybe three, missing in a storm that's going to kill anything it doesn't bury. Otherwise, I might have called in a search party to scour those woods. Do that now and all we'll end up with are more missing persons we may not find until the snow melts in the spring. Of course—"

Whatever Mort was going to say next was interrupted by the crackle of the dispatcher's voice over the radio.

"Dispatch to Sheriff Metzger."

He unclasped the mic and raised it to his lips. "Go for Mort."

"Sheriff, patrol just brought in Hank Weathers to keep him from freezing in the storm."

"So put him in a cell and let him sleep it off, Marge."

"He says he witnessed a murder last night, Sheriff. Out at the old Cabot Company factory."

Chapter Five

Mort drove back to the station as fast as he dared, careful especially to slow down well before we came to any intersections. Traffic was virtually nonexistent, and so far Ethan Cragg's plows were keeping up with the storm, which had dropped somewhere between three and four inches of snow at just past three o'clock in the afternoon, with the main event still hours away.

"That's our luck, Mrs. F.," Mort said as he eased the car to a halt in his reserved space, before it could slip into a skid. "We get a witness who drinks Jack Daniel's the way most of us drink water."

I climbed out of the SUV just ahead of him and pulled up my hood. "Let's hear what he has to say, Mort. You never know."

"You ever know Hank Weathers to get anything straight?"

"Well . . ."

"My point exactly." Mort's face grew somber. "Look, he's a fellow vet, Iraq as well as Afghanistan. I look at him and I think I could just as easily be looking at myself."

I nodded, already feeling the chill in the open air. You think you know people so well, there's nothing new you can learn about them. But Mort had just expressed compassion for the local town drunk whom no one else took seriously. I knew he was thinking that maybe this was the time Hank Weathers would get something right, something that might even help him regain his self-respect.

Mort pushed open the door, holding it against the stiff wind that threatened to slam it up against the station wall, and I trailed him inside. In a chair at a desk vacated by a deputy currently out on patrol, Hank Weathers was seated with a blanket wrapped around his thin, knobby shoulders. He was a fixture in Cabot Cove, known for doing odd jobs to make ends meet, although he was prone more to pouring liquor down his throat than to putting food on his table. He had a rough, ruddy complexion, his face spotted by too much exposure to the sun back when he'd worked for fishermen who needed an extra hand at the docks after he received a medical discharge from the army. He was sipping from a steaming Styrofoam cup no doubt filled with coffee from the single-serve machine Mort had recycled here after his wife, Adele, had purchased an upgrade.

Instead of taking Hank into his office, Mort spun a spare chair around and sat down facing him with me standing just to his right.

"How's the coffee, Hank?"

"What's she doing here?" he asked, crinkled face tilted in my direction.

"Just getting out of the storm, like you."

"That woman stiffed me on a job. A lot of people in this town stiffed me on jobs. I file reports but you don't do nothing about it."

Seth had warned me to stay clear of Hank Weathers because of his occasionally violent tendencies, a symptom of the PTSD that had followed him home from combat.

"You looking for a job, Hank?" Mort asked him.

"You hiring?"

"Depends."

"On what?"

"On what you saw at the old mill last night."

"I bunk there sometimes."

Mort nodded. "So I've heard."

"Cold last night. Couldn't get warm. Figured I'd try my luck somewhere else. That's when I saw him hurt that man."

"You saw who hurt what man?"

Hank Weathers looked genuinely scared. "He was big, Sheriff—I mean really big," he added with a hand raised well over his head. "A giant."

"And you saw this giant attack this man inside the old mill."

Hank nodded. "Hurt him bad."

"What did you see, exactly?"

"I hid behind one of those big plank posts when I heard the noise. The man came in and was standing in a spot I'd cleared out to bed down. Then I peeked around the post and saw the big man pounce on him, swallow him up."

"Swallow him up," Mort repeated.

"I got scared and ducked back behind the post. Didn't want him to hurt me, too. When I peeked next, the giant was dragging the man's body across the floor."

I looked toward Mort; much of what we'd gleaned at the Cabot Manufacturing Company was potentially confirmed.

"Did you get a good look at this giant?" I asked Hank Weathers.

Hank hedged. "Er, no. But I saw the man he hurt being dragged around the corner. Who else could it have been?" His gaze tightened, as if he was seeing me for the first time. "Did I ever thank you for that book, Mrs. Fletcher?"

I'd almost forgotten Hank stopping by the last Cabot Cove Library book sale I ran as chair of the Friends of the Library group. He was eyeballing a big coffee table book detailing every known breed of dog. He didn't have any money, but I let him have it for free.

"Yes, you did, Hank. What happened next?"

He looked confused. "Next?"

"After you saw the body being dragged across the floor."

"I was scared."

"I don't blame you."

"I went out through the back, a broken window, in case the giant was still there. Didn't want him to hurt me, too, because I realized who he was."

"Who?" Mort and I asked in unison.

Hank Weathers turned his gaze about to make sure no one else was in earshot.

"Bigfoot," he whispered.

Mort drove me back to Hill House through winds that rattled his SUV the whole way, threatening its precarious perch on the slick roads.

"So, what do you think about our star witness, Mrs. F.?"

"Well, he must have seen *something*."

Mort seemed to be enjoying himself at my expense. "But not Bigfoot."

"No, not Bigfoot."

He sighed. "I should have retired to a big city instead of a small town. I hate small towns."

"You left a big city."

"Well, maybe I should have stayed in New York."

"But then you never would have met me," I reminded him.

Mort dropped me off at the curb fronting Hill House and insisted on seeing me up the walk to make sure I didn't slip, with the storm really starting to intensify. The wind was practically lifting me off my feet, which left me glad I'd opted for my lace-up winter boots that morning.

"I'm going back to the station to do some more digging on Loomis Winslow before the storm gets really bad."

We were both kicking the snow from our path, feeling the snap of the biting wind we fought the whole way to the main entrance of the Hill House hotel. "What do you call this, Mort?"

*   *   *

I'd barely shaken my arms out of my bulky parka when I spotted a woman rising from one of the lobby's beautiful antique armchairs.

"It's true, then," she said, beaming. "You really do live here."

I glanced about to make sure she wasn't referring to someone else, then forced a smile. The woman had a casual elegance about her, expertly dressed and wearing fashionable heels in spite of the weather. If I didn't know better, I'd say she was dressed this way in expectation of making my acquaintance since, when I'd first spotted her upon passing through the entrance, she looked as if she was waiting for someone.

"Will you sign my book, Mrs. Fletcher?" the woman asked, extending a copy of my latest hardcover along with a pen.

I could tell by the bend of the spine that my fan had already read it.

"Nothing I enjoy more than signing a book after the fact," I said, smiling genuinely.

"I've read them all, each and every one. Some twice, a few even more times. When we scheduled the wedding up here in Cabot Cove, I swear I had no idea. Call it a fortunate coincidence." The woman's gaze drifted out the windows facing the front of the building. "Although this storm is proving to be anything but fortunate."

Then I remembered hearing Hill House had been rented out for a wedding currently scheduled for Saturday at the Cabot Cove Country Club. I say "currently" because this was

Thursday, and given the severity of the storm, there was no guarantee the club would even be able to open forty-eight hours from now. We Mainers might be a hardy bunch, but three feet of snow was certain to test even our mettle.

I stowed my wet parka over the back of another nearby chair, feeling instantly guilty for dampening the fabric. Pen and book in hand, I gazed down at the woman, who was several inches shorter than my five feet eight inches, even in her heels. She looked to be in her early to mid-sixties, though she boasted the platinum blond hair color of a woman half that age. The color looked natural on her and the designer clothes that I suspected were her normal garb, and not donned to impress me, fit her petite frame like a second skin. She had the look of money about her, balanced by a warm demeanor and pleasant smile.

"Who should I make it out to?" I asked her.

"Oh, of course. Listen to me, chatting away I'm so nervous. Constance Mulroy. Make it out to Constance, please. No, make that Connie, because that's what my friends call me."

I read the inscription out loud, since my penmanship suffered as a result of composing it while standing. "For Connie— Too bad you didn't save this for the storm. Here's hoping for better weather when my next book comes out! Keep reading! J. B. Fletcher."

She smiled from ear to ear as I handed her book back to her. "You just made all this worthwhile, even if the wedding has to be rescheduled. My son and future daughter-in-law," she added.

"I'd heard a wedding party had rented the place out, save for my suite, of course."

"I can't wait to tell the rest of the board of the library as soon as I'm home."

"Seems we have something in common, Mrs. Mulroy."

"Please, call me Connie."

"Well, Connie, I happen to chair the local Friends of the Library group here in Cabot Cove."

She grinned again. "And I'm vice-chair of the Library Advisory Council at Brown University. I must check to see if your first editions are housed in our collections at the John Hay Library."

I felt a bit smaller than I had just a few moments ago. "If not, I'm sure we could do something about that, and make sure they're all signed to boot."

"Really? You'd make me a star." She reached out and squeezed my shoulder with her free hand, the other clutching her signed book protectively against her side. "Thank you, Mrs. Fletcher."

"It's Jessica. And inscribing your book was my pleasure— believe me."

"I wasn't talking about that. I was talking about providing me some consolation in the wake of the debacle this whole wedding has become. I warned those kids not to tempt fate in February, but they wouldn't listen because none of the more obvious locales were available when my son popped the question just last month. Even said a bit of snow would add to the occasion."

Her gaze drifted out the window again, the snow beginning to cake over the edges of the glass, melting from the heat inside to form what looked like a crystal spider's web.

"Though I sincerely doubt this was what they had in mind," my newfound friend continued. "Would you believe they haven't even arrived yet, the future bride and groom, for their own rehearsal dinner?"

"Have you tried calling them?"

"I've misplaced my cell phone. Of all the times . . . I tried the landline in my room, but it went straight to voice mail." She gazed downward, suddenly looking shy and maybe a bit embarrassed. "I wasn't waiting for you in the lobby, Mrs. Fletcher—"

"Jessica."

"—I was waiting for them. Doing the nervous-mother thing, if you know what I mean."

I nodded politely, even though I didn't, save for my nephew Grady's wedding. Raising him through much of his youth alongside my late husband, Frank, was as close as I came to motherhood and remained one of the most fulfilling experiences of my life.

"They may end up getting married right here at Hill House with the twelve of us the sole attendees," Constance Mulroy continued.

"Twelve?"

"The wedding party. You wouldn't happen to know a priest, reverend, minister, or rabbi we could corral on short notice, would you?"

"No, but you could ask the hotel manager, Seamus McGilray. Perhaps hotel managers have the same power as captains at sea, at least during a blizzard."

She grinned. "I just might do that, Jessica. Looks like it's going to be just the immediate families and two of the couple's mutual friends anyway. All fortunately present and accounted for in preparation for the rehearsal dinner tonight, which was just canceled because of the state of emergency that's been declared."

"What about having it here at Hill House instead?" I suggested.

Constance Mulroy's eyes widened. "I hadn't gotten that far in my thinking, but what a wonderful idea. Could you introduce me to this Mr. McGinty?"

"It's McGilray, and of course I can. He keeps an apartment in the basement, so he's not going anywhere anyway. We can also see if he can brush up on his mastery of wedding ceremonies."

She switched the book from her right arm to her left and took my hand like an old friend. "On one condition, Jessica."

"What's that?"

"That you join us for dinner."

"I'd be delighted, Connie. Thank you. Now," I said, taking her by the arm, "what do you say we go find Mr. McGilray and see what can be done with the menu for tonight?"

Her eyes moistened a bit and she dabbed them with a tissue plucked from her shoulder bag. "I don't know how to thank you, Jessica—I just don't. With all that's happened . . ."

I let that unfinished remark pass and took her arm in both my hands. "You'll have a wonderful story to tell your grandchildren."

"Perhaps I could convince you to write it."

"Not unless there's murder involved, and that's one thing that won't be on the menu tonight."

Constance Mulroy smiled, and I smiled back.

If only we'd known . . .

Chapter Six

Constance Mulroy and I were still smiling, off toward the front desk in search of Hill House manager and part owner Seamus McGilray, when a tall, gray-haired man dressed in a sport jacket that showcased an ascot exposed under his collar brushed past us. I thought I heard my new friend Constance mutter, "Ugh . . ." before the tall man's voice drowned everything else out.

"I'm Doyle Castavette, and I'm most disappointed in the furnishings at your so-called hotel here," he snapped at the young woman alone behind the reception desk.

She forced a smile. "I'm sorry to hear that, sir. How can I assist you?"

Doyle Castavette produced a tiny hotelier-packaged soap from his pocket. When he laid it on the counter I could see the wrapping had been torn open and peeled back.

"Old and stale. I would think a hotel that purports to be a

luxury, five-star establishment could do better than this." His hand, defined by long, slender fingers that reminded me of a pianist's, dipped back into the same pocket, coming out this time with similarly tiny bottles of hotel-packaged shampoo and conditioner. "You notice these have been opened?"

"I do, sir," the young woman said, fighting to maintain hold of her smile.

"But they weren't opened by me. Tell me, young lady, is it the habit of this establishment to expect guests to use leftovers in the bathroom? Need I check the glasses to make sure they've been washed?"

The young woman, whose name tag identified her as JANE and whom I knew as Janey Ryland, remained conciliatory. "I'll let the manager know about both these issues and have replacements sent up to your room immediately, Mr. Cassavette."

"That's Castavette, and given what you're charging our wedding guests for rooms, I expect you should know the college from which I graduated and my entire bio from the latest *Who's Who*."

"Again, sir, I do apologize. Is there anything else I can do for you at this time?" Jane asked, clearly hoping there wasn't.

"Not at present, but I'm quite certain something will come up. I haven't checked the bed linens yet. I'm not expecting much."

"I'm at your service should anything with the linens or anything else arise."

Without uttering a speck of thanks, Doyle Castavette swung around in a huff, finding himself face-to-face with Constance Mulroy.

"Ingratiating as always, I see, Doyle," she said, the bite of her words tempered somewhat by her warm smile.

"Is it too much to ask for an establishment to handle the mere basics of its job?"

"Any word from your daughter?" Connie asked him.

"I was just going to ask you the same about your son."

"I'll take that as a no. I'm starting to find myself concerned that we haven't heard from them since just after their plane landed, the last one before the airport was closed."

"Could be Allison has tried to call, but I've been having trouble connecting to the hotel Wi-Fi," Castavette said, making sure his voice was loud enough for Janey behind the reception desk to hear, before his eyes fell on me. "Is this another member of the hotel staff you've acquainted yourself with?"

Constance Mulroy angled her frame to better introduce me. "Not at all. This is Jessica Fletcher, the famous mystery writer."

"Mystery writer?" Castavette said disparagingly.

"*Famous* mystery writer," Connie repeated for good measure, holding up her signed copy of my latest hardcover.

Castavette didn't give it a first look, never mind a second. "Well, someone has to write them, I suppose."

I extended my hand. "A pleasure to meet you, Mr. Castavette. And congratulations on your daughter's marriage."

"Save your congratulations," he said to me, before returning all of his attention to my newfound friend. "I'm starting to believe Allison finally wised up and realized she could do far better than that ne'er-do-well son of yours. How many scrapes with the law has he had, again?"

"Traffic tickets hardly qualify as scrapes with the law, Doyle."

"But one of them was a DUI, as I recall. Good thing your family owns an insurance company among its ambitious holdings. I'm sure that's the only reason he can still drive after the accident killed one person and crippled another."

I felt Connie stiffen next to me. "Daniel was exonerated of those charges."

"Then I guess it's also a good thing that the Mulroy family maintains an army of lawyers on call, though I suspect they're all busy tending to the mess left by your husband. I only wish I'd thrown him off the Brooklyn Bridge myself, given the fortune he stole from me."

I could feel Constance Mulroy tightening up at that, embarrassed. She had the look of a woman who badly wanted to be somewhere else in that moment—*anywhere* else.

"I was glad to see the authorities no longer consider you a person of interest," Castavette resumed.

"Thank you for that much, Doyle."

"You know how you can make good on this, Constance? By making me reasonably whole, like you promised."

Connie grew red faced at Doyle Castavette's raising that issue in front of an outsider like me, airing such dirty laundry in plain view.

"I told you I was doing everything I could, and I am," she said. "I've even—"

She stopped abruptly there, clearly about to share something better left between the two of them.

"And let's face it, Doyle," she resumed instead. "The only

difference between my husband's investment scam and your shenanigans in real estate is that Heath Mulroy got caught."

Castavette stiffened, looking like he badly wanted to respond, until his eyes fell on me again. And with that, he brushed past us, just missing my sweater.

"Pleasant man," I commented to Constance, after he'd disappeared into the elevator.

"You can't choose your relatives, Jessica, and you can't choose your in-laws either. I have to grin and bear it for my son. You've heard of the scandal," she said, her voice lowered to a tone that suggested regret and dismay. "That my husband swindled investors out of millions of dollars."

"You didn't say 'allegedly,'" I noted, indeed familiar with the case, though not making the connection with the name Mulroy until that moment.

"Because it's true. He was guilty and didn't have the courage to face his accusers. Jumped off the Brooklyn Bridge instead and left the rest of us—the twins and me—to clean up his mess."

I'd heard about that sad end to the story as well. "Your son Daniel has a twin?"

"Fraternal. They look about as much alike as you and I."

I smiled at her. "I'll take that as a compliment."

"Oh, I don't know. Your millions of readers must be more than happy with your appearance," Constance said, smiling as she spun the book around to flash the back-cover author photo my way.

"J. B. Fletcher," I said, referring to the name I wrote under, "doesn't age, so the fact that photo is over ten years old suits her just fine. *Jessica* Fletcher, on the other hand . . ."

I completed my remark with a shrug.

"I really am growing nervous about the whereabouts of Daniel and Allison, especially with the storm intensifying."

My new friend was right. Gazing out the spacious windows that adorned the lobby revealed a scene stitched solely in white. From this distance nothing else was visible—not a tree, neighboring building, or, of course, passing car, given the conditions. The storm had swept into our little hamlet with all the ferocity that had been predicted, no doubt feeding off the ocean to refuel itself to reach that dreaded forecast of upwards of three feet. Looking at the storm now, with the last of the meager light rapidly fading from the sky, I began to wonder whether that amount might yet prove an underestimation, given that at least ten inches had piled up already.

"Why don't I call our sheriff to see about reports of any accidents in the time since their plane landed that may have closed the main roads? How long ago was that now?"

Constance Mulroy's expression brightened. "Between four and five hours."

I started to reach for my cell phone, then remembered I'd left it inside the parka I'd draped across a nearby chair back. I was moving to retrieve it when a pair of sprightly older women pranced across the lobby in matching tracksuits.

"The Sprague sisters," Constance said softly, a bit put off by their approach under the circumstances. "First cousins I practically grew up with. As you can see, Jessica, twins run in the family."

"Identical, in this case."

Constance smiled. "You noticed."

She cleared her throat at the sisters' arrival. "Jessica, I'd like you to meet Olivia and Beatrice Sprague. Olivia and Beatrice, this is the famous mystery writer Jessica Fletcher."

"Liv and Bea to our friends, Mrs. Fletcher. I'm Liv."

"And I'm Bea."

They were indeed identical, right down to every woven curl and fabric seam. They'd even approached in lockstep, their hair dyed a uniform auburn shade that might well have come from the same bottle. In sneakers, they barely stretched to five feet tall, with bright smiles they seemed to flash in perfect unison as well.

"In that case, I'm Jessica," I said, shaking both their hands tenderly.

"And you write mysteries?" from Bea.

"What did Connie just say?" from Liv.

"That she's a mystery writer."

"Then why bother asking a question—"

"I already knew the answer. It was to make—"

"Conversation," Liv completed for Bea this time. "You're always making conversation. Perhaps you should try making—"

"Sense instead." Bea's turn. "You say that to me at least—"

"Once every day. And I'll keep doing so until you stop. Or—"

"Until we die. You say that every day, too. I hope I—"

"Go first. Sometimes I hope you do, too."

"Humph . . ."

"Humph . . ."

They both turned toward me, as if responding to some unspoken cue. Listening to them speak was like watching a Ping-Pong match, my head snapping from side to side to follow each.

"Nice to meet you, Jessica," they said in unison before turning their attention back to Constance Mulroy.

"We've been to the gym, dear," Bea told her.

"We moved our daily constitutional inside," Liv added.

"On account of the weather."

"It's frightful out there."

"Any word—"

"From the kids?" Liv completed this time.

"Not a peep. But I'm sure they'll be arriving soon," Connie said, sounding as brave as she could manage. "After all, who misses their own wedding?"

"Rehearsal dinner, in this case," Bea corrected. "And we're—"

"Famished already. But where will we be—"

"Eating, with the original venue closed for the evening?"

The Sprague sisters looked at each other before both turned back toward their first cousin.

"Mrs. Fletcher and I are working on that now."

"We're hoping to arrange the dinner here in Hill House's Sea Captains Room," I picked up when Constance finished; I realized we were copying Liv and Bea's speech cadence.

"We'll let you get to it, then," Liv offered.

"Yes, we will." Bea nodded.

"Quite the show, aren't they?" Constance said after the Sprague sisters had taken their leave, still chatting away and completing each other's thoughts. "Neither ever married, and they've lived together their whole lives."

"They seem happy," I said, watching them enter the elevator.

"Why shouldn't they be, without a care in the world and with more money than they'll ever be able to spend?"

Constance gave me a look.

"My call to the sheriff—of course!" I said, and finally fished my cell phone from an inside pocket of my parka.

Before I could dial, though, Seamus McGilray emerged from the back office behind the reception desk with a snow shovel in hand.

"Seamus," I called to him.

He stopped halfway across the lobby and turned. "Ah, Mrs. Fletcher, nasty spot of weather we're having."

I approached him with Constance Mulroy riding my wake. "I wonder if I might add something of a complication to it."

He lowered the shovel to the lobby floor and leaned against it. "Anything that delays me shoveling the walk for the first of many times this evening is welcome, complication or not."

"You've met Constance Mulroy, of course," I said, stepping aside so she could draw even with me.

"Not personally, but Hill House is very happy to be hosting your family, miss, though I apologize on behalf of the state of Maine for the turn in the weather."

"That's what we'd like to speak to you about, Seamus," I picked up, "specifically about the possibility of moving the rehearsal dinner here to Hill House, with Cabot Cove Country Club closed."

I'd expected any number of responses from Seamus, all of them with some level of resistance to the added work my request would cause his staff. Much to my surprise, though, he grinned broadly and nodded.

"It would be our esteemed pleasure to stand in as your host, Mrs. Mulroy. Perhaps Mrs. Fletcher has told you about our splendid Sea Captains Room, and while we may have to be creative with the menu, I'm sure we can accommodate your family in a way that makes you proud."

Constance looked instantly lighter, so relieved she practically melted into the floor with a sigh. "I don't know what to say, Mr. McGilray, besides thank you, thank you from the bottom of my heart."

"Don't thank me until the meal is set, miss, because with no food order coming in today, it might be a tuna casserole for the lot of you."

"I'm sure whatever you serve will be wonderful, sir."

"How many in the party?"

"Fourteen," Constance answered. "Well, twelve now, but fourteen by the time dinner is served, once the bride and groom arrive."

I watched Seamus's gaze drift out the window over Constance Mulroy's shoulder, his look of concern saying it all before he banished it from his expression and smiled reassuringly. "Then dinner for fourteen it is."

She squeezed my arm. "I actually meant fifteen, since Mrs. Fletcher will be joining us."

"Only if it doesn't cause you any additional bother, Seamus."

"Fifteen it is, then!" he said happily, the smile slipping from his face as he readied his shovel for the rigors ahead. "Now, if you ladies would be kind enough to excuse me, duty calls. Got to make sure the walk is clear when the bride and groom arrive, don't we? This might be as close as they come to walking up the aisle for some time, if the forecast holds true."

I had to admit that the opportunity to attend the dinner was far more appealing than the prospect of waiting out the worst of the storm alone in my room, and I found myself ever so grateful for my chance encounter with Constance Mulroy.

"Let me make that call to Sheriff Metzger," I said to my newfound friend and moved over to the lobby's side wall to view the storm from that angle.

The outside was already an unbroken sheet of white, the sky starting to dump vast curtains of snow in relentless fashion. I couldn't see much beyond ten or so feet and could only imagine the same scene once all the light faded from the sky. Nothing moved outside except for what shifted in the wind, which would pick up once the storm hit its peak that evening. I tried to envision how I'd describe such a scene in one of my books and drew an utter blank. It was almost as if the world beyond the window didn't exist anymore, was not just buried but swallowed up.

I shook myself from my trance and dialed Mort's cell phone. When it rang unanswered, I waited for a few moments and tried again, then a third and fourth time, before he finally answered.

"I'm a little busy here, Mrs. F.," he finally responded in a gruff, impatient voice. "In case you haven't heard, we could be looking at four feet of snow now. Tell me again why I took this job?"

"Sorry to pile more onto your plate, Mort, but we've got an issue here likely related to the storm."

"Where's 'here'?"

"Hill House. Did I tell you about that wedding party that's making this home through the weekend?"

"No."

"Well, the bride and groom haven't shown up for their own rehearsal dinner yet. According to the mother of the future groom, the last time they checked in was after their plane had landed in Portland, going on five hours ago now."

"Storm was just getting started then."

"That's the point," I told him.

"Wait, Mrs. F. You said they flew into *Portland*?"

I felt something flutter in my stomach. "What's going on, Mort?"

"Remember the Lexus SUV we found abandoned?"

"With Pennsylvania plates? Sure. Why?"

"It's a rental, registered to Hertz."

Chapter Seven

T he jetport in Portland has a Hertz," I said softly.

"But it's closed, along with the jetport itself, thanks to the state of emergency and travel ban issued by the governor. I'll see if I can get anything out of Hertz's eight hundred number, but I'm not expecting much based on my past experience pumping some call service tech in the Philippines or India for information related to a potential crime scene," Mort said.

I looked across the lobby to find Constance Mulroy conversing with another woman, who must have been part of either her or the bride's family. Her back was to me, which spared her from seeing the drawn look of concern that had claimed my expression.

I did some quick figuring in my head. "The timing checks out perfectly, based on when Constance Mulroy said she last heard from her son."

"Who's Constance Mulroy?"

"Mother of the groom."

"That's not good. But we can't be sure, Mrs. F., not yet."

"And a few hours from now, if the couple still hasn't shown up?"

"I can't order a search of the woods, not in this storm. I already told you that."

"What were they running from, Mort?" I asked myself as much as him. "Where did they go?"

"And who was sitting in the backseat, dragging gravel on his shoes that matched the Cabot Manufacturing Company parking lot?"

"Or *her* shoes," I corrected.

"Point taken."

"Murder doesn't discriminate between genders," I reminded him.

"Of course, according to Hank Weathers, we're actually looking for Bigfoot." I could feel the weight of the storm in his voice then and in the guttural groan that followed. "You need to keep this quiet, Jessica, at least until we're able to gather more information."

I gazed across the lobby at Constance Mulroy. I could feel the icy chill permeating through the window at my back, could feel the whole frame buckle under a sudden gust of wind that lashed a fresh blanket of snow against the plate glass.

"And how long will that take? The wedding's scheduled for Saturday, and the rehearsal dinner for the immediate family is tonight."

"Where?"

"Seamus McGilray's going to host it right here at Hill House, thankfully."

"Please tell me everyone's accounted for."

"Everyone except the guests of honor."

"I know what you're thinking, Mrs. F.," Mort said after a pause.

I was still gazing across the lobby at Constance Mulroy, wondering exactly how I was going to keep this news from her. "We need to find out who rented that Lexus SUV from Hertz, Mort," I said to him, fearing it had indeed been the missing couple, Daniel Mulroy and Allison Castavette.

"I could get the president of the country on the phone quicker than the president of Hertz. I'd wager somebody had good reason to remove the contents of the Lexus's glove compartment, which must have included the rental agreement."

"Same man who killed Loomis Winslow, Mort?"

"Or woman," he quickly corrected, just as I would have.

"Or Bigfoot, in the mind of Hank Weathers," I added.

"I can't see us learning much more until the storm subsides tomorrow. Wherever people are hunkered down now is where they'll be staying for a while. That includes this wedding party. No reason I can see for scaring these people more than they must already be with the bride and groom both no-shows."

"I wouldn't even know what to say to the parents." I stopped, recalling the squad car's flashing lights illuminating the Lexus abandoned on the side of the road with its front doors open and gravel on a backseat floor mat. "Why'd they run, Mort?

What or whom were they trying to get away from, risking ending up lost or stranded in the woods during a storm like this?"

"We don't know it was them, Jessica," Mort reminded me. "There were plenty of other flights that landed before the jetport closed. Any number of those passengers could have just as easily rented that Lexus."

"And how many of them would have reason to come all the way to Cabot Cove with a killer blizzard bearing down?"

"Need I remind you that you've been wrong before, Mrs. F.?"

"Not about something like this."

Fearing the worst, I put on the bravest face I could before approaching Constance Mulroy, just as her conversation with the woman she'd been speaking with looked to be ending.

"And who have we here?" the woman asked behind a blinding sheen of ultrabright teeth.

"This is Jessica Fletcher, Henley," my newfound friend said to her, "the famous mystery writer. We have Mrs. Fletcher to thank for the ability to use Hill House for the rehearsal dinner tonight."

"You have the hotel manager, Seamus McGilray, to thank far more than me, but it's greatly appreciated nonetheless."

"Jessica, this is Henley Lavarnay, Doyle Castavette's wife."

"Ex-wife," the woman hastily corrected, smiling pleasantly, in stark contrast to her former husband's demeanor. "Doyle and I are thankfully divorced. It's not like my daughter not to call," she continued with an anxious edge creeping into her voice. "Constance here was just telling me you hoped to inquire about the children with your local sheriff."

"I have, and there's no news. That's a good thing, given that if Sheriff Metzger had anything to share it would normally be something bad at this point," I informed the mothers of the bride and groom, letting go unmentioned for now the unsubstantiated facts involving the vehicle the missing couple might have rented at Portland Jetport.

"And what time do you expect Hill House will be prepared to serve our dinner?"

"I believe the hotel manager, Mr. McGilray, mentioned something about eight o'clock, just over three hours from now. And I'll bet the bride and groom will be accounted for by that time."

It was a bet I would have lost.

I finally returned to my suite and found myself staring out the window into the storm as night solidified its hold over the scene. Our childhood memories inevitably exaggerate the size and scope of the storms we watched through the window in the same fashion I was doing now. Part of that tendency is due to childhood exaggeration, but an equal part is because we were smaller and a foot of snow seemed like a lot more than a foot.

Watching Hill House's outdoor floodlights struggling to make a dent in the snow-swept scene brought my mind back to the fate of the missing bride and groom, Allison Castavette and Daniel Mulroy. Their being on the road as the storm began to intensify was cause enough for concern on its own. And now Mort had added the very real possibility that they had been the people who'd fled the front seat of the rented Lexus abandoned on the side of the road. Had they been running from whoever was seated behind them? Could it have been Loomis Winslow's killer? And I don't mean Bigfoot either.

Something about that thought stoked a memory of something awry in the Lexus's backseat, something I couldn't quite hold on to then or recapture now. I was starting to think the key to this whole mystery, perhaps including the disappearance of Daniel Mulroy and Allison Castavette, was whatever Winslow was investigating and who'd hired him to do so. Harry McGraw hadn't come up with much yet on his fellow private investigator, but the fact that Winslow specialized in the forensics side of financial misdeeds was plenty in itself. Indeed, it was Socrates who once said, "He who is not contented with what he has would not be contented with what he would like to have." In my experience, greed trumps revenge or passion as the primary motive for murder, and I steadfastly believed that Winslow must have been onto something likely connected to the financial scandal that involved Constance Mulroy's husband and had led to his suicide.

I turned on the television and went to the Weather Channel, noting the feed at the bottom of the screen read FOUR FEET OF SNOW PREDICTED FOR MAINE AND NORTHERN NEW ENGLAND. I'd just plopped down on the couch to watch the storm both on the television and out the window when I heard the door to my suite rattle. I figured the rattle must be a product of the wind, until there was a click of the locking system engaging, and then the door slowly opened.

I bounced up off the couch and spotted a man in his late twenties, early thirties maybe, easing himself through the door, only to freeze when his gaze fell upon me.

"Oh," he said, sounding genuinely surprised, "I must have the wrong room."

I looked at the key card still clutched in his hand and made sure he could see me reaching for the hotel phone, ready to press zero. "Yes, that must be it," I said, opting for discretion as opposed to valor, given the circumstances. "They've been having trouble with the computer at the front desk lately," I added as nonchalantly as I could manage. "Checking guests into rooms that are already occupied."

The young man slipped the key card into his pocket. "Well, that explains it. Terribly sorry to have startled you. I think I'll go raise some trouble down at the front desk."

"Are you here for the wedding?" I asked him.

"Wedding?" He shook his head. "No, ma'am, I'm just a stranded traveler who found his way here just in time. No night to be going anywhere."

"You're lucky you made it this far. But if you don't mind . . ."

The man realized he was still halfway through my door. "Yes, of course. A thousand pardons again," he said, bowing slightly. "I hope I don't find a stranger in my own room, once I'm properly checked in."

I smiled at him, glad he couldn't see my knees shaking, and

I stormed to the door and bolted the lock as soon as it closed behind him. My heart was hammering against my chest and I felt suddenly short of breath. Though I'm not easily startled, having a stranger trip my lock and find his way into my suite was unnerving, to say the least. The wrong-room story might have made some sense if he'd had any luggage with him. Not only that, but the man wasn't wearing a coat, indicating he must already be settled in the hotel. I'd heard only members of the wedding party had kept their reservations, but it was conceivable Hill House had rented out a few rooms to strangers like this, given the storm's severity bearing the very real potential of stranding travelers at its doorstep.

I knew I should call and report the incident to Seamus McGilray right away, but I didn't dare disturb him, given his commitment to fashion a dinner party for thirteen—fifteen, hopefully—at the last minute. I didn't bother calling Mort either since he, too, already had enough on his hands, more than he could handle. Gazing out the window at the snow piling up fast and hard on the road fronting Hill House beyond, I pictured Ethan Cragg's famous fiery temper being stoked by his best-laid plowing strategy going for naught. No plan could keep up with the fall of snow the Weather Channel was saying could reach five inches per hour at times overnight. And I think I caught the meteorologist currently on-screen showcasing a map of New England with certain areas of Maine now caught in a snow band capable of dumping even five feet of snow, never mind four.

And Cabot Cove was located smack-dab in one of those areas.

I retrieved my cell phone from the desk where I'd placed it and I pressed the number for Harry McGraw.

"You must be lonely," he greeted.

"What makes you say that?"

"Why else would you call me in the middle of a blizzard? I hear you could be looking at five feet now."

"Are you watching the Weather Channel?"

"No, that's on cable. I can't afford cable anymore on account of too many clients who don't pay their bills."

"Please tell me you've uncovered something more on Loomis Winslow."

"I've uncovered something more on Loomis Winslow."

"Really?"

"No, but you asked me to tell you I had. And we only spoke, what, a few hours ago?"

"Things have gotten a bit more complicated in those few hours."

"You mean, besides the storm that's hammering you?"

Stressing the possible disappearance of the bride and groom, I filled Harry in on everything I'd learned since we'd spoken that afternoon at the scene of the abandoned Lexus.

"Hey, if I'd known what marriage was going to be like, little lady, I would have hightailed it before the *I do*s, too."

"This couple apparently hightailed it together."

"But you can't even be sure it was their rental, at this point."

"The rental was a Lexus, Harry. That's rarefied air, and I get the feeling from the wedding party that both sides are no strangers to money."

"Hmm," Harry uttered. "Loomis Winslow?"

"Does tend to be moving in that direction, doesn't it? I believe we're on the same page," I told him.

"Except I don't write. I barely read. I'm more of a movie guy, and right now I'm seeing the same thing you're seeing."

"There's something else, Harry," I said, and proceeded to tell him what I'd been able to gather from Constance Mulroy and Doyle Castavette's tense conversation in the lobby, specifically the notion of her future in-law being swindled by her late husband.

A pause followed, during which the connection may have been broken, but his voice returned. "You want to tell me what else is bothering you, little lady? Besides this murder, the storm, and these financial shenanigans, I mean."

"How do you know there's something else bothering me?"

"Well, I am a detective, so it's kind of my business to know things."

I took a deep breath, amazed by Harry's intuitive skills, which were second only to his investigative ones. "Someone just walked into my room."

"What do you mean, walked into your room?"

"He used what must have been some kind of master key card. Claimed he'd just gotten the room wrong, which of course doesn't hold any water at all. Is that even possible—the master key card, I mean?"

"Not only possible, Jess, but becoming increasingly common," Harry said in his professional, as opposed to typically dour, voice. "Cybersecurity experts have only recently begun to acknowledge a new hack whereby millions of hotel rooms around the world have become vulnerable to exactly what you just experienced. Did you know a single lock manufacturer is responsible for the electronic locks that secure the bulk of the world's hotel rooms, including the major chains?"

"To tell you the truth, I never even thought about it."

"Of course not, because like everybody else you swipe or flash your card and the door opens. What you don't know is that a thief could do the very same thing. It isn't exactly rocket science either. Pretty simple process that involves finding a key card, any key card, of the hotel in question, using a cheap piece of hardware combined with custom-built software to read the card and search for the master key code, and then copying the master key information onto a new or existing card. That card is specific to an individual hotel and would allow a thief to access any room in the building."

I was about to respond, but Harry kept right on going.

"These thieves, hackers, or whatever you want to call them have become experts on knowing exactly when to enter a room and which rooms are empty at any given time."

"That wasn't the case with my thief."

"Good thing it was amateur hour. You tell Mort about this?"

"He's got a bit on his mind right now, Harry, and I don't think he could even get to Hill House from the sheriff's station if he wanted to."

"Maybe I should take a drive up."

"You wouldn't get past the New Hampshire line."

"Then I'll ski my way from there."

"You don't know how to ski, Harry," I reminded him.

"First time for everything, little lady."

*　　*　　*

Harry was right. I'd called him because I was nervous, un-settled. I suppose I'd called in the hope of gaining new infor-mation that would take my mind off a man using a hacked key card to break into my suite. I tried to imagine the kind of thief who targeted wedding parties and other venues where people were likely to gather with expensive jewelry, gifts, and plenty of cash. Wait for everyone to depart for dinner and then sweep up their valuables while they were gone. Of course, he couldn't know who was whom or in which exact rooms they were stay-ing. The young man's mistake had been not to knock to ensure the room's real occupant, me in this case, wasn't present.

I realized I really should call Seamus to report the incident, given all the potential targets staying at the hotel right now. Just as I suspected, though, according to Janey at the front desk, he was busy in the kitchen supervising dinner prepara-tions and hadn't even taken his walkie-talkie with him. I'd bring him up to date at dinner, hoping the thief, whose ap-pearance I'd committed to memory, didn't use that same mas-ter key card to access any other rooms before then.

I needed to shower and change clothes before dining with the wedding party, but I couldn't separate myself from the Weather Channel. Jim Cantore, the network's extremely rec-ognizable correspondent who based himself in the center of the worst America's weather had to offer, was doing spots live from right here in Maine, fifty miles down the coast from Cabot Cove. As bad as it looked outside my window, it looked even worse from his vantage point, and as ominous and fore-boding as it got, forecasters were in 100 percent agreement on one thing:

The worst was yet to come, and that worst was going to be something truly historic.

One good thing about my house still being reconstructed in the wake of the fire that had nearly claimed my life was that I wouldn't have to worry about getting my walk shoveled and driveway plowed. I have any number of friends and acquain-tances who've traded homes like my beloved one for condo living, and times like this made me better understand the na-ture of their decisions.

As night tightened its hold over the windswept snows, I finally pulled away from the television and readied myself for the evening to come. I was used to being in rooms where I knew practically no one and was actually looking forward to this particular occasion not being focused on me as a typical signing, talk, or benefit would be. I was grateful for Constance Mulroy's invitation even more than I had been initially, as I needed a break from the storm I knew would remain all con-suming for several days to come.

Just before eight o'clock I took the stairs down to the first floor, where the Sea Captains Room was located off the lobby just down the hall from the elevators, hoping against hope that the bride and groom had finally arrived. As I entered, though, my quick count put the number already gathered for cocktails and hors d'oeuvres still at ten, which told me they hadn't and that, in fact, two of the guests already registered had yet to arrive as well.

I surveyed the room, cataloging whom I knew from the lobby earlier, and spotted someone I recognized for another reason entirely.

It was the young man who'd used that master key card to enter my suite!

Chapter Eight

J essica!" I heard and turned with a start to see Constance
Mulroy approaching, forcing my eyes off the young man I
was convinced was a thief.

"Connie, you look absolutely lovely," I managed.

She forced a smile. "Well, I don't feel it. But there is some
good news to report."

"What's that?"

"Mark heard from Daniel!"

"Mark?"

"Oh, that's right, you haven't met the groom's twin brother.
That's him over there," Connie said, tilting her gaze toward
the bar.

I turned in that direction and spotted a man with shapeless
clothes and two days of beard growth handing his glass to the
bartender for a refill. The bartender had barely extended it
across the portable bar when Mark Mulroy snatched it from

his grasp and guzzled it down in one single, fluid motion. I also swept my gaze across the Sprague sisters, Doyle Castavette, and his former wife, Henley Lavarnay, and did my best to avoid the gaze of the thief on the other side of the room, who I didn't believe had noticed me yet. That meant I was now acquainted, at least visually, with half the members of the wedding party so far in attendance.

"So, where are they?" I asked her. "The future bride and groom, I mean."

"That's just it, Jessica. The future's no longer so certain. According to Mark, Daniel and Allison got stranded forty miles short of Cabot Cove and checked into one of those roadside motels. That's the good news. The bad news is, Mark says his brother told him they're, quote, reassessing the situation."

"What does that mean?"

"The wedding being in jeopardy, I imagine, as if one or both of them have gotten cold feet."

I nodded. "Literally, as it turns out. Well, if nothing else, that explains why neither of them contacted you or Allison's parents directly," I said, not bothering to add how relieved I was to learn they weren't the two people who'd fled that abandoned Lexus SUV.

"I made Mark promise not to tell anyone else," Connie confessed to me, "at least until the two of them come to their senses. But I can't help fearing the worst."

If only she knew what the worst could have been, I thought to myself.

"To be expected," I said, consoling her. "After all, you're the groom's mother, with an awful lot invested here."

"Not as much as the Castavettes . . . They're footing the bill for the entire wedding." She lowered her voice a pitch. "My late husband left me in a bit of a bad way, Jessica, as you probably got a sense of down in the lobby earlier."

I tried to ease her clear discomfort at broaching the issue. "I'm not all that familiar with what happened and I don't need to be."

"There's not a lot to tell that you couldn't have read in the papers. My husband committed suicide by jumping off the Brooklyn Bridge after his role in a Ponzi scheme was revealed. It hasn't been easy this past year or so, and to add insult to injury, the fact that his body has never been found has kept the whole mess going in a circle. The authorities are convinced he faked his own death to stage an escape."

"And what do you think?"

"That he wasn't smart or brave enough to do any such thing. He killed himself because he was weak and a fraud. I guess I knew that all along, but never let myself admit it. And you know the worst thing? He made my son Daniel complicit in his scheme, too, whether Daniel realized it or not. Heath jumping off that bridge left our son holding the bag and having to deal with the FBI and the Justice Department, who are threatening to prosecute him instead of Heath."

"Mark didn't work in the business, too?"

"He tried, but it wasn't the right fit. He just doesn't have a mind for numbers or money."

"Well," I said casually, "I can certainly relate to that."

"I had the good sense to keep our apartment in my name, since I inherited it from my parents. And I kept their modest trust fund out of his greedy hands as well. Not the product of ill-gotten gains, in other words."

"Thankfully, Connie." I squeezed both her shoulders tenderly. "We're two of a kind, both of us letting ourselves see only the good in people, even if we have to squint really, really hard to do so."

Constance Mulroy sighed, then settled herself with a deep breath, her eyes holding mine warmly as if we'd known each other for far longer than a few hours. It was a good time to change the subject.

"Who's that across the room talking to Beatrice and Olivia?" I asked her, nodding toward the man who'd used that master key card to enter my room.

He was dressed like a cover model and boasted the rugged, harshly masculine looks of an actor.

"Oh, him. That's Doyle and Henley's son, and Allison's brother, Tyler Castavette."

"Your tone suggests you're not a fan, Connie."

Her expression flattened out. "He was born with a silver spoon in his mouth that turned out to be plated instead of sterling. Every family has its own black sheep, and Tyler fits that description to a T," Connie said, lowering her voice as she drew closer to me with a look of concern, and something else I couldn't quite identify, dawning on her features. "Can I confide something in you, Jessica?"

"Of course you can."

She was nearly whispering now, close enough for me to smell the gin on her breath. "Actually, I need your expertise on a sensitive matter, something rather personal involving family."

"I'm hardly the person to ask about that, given I have so little family about myself, at least close by."

"Family secrets, to be specific. I believe you are something of an expert when it comes to secrets."

"Mysteries are full of them, both real and made-up. So are families," I added.

Connie scanned the area about us, as if afraid someone might have overheard that particular comment. "That's what I need to speak with you about," she said, her voice still hushed.

"Of course, but I'm hardly the right person to discuss family secrets with."

"I believe you are in this case, especially given your real specialty."

"Writing mysteries?"

"I was speaking more about solving them. Tell me, Jessica, have you ever solved a crime before it happened?"

"I'm not sure I know what you mean."

Her gaze, suddenly taut with anxiety, bored into mine. "You see, I fear my life may be in—"

"Aunt Constance!" a voice boomed, stopping her from finishing her sentence.

I recoiled as the muscular shape of Tyler Castavette swallowed Connie in a hug without a drop of his drink being spilled.

"How is it I haven't even seen you today until now?"

"Just lucky, I guess," Connie said awkwardly, before her

eyes fixed on me again. "And this is Jessica Fletcher, the famous mystery writer."

Tyler turned my way, not bothering to hide the spark of recognition flashing in his eyes. "We've already met, actually."

"Really?" posed a clearly curious Constance Mulroy.

Tyler responded with his gaze focused on me. "Would you believe the front desk checked me into Mrs. Fletcher's suite by accident?"

"You're kidding!" Connie said, eyes on me again. "Jessica, why didn't you tell me?"

"I was just about to. And we didn't actually meet, did we, Tyler?" I asked, choosing not to mention he'd had no luggage with him when he'd entered my suite.

He extended his hand, bubbling over with charisma to make up for whatever Connie believed he lacked. "Well, we are now. A pleasure, Mrs. Fletcher. I didn't know there was a celebrity staying at the hotel."

"Mrs. Fletcher is living here for a time, while her house is being renovated. We met in the lobby and I invited her to join us for dinner."

"Misery loves company," I said, forcing a smile, "and this storm certainly qualifies there."

"Not to mention being to blame for the bride and groom being no-shows. Did Mark speak to you, Aunt Connie?"

"As a matter of fact, he did, but I wasn't aware he'd shared his phone call from Daniel with anyone else."

"No worries. My lips are sealed," Tyler said, zipping them up with a slash of his finger across his mouth.

He was the kind of young man I'd always had crushes on in my school days, the charming bad boy who carried himself with a swagger that belied his lack of achievement. I found myself glad I hadn't found an opportunity to inform Seamus McGilray about the intruder in my room. The fact that Tyler Castavette was part of the wedding party, brother of the bride-to-be, was reason enough to give him a pass for now, especially in light of my new friendship with Connie. But at some point I'd have to tell her what had transpired, though I wasn't thinking about when.

The hors d'oeuvres table featured a sumptuous selection of the sort that would have taken significant planning to prepare. I had no idea how Seamus and the Hill House kitchen had managed that task while also fashioning an appropriate dinner menu. The help who'd stayed on would now surely be stranded here for the night, as those who remained were fiercely loyal to Seamus and Hill House because the hotel had continued to employ them, going without layoffs even during the most turbulent financial times. The hotel maintained all but its dedicated summer staff year-round, relying on the big bump it received during the summer tourist season to make up for the depleted revenue during the winter months. I doubted Hill House turned much of a profit after the busy season ended; Seamus McGilray probably would've been happy to break even.

For my part, I spent the remainder of the cocktail hour familiarizing myself with the identities of the remaining wedding guests who'd come in early for a rehearsal summarily canceled by the storm. This while the bride and groom were discussing putting a halt to all the festivities. Being cooped up at some roadside motel, imprisoned by the storm, was no way to work out their differences. But who knows? Maybe the opposite extreme would come into effect and the overall impact of being alone and isolated would bring them close together again.

Prepared to crane my neck to keep up with their repartee, I greeted the Sprague sisters, and said a quick hello to both Doyle Castavette and his ex-wife, Henley Lavarnay. I could now cross Tyler Castavette off my list of those I'd yet to meet, and I introduced myself to Daniel's brother, Mark. I also had the opportunity to meet Doyle Castavette's date for the festivities, a woman quite a number of years younger than he whom I found to be surprisingly pleasant. Her name was Virginia Da Salle, and I thought she looked familiar even before I learned she'd carved out a decent career for herself as an actress, playing supporting roles in more than a hundred and fifty films.

"I was actually born Desalle, one word, but switched to two because my first agent thought it would help my career," she confessed.

"Did it work?"

"I didn't land a single role until I found another agent."

Henley's date, meanwhile, arrived late, explaining that he was in the midst of a difficult legal case back home in New York. He walked with the aid of crutches, and I thought I also spotted the telltale bulge of leg braces beneath his baggy trousers. Henley introduced him as Harrison Bak and made it a point to add that he was an esteemed lawyer with any number of high-profile cases and clients to his credit.

"A pleasure to meet you, Mrs. Fletcher. I'm sorry I haven't actually read any of your books, but it's nice to see a face I recognize," he said, no doubt referring to the fact that, like me, he was a virtual stranger here.

"Then I hope you'll sit next to me for dinner, Mr. Bak," I suggested.

"I'd love to. Since neither of us knows the bride and groom very well at all—"

"*Not at all* in my case," I corrected.

"—we'll have to busy ourselves talking about other things. Our many adventures, perhaps."

"I'm afraid mine take place only in my head."

"And mine," Harrison Bak said, casting a subtle glance toward his cane crutches, "are limited to the courtroom. Ever pen a courtroom thriller?"

"Not precisely. But I'm always game for listening to new ideas."

He grinned. "It's settled, then. Perhaps I can serve you up an idea for your next book by the time the main course is served."

That left only three more guests with whom to acquaint myself, two of whom had yet to make their presence known. Before I could approach a young woman who bore a strong resemblance to Constance Mulroy, my attention was drawn to a projection screen flashing a constant loop of pictures featuring both the missing Daniel Mulroy and Allison Castavette from their infant and toddler years onward. One shot that especially grabbed my attention was of fraternal twins Daniel and Mark standing up happily in their respective cribs in the nursery they must have shared. It was a wonderful shot that showed them bubbling over with happiness, distinct in their looks even then.

Just before the slideshow flashed to another picture, something caught my eye. It was some kind of shadow just beyond the farther crib, in which the toddler I had pegged for Mark was standing with his hands grasping the crib's top safety rail. The shadow looked equidistant between his crib and his brother Daniel's. I moved in to see what about the shadow had captured my attention but the loop had moved to the next picture, so I went back to watching the dueling family photos come one after another.

I probably would have waited for the crib shot to come back around, but Seamus McGilray entered the room to ring a traditional dinner bell.

"Dinner," he announced, "is served."

And with that, a procession of the staff who'd stayed on to prepare and serve this meal entered the Sea Captains Room in single file, each bearing a tray holding cups of a luscious lobster bisque as the appetizer. I looked at Seamus and just shook my head in amazement at what he'd managed to pull off. I wondered whether cost had even been discussed with our host for the evening, Constance Mulroy. Seamus was old-school when it came to the treatment of guests, and the hospitable tone he set for Hill House was what had made it feel like a home to me for a number of months.

Under the circumstances, I don't think I've ever enjoyed a meal more, and I knew the experience wasn't one I'd easily forget, given the backdrop of the storm. Luckily the Sea Captains Room had no windows, sparing us the view of nature's wrath in full swing beyond. It was an oasis of sorts, especially for me, since I would otherwise have been stuck in my suite watching both the weather and the Weather Channel, with Jim Cantore as my only company.

I managed to grab a seat next to Harrison Bak, whose late wife, it turned out, had been a big fan of mine. Wealthy beyond imagination, he claimed, but someone who took all her books from the library because she loved going there and had since she was a little girl. I shared my own experiences as chair of the Friends of the Library group in Cabot Cove, and he promised to make a trip here next summer with Henley when the weather promised to be far better.

Summer . . .

It was hard to even picture such a thing in the dreaded conditions of this night.

I managed to check a tenth guest off my list in the person of Lois Mulroy-Dodge, Connie's late husband's niece, whose own husband, Taft Dodge, had perished during a boating accident that had left the newlyweds stranded at sea, found by the Coast Guard too late to save her husband's life. Connie introduced the young woman as the daughter she'd never had, something clearly welcomed by Lois since I'd later learn both her parents had died in a car accident, after which she'd been raised by her aunt and late uncle and been a virtual sister to the twins. I had seldom witnessed a family struck by so much tragedy, the Kennedys, of course, being one that came to mind immediately.

The incredible lobster bisque was followed by a lavish salad of mixed greens, with the promise of Hill House's specialty, sliced tenderloin, still to come. I had no idea how Seamus had come up with such an extravagant menu, and I guessed the only compromise he'd made under the circumstances was not to offer a vegetarian option. None of the guests seemed particularly irked by the presence of two empty chairs at the far end of the table. By my count, we were missing the two parties I believe Connie had referred to as mutual friends of the bride and groom. And I applauded Seamus's good judgment to remove the additional two chairs when it became clear that Daniel Mulroy and Allison Castavette would not be joining us.

Just as I formed that thought, the double doors to the Sea Captains Room burst open and a young couple burst in, covered with snow. The young man's hair was longer than the girl's, and the dampness of their hair and clothes indicated they'd probably been out romping in the storm.

"So sorry we're late," said the young man, his snow-moistened hair bouncing with every stride.

"It's just beautiful out there," the young woman added.

"Faye and Ian," Harrison Bak whispered in my ear, in a somewhat disparaging tone. "Best friends of the bride and groom. Ian's the best man and Faye's the maid of honor."

That surprised me. "Daniel didn't choose his own brother to be his best man?" I asked, gaze tilted toward Mark, who was seated on the other side of the table.

"Ian's the best man," Harrison repeated, leaving it there.

"Any word from the happy couple?" Ian asked those at the table. "Don't tell me they're having second thoughts."

He was looking at Constance Mulroy and her son Mark as he said that, realizing from their expressions that he'd just touched on a clearly sore subject.

"Oh," he added, and then, "I'm sure they'll come to their senses," as if to redeem himself.

"Is there a problem?" Beatrice Sprague posed.

"There's always a problem with young people," her twin sister, Olivia, chimed in.

"How do you know, when you were never—"

"Young? Yes, I was. It was you who was born old."

"At least I had a boyfriend." Olivia.

"No, you didn't." Beatrice.

"Yes, I did."

"Then what was his—"

"Name? I don't remember."

"If he was real, you'd remember." Beatrice looked across the table for a sympathetic eye and caught Lois Mulroy-Dodge's gaze. "I guess making him up was better than nothing."

"How would you know?" Olivia challenged. "You never even tried."

"Now, now," the ebullient Ian soothed, crouching between the sisters and dripping melted snow down on the carpet. "This is what always happens when you girls drink too much wine. And you'd still be fine catches for any man worth his salt."

"You really think so?" the twin sisters said in unison.

"If my father were still alive, I'd set you up with him."

"Which of us?" Olivia asked, after stealing a glance at Beatrice.

"Both," Ian said, without missing a beat, "just to see how long we could get away with it."

He stood back up and tossed an arm around Faye's shoulder, and off they went toward their seats at the far end of the table.

"Thank you for having us, Mrs. Mulroy," Faye said, stopping to give Constance a hug from behind.

"Yes, well, I only wish Daniel and Allison weren't stranded miles from here so they could be with us. You were my son's best friend when you were kids, right until you both went off to Brown together."

"Where I met Ian," Faye said, tossing her arm back around the young, long-haired man's shoulder. "And Daniel met Allison."

"She should have gone to Harvard," Doyle Castavette muttered under his breath, then cleared his throat when the entire table heard him.

Harrison Bak leaned in closer to me. "Long story," he whispered. "Suffice it to say that the Castavettes don't believe the Mulroys are good enough for their daughter. After the scandal and all."

"That money thing," I whispered back, "what led Connie's husband to take his own life."

"How does *Anna Karenina* begin? Something like, 'All

happy families are alike; each unhappy family is unhappy in
its own way.'"

"I'd prefer an Agatha Christie quote in this case: 'Money is
always the great clue to what is happening in the world.'"

Harrison toasted me with his wineglass. "Well said." He
clinked my glass. "I must read one of your books, Mrs. Fletcher.
Which one would you suggest?"

Before I could answer, the loud shattering of a glass drew
everyone's attention to the bar, where Mark Mulroy, Connie's
son and the groom's fraternal twin, had dropped his just-
poured drink. He shook his hand in the air and then wrapped
a cloth napkin around it as if he'd cut himself, which must
have been minor since I spotted no blood.

"I always recommend the latest," I said, turning my attention back to Harrison Bak.

With all the guests now present, the main course, that
sumptuously flavored sliced tenderloin broiled to perfection,
was served to actual applause and wolfed down with fervor.
After we'd all devoured our meals and conversations had resumed in earnest, Constance Mulroy rose from the head of the
table, tapping a spoon against her water glass to get everyone's
attention.

"I'd like to propose a toast to the bride and groom," she
said, raising her glass of red wine into the air. "Though they've
been waylaid by the storm, we're all here to celebrate them on
this wonderful occasion that sees us—that sees us . . ."

Connie's voice drifted off there. She looked confused,
stumbling over her words as her gaze went first distant and

then blank. She tried to sit back down, and I saw that her eyes were starting to roll back in her head. I bounced up out of my chair instinctively, and was halfway to my new friend when Constance Mulroy fell over forward, landing facedown on the dinner table.

Chapter Nine

I could see immediately that Connie was convulsing horribly in the grip of a grand mal seizure, the kind normally associated with epilepsy. Glasses, plates, and silverware went flying in all directions from the head of the table, some of them shattering at the same time my eyes recorded other guests rushing to her aid ahead of me. For the present, Tyler Castavette and her son Mark tried to hold her down, especially her arms, so she couldn't harm herself.

I felt helpless standing there, watching Connie's convulsions continue, spittle foaming up at the sides of her mouth. When it was clear no one at the dinner had any medical training, I drew my cell phone from my bag and hit Seth Hazlitt's number.

"How's the storm keeping you, Jess?" he answered, after the first ring.

"Someone's having a seizure! I need to know what to do!"

"Did you say you're having *a seizure*?"

"Not me! Someone else, here at Hill House! Tell me what to do!"

"Where is he?"

"It's a she, and currently convulsing atop a table, legs kicking in the air."

I could hear the tone of his voice change to doctor mode. Seth might be a crusty curmudgeon who lamented his status as no more than a small-town general practitioner, but in truth he was an excellent doctor who kept himself well schooled on the most recent tricks of the medical trade.

"Okay, first thing," he said as I made my way to the head of the table, sliding right up to Connie's side next to her son Mark, who was straining to hold her down, "you need to stabilize *her*." Seth seemed to catch himself in the midst of that thought. "You're not alone, are you, Jess? There are others, I assume."

"Twelve," I told him, the count frozen in my head. "Eleven able-bodied. A wedding party."

"A *what*? Never mind. The woman's being tended to, then?"

"Held down, anyway."

"Tell whoever's holding her down to get her onto the floor, gently onto one side to help her breathe."

"Mark, Tyler!" I called, and proceeded to repeat Seth's instruction.

They saw the phone in my grasp and didn't protest, having rightfully concluded I was speaking to someone well versed in medical matters. I watched the two young men do as Seth had prescribed, no easy task given Constance Mulroy's constant thrashing.

"She's still convulsing, Doctor," I said, addressing Seth that way to provide everyone a signal as to my intentions.

"Make sure the area is clear of any hard or sharp objects, anything she might cut or smack herself on."

There were only a few pieces of dinnerware in the area, some in pieces and some whole, and I kicked all of them away from Connie's jerking hands and legs.

"Okay," I said to Seth.

"Now put something soft and flat, like a folded jacket, under her head. And make sure to remove her glasses, if she's wearing any."

"She's not."

"Never a dull moment with you, is there, Jess?" Seth said, reverting to form.

Harrison Bak must have overheard the last of Seth's instructions, because he stripped off his jacket and balled it up as I watched. He handed it to me, and instead of passing it on I slid it beneath Connie's head myself, while Mark and Tyler did their best to hold her fast.

"She's still convulsing. There are two men holding her down. Is that okay?"

"Should be. Just make sure to loosen anything around her neck that could impede her breathing in any way."

"Her face is beet red, Seth. I'm not sure she's breathing at all. Should we perform CPR?"

"No!" he ordered definitively. "And don't put anything in her mouth either. That includes a spoon to keep the victim from swallowing her tongue. Little-known fact, Jess: a person having a seizure can't swallow their tongue."

"Well, that's a relief. What next?"

"How long has the seizure been going on?"

"How long have we been talking?"

"Just over a minute, I'd say."

"Then say somewhere around two minutes."

"Then the next step in normal circumstances would be to call nine-one-one, but these are hardly normal circumstances, given the storm."

"So what else *can* we do?"

While I waited for Seth to answer, my mind jerked back to the conversation I'd had with Connie during the cocktail hour.

I'm hardly the right person to discuss family secrets with.

I believe you are in this case, especially given your real specialty.

"Seth, are you there?"

Writing mysteries?

I was speaking more about solving them. Tell me, Jessica, have you ever solved a crime in advance, before it happened?

"Seth?"

I'm not sure I know what you mean.

You see, I fear my life may be in—

Seth's voice finally returned to my ear. "I'm here, I'm here. Just thinking. It's not every day I have to treat a convulsing patient over the phone."

"What else can we do?"

"Nothing."

"*Nothing?*"

"It should stop on its own."

"Should?"

"As long as it doesn't last longer than five minutes."

"It's been about that long now. Her face is almost purple, Seth. There's got to be something!"

I wonder how much of my desperation sprang from guilt over my having dismissed Connie's overtures during cocktails despite the fact that she clearly believed her life was in danger. I should have pushed her after we'd been interrupted, should have insisted she finish whatever she had to tell me. Perhaps if I had done that, she wouldn't be in these dire straits now.

And if she died . . .

I couldn't bear that on my conscience. Coupled with the fact that I genuinely liked this woman, I was left feeling weak and helpless, there being nothing more I could do.

"It's not stopping, Seth."

"Wait."

"It's not stopping!"

"Wait!"

And, sure enough, the next moment found Connie's convulsions ebbing, then stopping altogether save for a few last twitches of her arms and legs, the awful thrashing done.

"You were right," I told Cabot Cove's favorite physician.

"Of course I was."

"And she's breathing. A bit shallow and fitful, labored, but she's breathing."

"Is she conscious?"

"No."

"Once her breathing settles and her heart rate slows, she should regain consciousness. Otherwise . . ."

"Otherwise *what*, Seth?"

"Seizures of the intensity you're describing are known to induce comas. We'll deal with that if she still isn't awake in, say, an hour. Not a lot we can do under the circumstances, but the roads aren't going to be shut down forever."

"Your mouth to God's ears. What should we do now?"

"With no ambulance coming anytime soon, get her up to her room, onto her bed but not under the covers, and don't leave her alone until she regains consciousness, Jess." He seemed finished but resumed speaking almost immediately. "Wait—did you say *a wedding party*?"

Seamus McGilray had appeared at the tail end of my conversation with Seth and assessed the situation accurately enough to rush off and return moments later pushing a wheelchair. I watched Mark Mulroy and Tyler Castavette position themselves on either side of the now-still Constance Mulroy in order to ease her gently up from the floor and settle her into it, careful to support her head the whole time. A nasty bruise had begun to form across the top and bridge of her nose from where her face had impacted the table. I'd forgotten to mention that complication to Seth and wondered how a possible concussion might have affected his recommendation for treatment.

I need your expertise on a sensitive matter, something rather personal involving family.

Connie's words to me ninety minutes earlier felt like shadowy ghosts. I couldn't chase them from my mind, or rid my consciousness of their potential meaning.

Family secrets, to be specific.

What family secrets? And how might they be connected to the fears Connie had just begun to express to me about her life being in danger?

It was easy for me to linger while the others surrounded the wheelchair in a pack as Connie's son Mark wheeled the chair in which his mother's limp frame drooped from the Sea Captains Room toward the elevator down the hall back in the lobby.

I needed to be alone for a time to sort through what I was thinking and feeling. I stood in the very spot where Constance Mulroy had been when she'd risen to make her toast; I hoped it would lend me a perspective that would reveal something new.

Her wineglass had spilled over when she crashed forward. It was lying so its stem was hanging off the edge of the table. Something made me stand it back upright, so it wouldn't join all the broken dinnerware; I don't know why, but in that moment it seemed important to me to do so. And that's when I noticed a thin, chalky residue coating the sides and bottom of Connie's wineglass. Not everywhere and not all that pronounced, but enough to give me a notion as to what had caused her seizure:

Constance Mulroy had been poisoned.

At that point I was still alone in the Sea Captains Room, the memories captured in the slideshow projected against a screen in the far corner my only company. Prior to joining the wedding party upstairs in Connie's room, I called Mort Metzger.

"How you holding up, Mrs. F.?"

"You wouldn't believe me if I told you."

"Can I hang up now and send this call to voice mail? You're stranded in a mostly empty hotel in the midst of a killer blizzard. You can't possibly be calling to report a murder."

"Well . . ."

"Please tell me I'm dreaming this."

"Not a murder, Mort—at least not yet."

"We talking about those near newlyweds again who may have been inside that abandoned Lexus?"

"No, they've apparently turned up at the Roadrunner Motel, about forty miles down the road. This is something else— *someone* else. The groom's mother. I think she was poisoned, Mort. She suffered a seizure during dinner just minutes ago."

"This would be the dinner you weaseled your way into."

"I didn't weasel my way in—I was invited."

"So, you're eating gourmet through this muck while I'm surviving on reheated pizza and stale coffee. What's wrong with that picture?" He paused. "So, what's the prognosis for this potential victim?"

"Too soon to tell. Seth talked me through the process of stabilizing her and not doing the wrong thing. The family just brought her up to her room."

"And if she really was poisoned . . ."

I nodded, even though Mort was on the other end of the line. "The suspects aren't going anywhere anytime soon."

"You thinking this has something to do with the missing bride and groom?"

"I told you, they're not missing anymore."

"What happened to that suspicious nature of yours, Mrs. F.?"

He was right. I was taking Mark Mulroy's word that he'd gotten a call from his fraternal twin brother with the explanation of bad roads and second thoughts. If Mark had been lying about receiving such a call for whatever reason, Connie's potential poisoning would take on an entirely different context.

"I guess I just wanted those kids to be found for Connie. The missing groom is her son."

"Who's Connie?"

"The victim of that suspected poisoning. We'd become friends, or that's what I thought."

"Something changed?"

"Our meeting earlier in the day wasn't coincidental," I told Mort. "Constance Mulroy was staking out the lobby because she wanted my help with something, something involving family secrets. I think she had reason to believe she was in danger."

"That's what she said?"

"Not in those exact words, but pretty much, yes."

"Constance Mulroy," Mort repeated. "Could you spell that for me?"

I did.

"Okay, let me see if flagging her name brings anything back. And what'd you say the name of that motel was?" Mort asked me.

"The Roadrunner."

"Just off the highway, same exit you take to get to Appleton."

I hadn't thought in some time now of the town where Frank and I had spent a number of years raising our nephew Grady. "That's right."

"Power's down already in much of that area and I doubt I'd be able to get the place checked out, but let me put in a call to the State Police and see if they've got a cruiser that's still moving in the area."

"And we need to find out who hired that private detective, Mort. Loomis Winslow."

"The only connection to this wedding party is that abandoned Lexus SUV rental with its front doors left open. If those kids really did get stranded by the storm, we've got no reason to believe that Winslow, or Bigfoot, is related to this in the slightest."

"In other words, I'm barking up the wrong tree."

"Or trying to climb two at the same time, Mrs. F."

"Not in this weather, Sheriff."

A heaviness settled over the line, lingering long enough to make me wonder if we'd been cut off.

"Mort?"

"I'm still here. Just thinking that I'm not going to be able to get over there to help you on this one, Jessica. You're on your own."

If there was a criminal about—a potential murderer, no less— I didn't want to risk drawing undue attention to myself by remaining absent for too long. My call to Mort over, it was time to join the wedding party up in Connie's room.

On the way out of the Sea Captains Room, though, I couldn't resist stopping before the projection screen that was flush against the far wall and waiting for the picture of the nursery that had grabbed my attention earlier to come back around.

Because of that shadow that loomed at the rear of the shot.

It could have been, probably was, nothing. I can't describe why it had stuck in my mind or what its significance might be. This time, when the slide in question came around again, I hit the laptop's space bar to freeze the screen. I then studied the bouncy, happy forms of fraternal twins Daniel and Mark. The still shot had been taken either from the doorway or just inside it, sharply angled to keep the cribs in the foreground of the picture.

With no need to rush and no eye over my shoulder, I studied particularly that portion of the picture backlit by a light shining close to Daniel and Mark's cribs. The shadow that had drawn my attention earlier didn't look to be much of anything at all, as it turned out, and I was beginning to think it was no more than a trick of the light. Then I stepped back a bit to view the shot in the context of the nursery's two cribs. That perspective clarified at the far edge of the screen an object that wasn't a shadow at all.

And it was something that made no sense, no sense at all.

Chapter Ten

I headed up to join the others in Constance Mulroy's room with fresh vigor and a renewed spring in my step, albeit with a sense of anxiety and uncertainty added to the mix. If I was right about what I'd spotted in that seemingly innocent nursery photo, another potential piece had been added to the puzzle here.

First, Private Investigator Loomis Winslow had been found dead in what could easily have been passed off as a tragic accident.

Then that abandoned Lexus had been discovered with the occupants of the front seat nowhere to be found, and with whoever had been in the back linked to the original crime scene by gravel that had collected in the grooves of the Lexus's winter floor mat.

Now Constance Mulroy was unconscious following a seizure that may well have been induced by some kind of drug stealthily mixed with her wine.

I had the very real sense that all of these things were intrinsically connected. And I suspected there was far more afoot in the mechanics of what I was slowly uncovering than I could possibly realize at this point. The guest list made for an odd lot indeed, and I suspected that among those guests Tyler Castavette was far from the only one with both skeletons in his closet and secrets to bear.

With all that in mind, my first order of business once I got upstairs was to have a talk with Mark Mulroy. I needed to hear more about that purported phone call from his brother about the couple's decision to ride out the storm at the Roadrunner Motel around forty miles down the road. With his mother incapacitated, Mark was also likely the only person here who could definitively confirm whether my suspicions of what I was convinced I'd spotted in that video display slide were accurate.

My path to the lobby elevators took me past a bank of windows that revealed the power of the storm in all its glory. It looked as if another ten inches of snow had fallen since the time I'd left my suite for the dinner, bringing the total to somewhere around eighteen already in a blizzard that was just reaching its peak. I tried to picture in my mind what it might look like outside in the morning, since at present the snow was climbing the glass at a fever pitch and swirling winds conspired to hide the outside world from sight. I should have felt comforted by being safe and warm inside the confines of Hill House, a site that had weathered more than its share of storms and emerged from each and every one of them in remarkable condition.

There was a Cabot Cove legend that on the eve of the hotel's opening in 1888, Hill House had been blessed by a local priest revered by the townsfolk for his piety. He was also rumored to have a touch of healing power, and to this day many locals will tell you Hill House owes its nearly hundred-and-fifty-year existence to that blessing. Those who know our town's history best are fond of relating the tale of lightning strikes obliterating the buildings on either side of the hotel during a storm that didn't so much as scorch the hotel's structure. It had also weathered any number of expansions, growing to four times its original size in the past twenty years alone. So, too, had Hill House survived every financial crisis that had led to changes in ownership while never costing the facility its character.

Tonight, although I felt safe within its walls from the raging storm beyond, a different storm was brewing inside. Indeed, Constance Mulroy's poison-induced seizure left me filled with a deep sense of dread, not for the poisoning alone but for what it suggested might be to come. The continually deteriorating weather conditions might have made it increasingly difficult to discern the view beyond the windows, but the picture taking shape inside looked dark and ominous to me. The strange events of the day had given way to equally strange events of the night, starting with Constance Mulroy's believing her life to be in danger, apparently because of the "family secrets" she had mentioned to me on whispered breath.

As far as I was concerned, that left two things reasonably certain: that none of us was going anywhere and the worst of this night was yet to come.

*   *   *

By the time I got upstairs to join the remainder of the wedding party in Connie's room, she was resting comfortably atop the bedcovers with a spare bedspread covering her fully clothed form. Her breathing seemed to have steadied, and if I didn't know better I'd say she was no more than taking a nap. I cataloged the other eleven persons in the room—twelve, counting Seamus McGilray, who must have remained after supervising the effort to safely transport Connie to her room.

I had known not a single one of the wedding party until mere hours before, and now I felt tasked with determining the means by which the comatose woman had been poisoned and by whom. Given the lateness of the arrangements to hold the dinner here, certainly the wineglass she'd drunk from at the head of the table couldn't have been tampered with until that table was set, and likely not before the glass had been filled. So, standing there surveying those before me, I knew one of them had to be the culprit who'd poisoned Constance Mulroy.

"You look deep in thought, Mrs. Fletcher," the esteemed defense lawyer Harrison Bak said, suddenly alongside me, leaning awkwardly on his crutches. "A notion coming to you for a new book, perhaps? How about twelve people gathered for a wedding that's been waylaid by a blizzard?"

"Hardly original, given the Agatha Christie classic *And Then There Were None*."

"Never read it, I'm ashamed to say. And now I'd rather wait for your version."

"I'm guessing Henley Lavarnay is the only one you know among these people," I put forth.

"Well, I have met Tyler, and Doyle, of course, but otherwise your assumption is correct."

"What do you think of Tyler?"

"How frank would you like me to be?" Harrison Bak asked softly, even though we stood at the very rear of the room, close enough to the wall to note the slight bubbles in the wallpaper.

"As frank as possible."

He leaned in slightly closer to me on his crutches. "Then let me put it this way, Mrs. Fletcher. When I'm in Tyler's company, I always keep hold of my wallet. There's something—how do I say this?—well, slippery about him. Charming and charismatic to a fault. The kind of young man who greets you with a hug so he can pick your pocket."

I nodded, not afraid to show that Bak's impressions of Tyler Castavette mirrored my own. It would be some time before I relieved myself of the image of him entering my suite unannounced earlier that evening. And strangely enough, I was just thinking of that when Tyler turned from Constance Mulroy's bedside, caught my eye, and flashed the disarming smile that I'm sure he employed like a Halloween costume.

Of course, this didn't make him a murderer, but I had the distinct sense that someone in the room was.

It was determined that someone should remain with Connie all through the night on the chance that her condition changed, she awoke in some distress, or she just needed a telling of the events that had led to this point.

"Why don't I take the first shift?" I offered for my own reasons, when no one else stepped up.

"We saw Mrs. Fletcher with Constance," Beatrice started.

"Earlier in the day," her twin, Olivia, said, picking up her thought.

"And they were getting along wonderfully."

"Quite so."

"Then it's settled," said Doyle Castavette, asserting himself as the person in charge, especially as Connie's son Mark offered up no argument.

"I'll take the second shift, Mrs. Fletcher," Mark volunteered. "Since there are twelve of us, we can make the initial shifts an hour each. How's that sound?"

"Count me out, if you don't mind," insisted Doyle Castavette.

I quickly smiled and looked toward Mark, figuring I'd have to delay the questions I had for him until he came to replace me at the end of my shift. "I'll be here until you relieve me."

Mark gazed down at the still form of his mother. "I think I'll try out the hotel gym in the meantime. You know, relieve some stress . . . after I call my brother to tell him what's happened."

"I'll head downstairs with you," said Seamus McGilray. "Make sure all the equipment's in working order."

"Oh, Seamus," I said, trailing him out into the hall and drawing him aside slightly. "You'll note a wineglass missing when you replace the dinnerware. I promise to return it in good time," I added, patting my handbag to indicate where it currently rested, securely wrapped in the napkin I'd neglected to mention had also gone missing.

He caught the look in my eye. "Whatever you say, Mrs. Fletcher. Just tell me everything's okay."

I squeezed his arm as reassuringly as I could manage. "I promise to, just as soon as I can."

I closed the door once I was alone in the room with the peacefully resting Constance Mulroy and waited for a few moments to make sure none of the wedding party returned. Satisfied that they'd all gone to their rooms, I turned my attention to Connie. Maybe she'd magically wake up and finish the explanation of why she feared her life was in danger. Maybe she'd even have a guess as to who among the guests had poisoned her wine. No such dramatic moment ensued, and I was left with the same realization I'd faced too many times before—that crimes in real life were not as conveniently resolved as fictional ones.

I laid my handbag on the room's desk and removed my cell phone. Seth Hazlitt's number was already keyed up, and I pressed it again.

"How's the patient?" he greeted, upon answering his phone.

"Resting comfortably, by all indications."

"Are you up to doing some doctoring, Jess?"

"So long as it doesn't involve surgery."

"Is the patient in bed?"

"Atop it, covered in a light bedspread."

"On her back?"

"Yes."

"Safer for her to be resting on her side, in case she's concussed and comes awake vomiting."

I gauged the effort it would take to roll Connie onto her side by myself. "I don't want to disturb her, Seth."

"Understandable. The alternative is a very careful watch, something I assume has already been arranged."

"It has."

"Then I suggest when your replacement arrives, you turn the woman onto her side together."

"Will do."

"Now," Seth resumed, "move to her bedside. You're going to peel open one of her eyelids to check the reactions of her pupils to light, a flashlight preferably."

"I don't have a flashlight."

"Yes, you do. Your phone."

"Of course," I responded, thinking there might be a way for Seth to see for himself what he needed to. "You don't have FaceTime on your phone, do you?"

"Have you seen my phone lately?"

"No."

"Then suffice it to say I don't have FaceTime. And when did you become such a technology maven, Jessica Fletcher?"

"You don't have to be a maven to know about FaceTime, Seth."

"I suppose, if you say so. Now, shine your phone flashlight beam directly into her eye and then tell me if the pupil reacts or remains fixed and dilated."

I carefully peeled back Connie's eyelid and did exactly as Seth Hazlitt had instructed. "Fixed," I said, iPhone back at my ear with flashlight feature disabled.

"That confirms the coma. My impression is that it's moderate in nature. Can you check her pulse for me, Jess?"

I put the phone on speaker and felt for a pulse in the spot that was always easier for my characters to locate than me. "Feels steady," I said. "Hold on. . . . Heart rate is around sixty-five," I reported after a minute had passed.

"I don't believe she's in any immediate danger, but she will still need *professional* medical attention as soon as the roads allow."

"I believe I've already found the cause of her seizure."

"Have you really, *Doctor* Fletcher?"

"I think she was poisoned, Seth," I said, and proceeded to tell him about the residue I'd spotted on her wineglass.

"Murder really does follow you around, doesn't it, Jess?"

"Any way of determining what she was poisoned with?"

"What color was the residue?" Seth asked me.

"A kind of yellowish white, with specks of red from the wine."

"You said *yellowish* white?"

"I did."

I could feel Seth perking up on the other end of the line. "Okay, Jess, I want you to check the bathroom."

"For what?"

"Prescription bottles."

I took the phone with me as I followed his instructions. "None I can see anywhere."

"Just as I suspected."

"Then why'd you have me look?"

"You'll see. Now check the woman's handbag and tell me what you find."

Sure enough, I located an orange prescription bottle right at the very top. "Found one!"

"Read me the name of the drug on the label."

Because I didn't have my reading glasses with me I had to squint, and even then reading it was a chore. "I can't pronounce it, Seth."

"Then spell it for me."

"B-U-P-R—"

"Bupropion," Seth interrupted, before I could finish.

"Yes. What is it?"

"An antidepressant, Jess. All antidepressants lower the threshold for seizures, but bupropion is the grand champion in the field. In fact, it's been reported that bupropion ingestion is the third most common cause of drug-induced seizures, after cocaine ingestion and benzodiazepine withdrawal."

I didn't bother quizzing Seth further on that.

"Is she an older woman?" he asked me.

"No older than I. What makes you ask?"

"Because elderly patients taking the drug are at a greater risk of suffering a seizure from chronic dosing. Any idea if the woman is taking any other prescription drugs?"

"I don't know. Should I check her bag again?"

"Not yet. Pop open that prescription bottle instead."

"Done," I said, once the bottle was open.

"Describe the pills inside."

"Solid yellow."

"That's the microencapsulation coating to make the medi-cation release over time, either twelve or twenty-four hours."

"The bottle says to take one pill in the morning with food."

"And if the pills were powdered to make them dissolve in the wine, the entire medicinal content would be absorbed into the bloodstream immediately. The fact that there was enough residue left on the glass for you to identify it so readily tells me several pills were mixed with the wine, as many as five or six."

"Looks like there's about fifteen left in the bottle."

"When was it filled?"

"Eight days ago. Thirty pills total."

"Then we're on the right track."

"Seven pills," I said, doing the math. "There are seven pills unaccounted for."

"More than enough to explain that chalky residue. In fact, I'd go so far as to say that's what saved the woman's life, at least for the time being. Had whoever poisoned her managed to dilute the pills entirely, the dose would almost surely have been fatal. Any thoughts on a suspect?"

"More of them than I can count on all fingers, Seth."

"Then you'd best be careful, *ayuh*. I'd head over there my-self, but the snow's already piled up past the tires of my old Volvo. Remind me to clean out the garage 'fore next winter, will you?"

"Even though you won't listen? Even though you'll probably

say something like, 'Never get another like last year's storm, *ayuh*'?" I said, doing my best Seth Hazlitt impersonation.

"You know," he responded, "this weather must be good for your constitution, because that's the best you've ever sounded. That said, I hope you take stock of this conversation, Jess, because whoever tried to kill this woman must have known she was taking these pills and exactly where to find them."

"Someone close to her, in other words," I said, completing for Seth the thought I'd already reached myself. "Maybe you should consider abandoning medicine for detective work."

"In that case, let me state something else you no doubt already know: There's a murderer among you there, Jess, and he or she may not be finished yet."

Chapter Eleven

T hat was the reason I'd volunteered for the first shift. If Constance Mulroy's would-be killer came back to finish the job while she was still in a coma, it would likely be sooner rather than later.

I sat back in the desk chair I'd placed at her bedside and ruminated on the logistics of her poisoning. When we'd last spoken, when she'd been on the verge of telling me why she feared her life might be in danger, she was holding a glass of red wine in her hand. Since that was sometime more than ninety minutes before she'd risen to make her toast, it was clear that particular glass had not been the one contaminated with seven ground-up bupropion tablets.

I thought back to the particulars of our table setting. Since I seldom, if ever, drink, I normally don't notice the inclusion of a wineglass before me. But I was now able to conjure a wineglass in its customary place to the left of the water glass, as with every setting. I also recalled a male server carrying bottles of both red and white wine around the table at regular intervals. I'd demurred on each occasion, and the reason why I remembered the server so clearly was that he was wearing an ill-fitting Hill House smock that suggested he'd been pressed into action for the evening's storm-bred contingency plans.

That server had filled Connie's glass with red wine on at least one occasion, and likely more. That added to the mystery, then, of how her would-be murderer had managed to mix the ground-up tablets into her glass. The residue indicated that he or she might not have had the opportunity to complete the work. In any case, I was at a loss to come up with a theory about how precisely that had transpired.

All my life, I've been a fan of magicians. To this day, I watch shows like *America's Got Talent* utterly amazed by their ability to make you believe their tricks might truly be magic, since there seems by all accounts to be no other explanation. I'm old enough to remember a time when critics claimed that magic as a performance art would never survive television, because you can't misdirect a camera. Especially now, with flat-screen televisions and the ability to slow a broadcast recording virtually to frame by frame—which, I confess, I've done myself, never once successfully gleaning how this magician or that was able to perform the impossible.

I felt the same way now. With the information I currently had before me, I could see no feasible way Constance Mulroy's wine could have been tampered with. And there was also the matter of the murdered private investigator, Loomis Winslow, to take into account here. Although nothing at this point indicated his murder was at all connected with the attempt on Connie's life, I couldn't chase away the possibility that someone among the wedding party had hired him to look into some issue pertaining to money, likely connected with the financial malfeasance committed by none other than Connie's husband, Heath Mulroy. Had the groom-to-be Daniel Mulroy not phoned his brother Mark to pass word on that he and the bride-to-be Allison Castavette were holing up for the night at the Roadrunner Motel, I'd be looking at the night's events from an entirely different angle. I might even now be assuming that whoever had dragged gravel from that old mill into the backseat of the abandoned Lexus was a member of this very wedding party and responsible for the coma in which Constance Mulroy currently rested, not to mention the murder of Loomis Winslow.

As soon as I sat down in the chair I'd set by Connie's bedside, I felt an immense wave of exhaustion wash over me. But I snapped alert moments away from drifting off, both by presence of mind and by the power of my imagination to wonder whether I might have been somehow poisoned, too, and was about to slip off into a slumber from which I might never awake. When was the last time I had a sip of anything? Who had handed me the glass? And what about the ginger ale I'd had refilled on multiple occasions, several by that server wearing the ill-fitting smock? I almost called Seth to ask him about symptoms beyond the fatigue that had nearly overtaken me.

But that fatigue was far more likely rooted in the stress,

pace, and mere length of this day that had brought me from Mara's to one murder scene and then, later, another potential one. Not to mention bearing witness to local drunk Hank Weathers identifying Bigfoot as present in the old mill where Loomis Winslow had been murdered. I was tired because, well, I was tired. Nothing Dr. Seth Hazlitt could do about that.

To keep myself alert for as long as possible, I proceeded to busy myself with a thorough check of Constance Mulroy's room, just to see if anything jumped out at me as amiss. There was nothing hidden in the bureau or desk drawers, nor was there anything concealed in less likely locations of note, like the back of the toilet tank or behind one of the room's paintings. I even did a thorough inspection of the drawn window blinds to see if Connie might have hidden anything there. Finally, just for good measure, I checked under the bed as well, and then searched both the in-room refrigerator and the microwave, the kinds of places those not necessarily used to concealing something might choose.

I guess you could say I was looking for a secret, something that might explain why someone would have tried to kill her. But the only anomaly I found was inside the closet, in relatively plain view. It was there that I spotted a set of luggage that matched Connie's designer handbag; Hermès, Louis Vuitton, or some other upscale brand. There was a large suitcase, and a medium-sized one resting next to it, indication that for the weekend of her son's wedding Constance Mulroy wasn't traveling light. The anomaly lay in the fact that there was a noticeable gap between the medium-sized suitcase and an old-fashioned cosmetics case that similarly rested on the closet floor. I imagined the set came complete with a matching soft tote, which would have neatly filled the empty slot but was nowhere to be found. That left me thinking what the potentially missing tote may have contained and why another member of the wedding party might have absconded with it.

I laid my cell phone down in my lap to make sure an incoming call from Mort or Seth wouldn't go unnoticed if I happened to nod off while fulfilling my shift's duties. I was just thinking of calling Harry McGraw when it rang with his name lighting up at the top of the screen.

"I'm working on something," he said after I'd greeted him.

"Care to tell me what?"

"No."

"Then why are you calling me?"

"To tell you I'm working on something. Besides, I couldn't tell you even if I wanted to, because I'd risk making you an accessory to a crime."

"What crime would that be, Harry?"

"I'm not sure. Bearing false witness or giving false testimony, maybe. Or impersonating a detective."

"You are a detective."

"I mean a *real* detective."

"You are a real detective," I told him.

"I meant a police officer. I'm not that, according to my ID. Then again, according to my ID my name is Marvin Linquist, on account of the fact that he doesn't have any outstanding parking tickets or tax bills, while Harry McGraw has a mountain of both."

"So sorry to hear that, Harry."

"That's what happens when you've got deadbeat clients," he told me wryly. "Anyway, stay tuned for my surprise."

"What surprise?"

"If I told you, it wouldn't be a surprise, but there is something I need from you in order to make the surprise happen."

I had no idea where Harry was going with this, but I decided to play along. "Okay, what do you need?"

"It's so simple, it's not even worth charging you for."

"Can you just tell me what you need, Harry?"

"The names of all the guests who make up the wedding party and are currently staying at Hill House."

"What on earth for?"

"Again, for the surprise I'm putting together for you."

"Can you at least give a hint?"

"It's a surprise, Jessica, but okay," he relented. "If my instincts are correct, the information I'm this close to getting will tell us who hired this private eye Loomis Winslow for a job that very likely got him killed. I guess we should be thankful for one thing."

"What's that, Harry?"

"That whoever it was didn't hire me instead."

It seemed I'd barely finished texting Harry all the names of those in the wedding party when my phone rang again, this time with a call from Mort Metzger.

"What's the latest, Mrs. F.?"

"Good evening to you, too, Mort."

"What's good about it? I'm stuck here at the station, fielding any and all emergency calls, and just heard from Dick Mann that his trucks can't maneuver in this amount of snow. I stuck a yardstick in the ground outside the station I'm about to file a missing-persons report on. Ethan Cragg has pulled the plows that aren't already stuck off the road and the Weather Channel just mentioned Cabot Cove by name as being the actual vortex of the storm, whatever that means. Maybe it's all connected."

"Maybe all *what* is connected?" I asked him.

"That there really is some weird cosmic convergence in this town that makes bad things more likely to happen. Speaking of which, I just heard from Harry."

"I got off the phone with him barely a minute ago."

"And I was already keying your number up when I saw his in the caller ID, Mrs. F. When were you going to tell me about the connection between Loomis Winslow and someone in this wedding party?"

"When I confirmed there was one."

"Quite the wordsmith, aren't you?"

"It is how I make a living."

"My point exactly. As hard as it might be to believe, you don't make your living solving murders. And since I'm not there for you to advise me after I ask for your advice . . ."

"Hill House is three miles from the Sheriff's Department, Mort. It's not like it's in another country."

"It might as well be tonight, Mrs. F. I need you to stay in touch with me through the night on any new developments, and I mean *immediately*."

"What makes you think there are going to be any new developments?"

"Because we're inside the vortex that is Cabot Cove."

Speaking with Mort had lent an air of normalcy, if you could call it that, to the events of the evening. Our conversation had also served to focus my mind not so much on the foreboding sense of more bad turns in the offing, but more on the investigatory aspects with which I was at home.

My next thought was to reach out to the groom-to-be, Daniel Mulroy, myself. I had no evidence, after all, that Mark Mulroy had ever actually spoken to his brother, besides his word, and I resolved to press the young man further on that as soon as he came to relieve me at the close of my shift. For all I knew, he had made the whole story up for reasons yet unknown. So I googled *ROADRUNNER MOTEL MAINE* on my phone and tapped the number that loaded with the profile.

Unfortunately, the call didn't go through, didn't even produce a ring. I tried again, then a third and fourth time, all with the same results. But the fifth provoked a different result—no rings, but a monotone message.

"Your call cannot be completed at this time. Please try your call again later. Operator—"

I ended the call before the voice had completed identifying itself by number. Given the storm's battering assault, it was hardly surprising lines were either down or overloaded, as was the case during any true emergency. And if either the mounting snows or gale-force winds accompanying the storm had put a cell tower or two out of commission, other towers would be hard-pressed to compensate for the decline in service. I remembered all the terrible stories that had emerged out of 9/11 in this regard and got a chill just thinking of all the people trying desperately to reach loved ones lost after the Twin Towers fell.

I resolved to keep calling the Roadrunner every few minutes and, in the meantime, tuned the television in Constance Mulroy's room to the Weather Channel so Jim Cantore could keep me company. He was broadcasting live from a nearby site when I must have drifted off, and he was on-screen again when a rapping on the door drove me from my inadvertent slumber.

I awoke with a start, my eyes going immediately to Constance Mulroy once my disorientation passed. She looked exactly as she'd been when I'd nodded off what must have been nearly an hour ago. I cleared my throat, shook the sense back into myself, and moved to answer the door.

"Mrs. Fletcher," a young woman greeted me once I opened it.

For a moment I had no idea who she was, until I recalled briefly meeting Lois Mulroy-Dodge, Connie's niece, in the waning moments of the cocktail hour.

"Ms. Dodge, so sorry I didn't . . ."

"It's me that's sorry, Mrs. Fletcher. I came up to see if Mark needed anything. This is his shift, isn't it?"

Indeed, my hour had ended as much as a half hour ago, and Connie's son Mark had not appeared to replace me.

"It's supposed to be," I affirmed. "Something must have delayed him."

Lois Mulroy-Dodge flashed her phone. "I've tried calling him, but he's not answering."

I remembered Mark mentioning something about going to the gym to calm his nerves. "Would you mind staying with your aunt while I go and look for him?"

"Well, my shift's the one immediately after his, so it'll be like just starting a bit early. I'll bet he fell asleep or something. It would be just like Mark."

"You'd be about the same age, wouldn't you?"

She nodded. "We're practically brother and sister."

I recalled how she had been raised by her aunt and uncle following the death of her parents when she was a young girl. Given her closeness to the family, I thought about asking Lois Mulroy-Dodge about the odd thing, the anomaly, I'd spotted in Daniel and Mark's nursery amid the slideshow, but it didn't feel like the right place or time. Besides, Mark Mulroy himself would be far better positioned to answer my questions.

"I was terribly sorry to hear about your husband," I said instead, recalling that Constance had told me the young woman had lost her husband to an accident at sea.

Her expression turned stoic. "He wasn't nearly as good at piloting a sailboat as he thought, Mrs. Fletcher. We never should have gone out that day, even if that storm did spring up out of nowhere. The mast cracked and landed on him while he was trying to protect me. He died hours later while I was holding him."

"I'm so sorry, Lois."

"I wake up some nights in bed and can still feel him sleeping next to me. Is that unusual?"

"Are you asking me as a writer?"

"As an expert in such things, I suppose." The young woman shrugged.

I opted not to ask her what she meant by that, and for the simplest of responses. "No, Lois, it's not unusual at all. In fact, it's totally normal, what those far more expert than I would call the lingering effect of shock and grief."

It didn't appear my words had worked much as a reassurance.

"Thank you, Mrs. Fletcher," she said anyway, as I stepped aside so she could enter the room. "I'll be waiting up here when you find Mark."

Over my months residing at Hill House, I'd trodden a well-worn path to the hotel gym that was located in a newly renovated area of the basement level that also included a business center and a pair of conference-style rooms. The minor upgrades allowed the hotel to attract at least modest conference business of up to fifty attendees. That didn't do that much for Hill House's bottom line, but it did serve to boost revenue during the normally slower winter months.

I retreated to the gym regularly during the colder months, when my bicycle was tucked away in storage. I preferred the elliptical machines and was also no stranger to the pair of treadmills with a television hanging between them. The two ellipticals, meanwhile, had television screens built in. For the record, I'd also gotten to know my way around some light weight-lifting exercises.

I used my key card to enter the gym. One of the televisions was on, tuned of course to the Weather Channel, but there was no sign of Mark Mulroy anywhere about, until I spotted a figure lying supine on a bench positioned under an assisted weight assembly I think is called a Smith machine. The Smith machine operated on a cable-and-pulley system that maximized safety for whoever was using it.

"Mark," I called out. "Mark, it's Jessica Fletcher. I was just wondering if—"

I froze halfway across the floor, realizing Mark Mulroy's arms had dropped to his sides, fingers nearly scraping the floor. He wasn't moving, wasn't breathing, and as my vision adjusted to the lighting and the mirrored far wall, I saw that the stationary barbell supporting the weight stack was pressed against his neck. I made myself move forward until I was close enough to confirm what I'd already suspected.

Mark Mulroy was dead.

Chapter Twelve

My breathing settled again after a few seconds, at which point I called Seamus McGilray on my cell phone. I figured as part owner and manager of the hotel he had a right to know first.

"Jessica?"

"I'm in the gym, Seamus. You need to get down here."

"Problem?"

"Putting it lightly, yes."

Through the gym's glass walls I watched him coming down the basement hall inside of three minutes later. As soon as he stepped through the gym door I held open for him his eyes traced the same path mine had, and immediately fixed on Mark Mulroy's still form.

"Is he—"

"Yes," I said.

"Oh my, what an awful night this has become," Seamus muttered, shaking his head.

He approached the weight-lifting bench where Mark Mulroy lay dead. Drawing closer in his wake, I could see the blanching and purple bruising of the young man's face, indicative more of death by asphyxiation than a broken neck from the force of two forty-five-pound weights on either side of the bar crashing down on him.

Seamus seemed to read my mind. "The whole purpose of this piece of equipment is to minimize risk to the user. That's why it's here."

"So the weight didn't fall and crush his neck?"

He positioned himself behind the young man's frame atop the weight bench, and looked as if he was prepared to lift the weighted bar upward. "The bar is resting on the neck, but given the design of the machine, it's virtually inconceivable that it could have crushed it. Looks to me instead like somebody stood about where I am and pushed the weight downward, holding it until the young man suffocated to death."

"How terrible."

"Indeed."

I considered the scenario Seamus had proposed, recalling Mark Mulroy's appearance and how he carried himself. "He was clearly in fine shape and quite muscular. If you're right, we're looking for someone at least as strong as him, and likely stronger."

"Not necessarily, Jessica," Seamus told me. "Whoever held the bar down against his windpipe wouldn't need to be all that strong, because he, or she, would've had the advantage of leverage." He imitated the positioning and motion it would have taken. "The killer would only need to be standing where I'm standing and push down on the bar here and here, until the deed was done."

"Murder, then."

"I'd say most certainly, but I'm hardly an expert on such things," Seamus said, the tone of his voice implying that I was.

I let that part of his comment hang in the air and resolved to take some pictures on my phone, which I could then forward to Seth Hazlitt so the good doctor could confirm Seamus's conclusions as to the means by which Mark Mulroy had been killed.

"We need to seal this room, Seamus," I said, hearing my own voice as if someone else was speaking. "Nobody else allowed in."

"I can take it off-line, so no one else's key card will work in here."

That made me think of Tyler Castavette's unwarranted entry into my room, something I'd yet to share with Seamus. "Something else," I told him. "One of the guests upstairs has a master key card of some kind."

"For all of Hill House, you're saying?"

I nodded.

Seamus's expression bent into a scowl. "Please point him out to me. I need to have a word with this guest."

"I don't think that's a good idea at this point when we should be focusing all our energy on one successful murder and one attempted one. That starts with gathering the ten remaining guests in the lobby to tell them what's transpired and continue our investigation."

"*Our* investigation, Mrs. Fletcher?"

"Didn't you mention to me once that you had some police experience in your native Ireland, Seamus?"

"As a constable directing traffic—murder wasn't exactly in my job description."

"It is now."

Before closing off the hotel gym, Seamus and I checked it carefully for Mark Mulroy's personal items, which might be important to the investigation into his murder. If I've learned anything about cell phones, it's that their detailed call logs can be a godsend in determining a murder victim's final words, plans, and intentions. But Mark Mulroy's cell phone was nowhere to be found, either on his person or anywhere inside the small gym. Neither was his wallet or even the key card to access his room, and it was a safe bet that his murderer had made off with all of that.

While Seamus retreated upstairs to begin the process of rounding up the rest of the wedding party, I remained outside the gym to call Mort. I have to admit that the prospect of being alone anywhere in the hotel right then was hardly pleasant. I made sure to ring Mort with my back pressed against a wall and with a clear view of the hall beyond, stretching past the hotel business center and conference rooms all the way to the elevator and stairwell.

"Any updates, Mrs. F.?" he said, by way of greeting. "I was just about to call you with some news of my own."

"Yes, there is indeed, Mort, if you include murder."

I heard him sigh on the other end of the line. "The woman who was poisoned passed?"

"No, it's her son," I said, and proceeded to fill him in on what I'd found inside the hotel gym, adding for good measure the conclusions Seamus had reached. "Mort?" I said after he'd stayed silent for too long once I'd completed my report.

"You know the conditions when the crime rate was the lowest in New York City, Mrs. F.?"

"Blizzards would be my guess," I told him.

"Any measurable snowstorm, actually. The crime rate literally fell in direct correlation with the amount of snow accumulated. Apparently, that unwritten rule doesn't apply in Cabot Cove. No rules of crime apply in Cabot Cove."

"Not when it comes to murder," I said, from outside the Hill House gym while Seamus went about the chore of rounding up the remaining ten guests to gather in the lobby.

I filled Mort in on the details of Mark's death, drawing a hefty "Ugh" from him when I suggested murder was the only rational explanation, though a weight-lifting accident was still a remote possibility.

"If you're right, Mrs. F.," Mort pronounced grimly, "it means you've now got a murderer loose at the hotel. Good news is they're not going anywhere."

"What's the bad news, Mort?"

"That they're not going anywhere until their work is done."

"Could be it already is, if mother and son were the targets."

"So far, you mean. Who else is present from that side of the family, in terms of direct relatives?"

"Just a niece," I said, thinking of Mark's cousin Lois Mulroy-

Dodge, the young woman presently standing vigil over Constance Mulroy up in her room. "Oh," I said as an afterthought, "a pair of elderly twin cousins: the Sprague sisters, Beatrice and Olivia."

"More twins?"

"It seems to run in the family, along with tragedy."

"And murder."

"Unfortunately."

I could feel Mort thinking on the other end of the line. "Did I tell you that Cabot Cove maintains a small fleet of snowmobiles for just this sort of emergency?"

"I remember it coming up in the emergency town meeting earlier today. Was that the news you said you had to share with me?"

"No, that's something else. Anyway, Dick Mann pulled them out of storage at the fire station and found them to be in fine working order once he gassed them up."

I gleaned his intentions immediately. "Have you ever driven a snowmobile, Mort?"

"Have you ever driven to a crime scene through New York City rush hour traffic?"

"I've never driven anywhere, period."

"Then take my word for it—after twenty years doing that, driving a snowmobile will be a piece of cake. If you can just hold down the fort long enough for me to get there, Mrs. F. . . ."

"You've got an entire town to watch over during a record snowfall, Mort," I reminded him.

"And now I've got at least one murder to solve as well."

"I told you the initial victim is still resting comfortably."

"But she wasn't really the initial victim at all, was she, Mrs. F.? There was that private eye this morning, and then the soon-to-be newlyweds who might well have fled that abandoned Lexus this afternoon."

"Except they're apparently present and unaccounted for now, remember?" I said, thinking of the message the late Mark Mulroy had received from his twin brother, Daniel.

"Well, it turns out they're not, not at all. That's the news I had to share with you," Mort told me. "You see, I finally tracked down the owner of the Roadrunner Motel. Turns out, he closed the place down at noon today with no guests whatsoever on the premises."

That left me considering in an entirely new light what we were facing here tonight. I had wanted to get to the lobby before any of the wedding guests arrived, in order to study their reactions even as they emerged from the elevator. But I had to process what Mort's news meant before proceeding upstairs.

First off, obviously I needed to view the Lexus that had been abandoned on the road with its front doors still open in the context I'd originally feared. While Mort still hadn't received confirmation that this particular Hertz vehicle had been rented at the Portland Jetport, it was difficult not to consider the obvious. And with the obvious came the connection, through that distinctive gravel left on the SUV's backseat floor mat, with the murder of Loomis Winslow. That left me considering the worst-case, and now most likely, scenario.

First, the private investigator had been murdered, though not by Bigfoot as our lone witness claimed.

Then, the Lexus SUV had turned up, its driver and passenger having fled and the presence of that gravel in the backseat indicating the same killer might have been responsible.

Next, Constance Mulroy had somehow been poisoned at dinner, and then her son Mark was murdered in the hotel gym.

That, of course, raised the question of why exactly Mark had lied about his brother having contacted him. I wanted to believe it had been to assuage his mother's fears, to give her and everyone else one less thing to worry about, given the promise of an already-frightful night. But what if his intentions had been more nefarious? And did those intentions explain why his cell phone was missing from the hotel gym? Surely he wouldn't have ventured down there without it, under the circumstances. Without it, meanwhile, we'd be unable to ascertain whether he'd actually spoken to his brother Daniel at all or learn the identity of anyone else with whom he might have been in contact.

I remembered in that moment that, while upstairs with Constance Mulroy, I'd texted Harry McGraw the names of all members of the wedding party, the late Mark Mulroy included. I still had no idea what he needed them for and resolved to call him for an update after the meeting upstairs in the lobby with the remainder of the wedding party was concluded. I now had Constable Seamus McGilray to serve as my deputy, and I fully expected to receive a call from Mort Metzger fairly soon that he was about to set off for Hill House via snowmobile.

Just as I was finally heading for the elevator, my caller ID lit up with *SETH* at the top of the screen.

"You didn't call to tell me," he snapped angrily.

"Tell you what?"

"That there's been another murder there."

"The first victim's still alive—remember?"

"All the same, I have to learn such news from Mort?"

"He called you?"

"I called him. In case you've forgotten, I am chief emergency medical official of Cabot Cove. I just thought I should check in, and what do I learn? That Jessica Fletcher is stranded at Hill House alone with a killer."

"I'm hardly alone, Seth. There's the rest of the wedding party, in addition to Seamus McGilray."

"Whatever that means. Mort was slight on the details."

"I didn't provide many."

"He said something about asphyxiation in what originally might have been deemed a weight-lifting accident. Broken neck as well?"

"No. By all accounts," I corrected, not going into all the details, "the young man's killer pressed the barbell down against his throat and held it there until . . . Anyway, I was just about to e-mail you some pictures so you could confirm that diagnosis."

"So now you're a medical examiner *and* a doctor? A more suspicious type might think you were out to replace me. Good thing Mort will soon be on his way to sort everything out."

"He's really going to try to make his way here? He told you that, Seth?"

"Indeed, he did, *ayuh*. Coming by snowmobile, he said, of all things. Says he's gonna try to make it to the fire station in his SUV and ride over to Hill House from there. I was almost tempted to ride along with him."

"What stopped you?"

"Survival instinct, I suppose, Jess. Have you ever known me to ride in any moving vehicle other than one of my trusty Volvos?"

"As a matter of fact, no."

"Then why start now? But I find myself worried over my favorite pinochle partner and fellow Mara's pie enthusiast."

"I'll be fine, Seth. Like you said, Mort will be on his way shortly."

"Right, riding a snowmobile," Seth repeated. "Might as well be coming from Boston. Don't forget to send me those pictures so the real de facto medical examiner of Cabot Cove can have a look."

Upstairs in the lobby, I left my phone on in case a call came from either Mort or Harry McGraw, whom I was expecting to hear from. By the time I got there everyone had been assembled, having been shepherded accordingly by Seamus McGilray and placed in a makeshift sitting area that had called for a repositioning of much of the lobby furniture into a neat circle. Seamus had left one of the staff members riding the storm out on the premises to watch over Constance Mulroy upstairs, and the ten remaining wedding party members gathered here along with Seamus and me.

Make that eight, I realized, quickly ascertaining that Ian and Faye, best man and maid of honor respectively, were missing.

"Couldn't rouse them from their room, Mrs. Fletcher," Seamus whispered to me. "They said they'd be down in good time."

I could tell by the teary reaction of Mark's cousin Lois Mulroy-Dodge that Seamus had already shared the news that Mark Mulroy had been found dead, most likely murdered, in the hotel gymnasium. The young woman's tearful reaction was consistent with what I would have expected given the circumstances of her upbringing, Mark much more like a brother to her.

Now, though, I needed to bring the remaining guests up to speed on the second tragedy that had struck here. I would certainly inform them of Mark Mulroy's likely murder, but I saw no reason at present to tell them of my suspicions about what may have befallen the future bride and groom.

All of their eyes were rooted on me as I approached, while my gaze fixed on the incredible scene continuing to rage in the world beyond the walls. I'd kept thinking this whole evening that the storm couldn't get any worse, but it had ideas of its own. If this wasn't its zenith, it must be close, because nothing was visible outside the windows besides a blinding curtain of white that gave up nothing through the spray of the hotel's outdoor floodlights. The windblown drifts made getting a fair estimate of how much snow had fallen difficult, but it was thirty inches easily, with hours more of snowfall to come, according to the latest forecasts. I even found myself fearing for Jim Cantore, who had weathered any number of major storms across much of the country, but never anything like this. He would certainly rue the day he'd opted for a live remote in the

storm's very worst track. Then I thought of Mort Metzger fool-
ishly trying to cover almost three miles through this treacherous weather to reach us, and I would have called to warn him
off if I'd believed there was any chance he'd listen to me.

Just as I was about to begin addressing those assembled
around me, my phone signaled an incoming text. I took a long-
enough glance to see it was from Harry McGraw and read simply, Have News. Call Me!

But Harry's news would have to wait, at least for a few minutes.

Chapter Thirteen

E ven though two members of the wedding party are currently missing," I started, "I see no reason for their absence to inconvenience everyone else further. First off,
thank you for your cooperation in coming down here. I can
see from your reactions," I continued, looking at the still-
sniffling Lois Mulroy-Dodge, "that you've already learned of
Mark Mulroy's tragic passing."

"Oh," interjected Doyle Castavette, as he loaded tobacco
into his pipe, "is that what you're calling murder these days?"

"Sir," said Seamus McGilray, "need I remind you that Hill
House is a smoke-free establishment?"

Castavette ignored him and lit up his pipe. "I should expect
it to be a murder-free establishment as well." He took several
deep puffs, which turned the pipe's tobacco packings fiery orange. "What are you going to do, kill me?"

Seamus, to his credit, let it go.

Beatrice Sprague was shaking her head. "That poor—"

"Boy," her sister, Olivia, completed for her. "So young and—"

"Charming," Beatrice picked up. "We watched him grow up, the family being so—"

"Close for a time."

Finished with their joint remarks, the sisters looked at each other and nodded sadly.

"Well, then," said Doyle Castavette between puffs on his pipe, "perhaps the non-Mulroys have nothing to fear. Perhaps whatever's going on here is aimed strictly at the Mulroys."

"I sincerely doubt that, Mr. Castavette," I told him. "Murder is more often than not a crime of opportunity, and Mark's trip alone to the hotel gym was likely to blame for his being the latest target."

"What about his mother?" Lois Mulroy-Dodge challenged in a whiny, nasal voice. "She wasn't alone. Whoever poisoned her drink could only have done it in potential view of a dozen witnesses, more if you include the waitstaff."

"True enough," I conceded.

"May I, Mrs. Fletcher?" started Doyle Castavette, making his son, Tyler—seated nearby, next to his mother, Henley Lavarnay—roll his eyes.

"May you what, Mr. Castavette?"

"May I speak?"

"Of course," I said politely, resisting all of the other terse responses that popped into my head.

"Would you mind explaining to me how it is that you've seized authority here, ordering us all about?" Castavette challenged.

His companion for the wedding, the actress Virginia Da Salle, nodded in support but the gesture looked forced and hardly convincing.

"It's a fair question," I acknowledged. "First off, you should all know that Cabot Cove's sheriff, Mort Metzger, is making his way here via snowmobile right now. In the meantime, Constable McGilray and I have taken charge because of our experience in such matters."

And with that, I met Seamus's gaze and came up just short of a wink.

"'Such matters' meaning murder?" Tyler Castavette said, looking sheepish, as if fearing I might ultimately report to the authorities his unwarranted entry into my suite.

"Regrettably," I told him, "yes."

"The ones you've made up or those you've actually solved?" posed Harrison Bak.

One of his crutches had tumbled over to the floor, and I retrieved it to save him the bother of straining to do so. "It's often difficult to tell them apart. But I didn't gather you all together to assume command. I gathered you all together so we could discuss how to survive the night without losing any more of your party."

Just then, Faye and Ian emerged from the elevator dressed as if they were headed for the ski slopes, except with backpacks slung from their shoulders.

"Hey, folks," said Ian. "I hope you don't mind us taking our leave of this circus."

"Are you mad?" Henley Lavarnay said caustically. "This storm's a killer."

"And there's one loose inside this hotel, too," Ian argued. "I think we'll take our chances."

"Is this why Daniel chose you as his best man instead of his own brother?" Tyler Castavette snapped. "So you could run out on everyone?"

"You'll have to ask him when he shows."

"To find you gone . . ."

"You really think the wedding will go forward with his mother in a coma and his brother dead? Show's over, dude. Live with it."

Tyler shook his head. "Daniel never was much of a judge of character."

"You know what they say," Ian snapped back at him. "You can choose your friends, but you can't choose your in-laws. Speaking of which, do your fellow guests know to keep track of their valuables with you in their company?"

The younger Castavette started to come out of his chair, only to be restrained with a firm hand and harsh look by his mother, Henley Lavarnay.

"I hope you freeze to death out there," Tyler shot at Ian instead.

"Better than dying in here." Ian swung toward me, Faye's head pivoting like a spindle in mirror fashion. "Two down, ten more to go, right, Mrs. Fletcher? But once we're gone, it'll only be eight."

"Look out the window," I warned him. "You won't get a hundred feet without losing your way in this."

"We'll take our chances—won't we, Faye?"

Still mute, Faye merely nodded.

"Good riddance," Lois Mulroy-Dodge hissed at them.

"Hey, Mrs. Fletcher, you should keep your eye on this one as a potential suspect. If she doesn't become the next victim, that is, given how much money she'll stand to inherit if Daniel turns up dead, too."

"How dare you?" the young woman, practically a daughter to Constance Mulroy, blurted out.

"This whole messed-up lot were no strangers to crime long before the bodies started dropping here tonight. No wonder the bride and groom are both no-shows. Come to think of it, Mrs. Fletcher, they just might be the prime suspects."

If only he knew, I thought, eager to change the subject.

"If you don't mind, Ms. Dodge, before Ian here departs, I was wondering if I might ask you a question I'd hoped to ask Mark Mulroy?"

"Of course, Mrs. Fletcher."

"In that slideshow that was on display over dinner, I noticed an unusual shadow in a shot of Daniel and Mark's nursery. On closer inspection, that shadow turned out to be a third crib," I said, finally getting to the point I'd been holding back. "My question is, why three cribs if there were only twins, and not triplets?"

Lois Mulroy-Dodge nodded slowly. "It's a sad story, Mrs. Fletcher, because there were triplets, but one of them died at birth. My aunt and uncle named him Owen and buried his remains in the family tomb."

The Sprague sisters were nodding in perfect synchronicity, obviously familiar with the story as well.

"You're right," I said to Lois, "a very sad story."

"Both these families seem consumed by them," noted Ian. "Now, if you don't mind . . ."

Before he and Faye could take another step for the door, eleven cell phones all buzzed practically in unison, including mine but not Seamus's. Like everyone else in the lobby but Seamus, I jerked mine from my pocket and found a trio of sour-faced emojis above a pair of Web links. I clicked on the first one, along with everyone else, all of us reading the same headline of a news report at almost the same time:

PRIVATE JET LANDS WITH ALL PASSENGERS DEAD
FOUL PLAY SUSPECTED

I stopped reading there and went back to the original text message to click on the second link instead of continuing. I could see others in the lobby doing the same thing, while some stuck with the first news story.

TEN GUESTS FOUND MURDERED IN PRIVATE
WILDERNESS RETREAT

Seamus had approached to read the content over my shoulder, everyone else perusing the articles at their own pace, with various utterances of shock and surprise.

Because the message from whoever had sent the text was clear: The killer wanted all of us to know that he or she had done this before and was doing it again.

Here, tonight.

*   *   *

"Madness!" exclaimed Doyle Castavette, laying his pipe down on the sill of an ashtray he must have carried with him.

"What are we going to do?" moaned Virginia Da Salle. "What are we going to do?"

I turned my gaze toward Seamus. We needed to read these articles more closely, but they changed everything by suggesting we were dealing with a serial mass murderer.

"It must be a game to him," noted Harrison Bak, "and now he's got us playing along."

"Well, we don't have to play, do we, Faye?" Ian asked the young woman by his side.

"No," Faye said, speaking finally. "Let's take our chances in the storm."

"Have you ever known such a thing, Mrs. Fletcher?" Bak asked me. "Someone who kills for sport, for the mere delight of it."

"Never directly," I told him. "But I think we're getting sidetracked. How, for instance, could such a killer have known we'd all be isolated here by a blizzard? That killer would have had a captive audience on that plane as well as at that wilderness retreat. Neither of those settings would be dependent on the weather for him to be assured his victims couldn't evacuate or flee."

"I think I read about this happening on one of those private yachts you can charter that was found floundering at sea," noted Henley Lavarnay. "A ghost ship, as they say, but quite literally, since no one was found on board and the remains of both the passengers and crew were deemed lost at sea."

"That would be in keeping with the pattern," her companion for the weekend, Harrison Bak, said, nodding. "But we're forgetting something, aren't we? This plot of his would require him to somehow round up all our cell phone numbers."

"Hardly a difficult task," noted Doyle Castavette, his voice ringing with derision.

"In most cases, I'd agree with you. But this," Bak explained, holding up his oversized smartphone, "is my work phone, not my personal one. I see no way the killer could have obtained it, no way at all."

"That's his game, is all," noted Tyler Castavette, with a knowledge best explained by his own experience. "Tonight is just the icing on the cake for him. The real fun came with getting to know us intimately, everything about us, so he could tease and taunt us prior to knocking us off one at a time."

"I'd listen to my son if I were you," his father told us all. "Tyler is, after all, well acquainted with the dark side of things. Isn't that right, son, given all your brushes with the law? When we get home, I suggest you begin looking for work that doesn't come from any of our various holdings. You've already burned all those bridges."

"*If* we get home," Tyler corrected. "Which is no sure thing, under the circumstances."

"You don't mean that, Doyle," said a stunned and embarrassed Virginia Da Salle from the other side of Tyler. "It's just the stress of the evening talking."

"When it comes to boorish behavior, it's not hard to figure who our son takes after, is it?" Henley Lavarnay challenged her ex-husband, as she looked toward Tyler. "I'll help you find something suitable with my contacts. Your father's not wrong, just misguided and heartless. You don't need him any more than I did."

"That's fitting," spat Doyle Castavette, "since if you hadn't spoiled him as much as you did, he wouldn't have made such a mess of his life."

"I think we're missing the point here," Henley Lavarnay said, turning away from her ex-husband in disgust and fixing her gaze on me. "Why bother with all these recriminations when we now have reason to believe we're the targets of a fiend who kills for sport?"

"We have reason to believe that because he wanted us to know," I reminded them.

"I'm not sure I understand your point."

"Well, Ms. Lavarnay," I said, taking a few steps closer to her, "in my experience it isn't a killer's habit to announce themselves. And when they do, it's normally more for distraction than for anything else."

"That's one heck of a distraction," noted Tyler Castavette.

"At last, intelligent words from my deadbeat offspring," said his father, the lament palpable in his voice. "They say if you leave a chimpanzee at a keyboard long enough, eventually he'll type the complete works of Shakespeare. Son, I do believe you've just proved that theory."

Tyler Castavette, for all his bravado and charisma, swallowed hard and leaned back in silence, not daring to cross his father, whom he must have relied on for funds to supplement the income gained from breaking into people's hotel rooms.

"None of this matters," I told them all, "none of it. All that does is that we survive the night. With any luck, the sheriff will be here soon, at which point he'll take charge and restore order. In the meantime, Constable McGilray and I will escort all of you back to your rooms on the second floor. We will see you safely inside one at a time after a careful check of the premises and wait until you lock the door behind you before we move on to the next. Once everyone is secured in their rooms, I'll return downstairs to await the sheriff's arrival, while the constable keeps watch of the hall."

Doyle Castavette lurched from his chair, a portrait of impatience. "Anything else, Mrs. Fletcher?"

"Just one thing. During my shift watching over Constance Mulroy," I said, addressing everyone, "I noticed a gap in her closet that seemed to indicate a matching piece of luggage the size of a tote bag was missing. I trust no one here would mind if Constable McGilray searches their room for it."

No one voiced objection, until Ian spoke up with his customary flair.

"Except us. We're blowing this joint. Hope all of you make it through the night."

"Not before we search both of your backpacks," Seamus said, sounding very much like the real policeman I had suggested he was.

Ian tossed his to the floor, Faye following suit immediately. "Fine. Have at it. Just hurry it up so we can be on our way. Take our chances in the storm instead of with you bozos."

Seamus collected the backpacks in either hand. "In that case, we'll search yours last. You can make yourselves comfortable back upstairs in your room in the meantime."

He gave Ian a stare that left the young man's knees weak. I was starting to wonder whether there was more to Seamus McGilray's career as a constable than he was letting on. Either way, Ian forced a smile and mocked a salute.

"Whatever you say, Officer. Just get it done before the next victim drops."

Just then Hill House's ancient grandfather clock chimed midnight, giving us all a start and turning our gazes in its direction. I heard a gasp. Then something rattled to the floor, shaken loose from someone's grasp.

"Oh my—," Olivia Sprague started.

"Stars," her sister, Beatrice, finished.

Because the roman numerals for one and two on the grandfather clock's face had been crossed out.

Chapter Fourteen

Took you long enough, Jess," said Harry McGraw, when I finally called as requested in his text.

"I've been busy, Harry," I said, having just managed to recover my senses after the others had all left the lobby to return to their rooms.

I had turned away from the grandfather clock before placing the call, as I had no desire to keep staring at what was the strongest indication yet that a murderer was indeed among us, a murderer who clearly had no intention of stopping until all twelve roman numerals were crossed off.

"Another attempted murder?" Harry asked me.

"Don't ask."

"I just did."

"This one succeeded."

Harry hesitated, only the sound of his breathing telling me he was still there. His tone sombered when he resumed.

"What's Mort have to say about this?"

"I don't know. He's on his way here now."

"What do you mean, he's on his way? In this storm?"

"He's coming by snowmobile."

"Do we have a bad connection, or did you just say he's coming by *snowmobile*?"

"What is it you have to tell me, Harry?"

"See what happens when I'm not there to protect you? Maybe I should head up there, too."

"You're in New York."

"But I've always wanted to see what five feet of snow looks like. Imagine all the bodies you could bury in that. . . ."

"I don't have to imagine that," I told him. "I'm living it right now."

"Well, here's something that might help. Does privilege exist between a private detective and his client?"

"You know, I'm not sure."

"If it doesn't, we never had this conversation, okay? Because it involves breaking a whole bunch of federal banking laws."

"You've lost me, Harry."

"Then allow me to get you back. I have a hacker friend who specializes in bank accounts, brokerage statements, investment accounts—all that sort of thing. Anyway, he was able to hack into the checking account of a certain PI named Loomis Winslow."

I recalled texting Harry the names of all those comprising the wedding party and now understood why he'd needed them.

"Turns out there was a rather sizable check deposited from a certain trust account. Care to guess who the signatory of the trust was?"

"Can you just tell me?"

"Constance Mulroy."

Harry had just added yet another piece to an increasingly twisted puzzle. In the scenario I conjured, Connie's hiring of Loomis Winslow must have been connected with the funds her husband had fleeced from his clients, provoking the investigation that led him to jump off the Brooklyn Bridge on the eve of his arrest. If that were the case, I could also assume that whatever Winslow had uncovered had led to his death. So no longer was the detective's presence in Cabot Cove a mystery in itself; he must have come here to meet directly with his client but had somehow ended up at that old textile factory before he could do so. His presence inside the decrepit, crumbling structure, though, indicated he'd ended up meeting with someone else entirely before he was murdered.

And not by Bigfoot either.

So who? And for what purpose? And how might the murder of Loomis Winslow be connected with the murder of Mark Mulroy and the attempt on his mother's life?

Before signing off with Harry, I forwarded him the text message containing the links detailing how comparably sized and similarly isolated groups had been summarily wiped out one or two at a time. If we were being toyed with, if the serial mass murderer behind those incidents had staked his claim here, that would substantially change the nature of what we were facing. Solving a mystery starts with motive, but when that motive is in itself the pure joy of killing, there is no launching point for the investigation. That didn't appear to be the case here, but who's to say seeking pleasure wasn't part of this killer's modus operandi? Maybe all the victims in these other mass murders were associated with one another, with secrets to hide and scores to settle that the killer was able to seize upon. In that scenario, I might be facing the most challenging adversary I've ever come up against.

"There's something else," I told him, already picturing all Harry might be able to unearth about those two other murder sprees.

"Wait a minute while I work my cash register. . . . *Ka-ching! Ka-ching!* . . . Okay, I'm ready."

"How are you with birth certificates, Harry?"

"Well, I like to avoid my own because it reminds me I was born, but other than that, what do you need?"

"If I gave you names and approximate birth dates, could you track them down?"

"What about city and hospital of birth?"

I shook my head, even though he couldn't see me. "Sorry."

"Ka-ching! Ka-ching!" he said again. "The difficult I can deliver in five minutes. The impossible takes a bit longer and tends to be very expensive."

"Put it on my bill."

"Your bill's longer than one of your books at this point. So, what are these names?"

*   *   *

I needed to wait for Harry to learn what he could about the other incidents, along with the other hunch I was playing. I needed to wait for Mort to arrive by snowmobile to take charge of the investigation.

In the meantime, I took the elevator to the second floor to assist Seamus McGilray's efforts in securing the guests in their rooms. I stepped off the elevator to find staring at me a bearded mountain of a man I'd never seen about Hill House before.

"You must be Mrs. Fletcher," said the man, who was wearing a Hill House kitchen uniform stretched at the seams by his vast bulk.

Bigfoot, I thought, as Seamus drew even with us. "I see you've met Eugene. I asked him to stand guard in the hallway to discourage anyone from leaving their rooms."

"How are things holding up, Constable?" I asked, finally lifting my gaze from the bearded mountain of a man.

"All guests secured in their rooms, having been advised that we intend to conduct searches in quest of Mrs. Mulroy's missing tote bag."

We started down the hall to begin that process.

"Tell me about Eugene," I said softly.

"He's a temp we brought on for the wedding-party weekend, as we call it. As you know, we're short staffed during the winter, and we needed to beef up a bit even before our responsibilities became increased by the stranding of our guests."

I glanced back at Eugene and tried to reconcile his appearance with Hank Weathers's claim to have witnessed Bigfoot murdering Loomis Winslow. "Nice to hear all of those guests cooperated," I said, returning my gaze to Seamus.

"They're frightened, Mrs. Fletcher—*terrified* might be a more accurate way of stating it. I think the bulk of them see you as their best hope to live through the night."

"That text message and the possibility that we're facing a killer who's done this before, several times, has definitely changed the equation."

Seamus's expression tightened. "You think it was the killer himself, or herself, who sent the text message, don't you?"

"In that scenario, we'd all be nothing more than pieces to be moved around the board of this game he's playing. But it could also be a distraction, someone covering their tracks in advance and making us chase something we're never going to find."

Before Seamus could respond, a figure I recognized as the actress Virginia Da Salle burst out from a door at the far end of the hall.

"Someone help me! *Help me!*" she cried out, before her eyes fell on Seamus and me. *"Please help me!"*

Seamus and I charged down the hall, as the doors along the hallway jerked open.

"Doyle's locked in the bedroom of our suite!" Virginia screeched, digging her fingers into both my arms, when we got to Doyle Castavette's suite. "Something's happening in there, something terrible!"

Seamus and I surged past her into the living room portion of their suite, swiftly followed by more of the wedding guests, trailed by Harrison Bak, maneuvering gingerly on his crutches, Henley Lavarnay riding his wake. The sounds of a terrible commotion emanated from inside the bedroom.

Seamus got to the door first and began pounding. "Mr. Castavette, Mr. Castavette, can you hear me? Mr. Castavette, it's Constable McGilray! What's happening in there? Open the door, man—open the door!"

The commotion continued, all manner of crashing and smashing sounds, including the distinct crackle of something breaking in whatever struggle was transpiring inside the bedroom. Who might be in there with Doyle Castavette? The increasingly annoying Ian and Faye were absent yet again, and I couldn't see Lois Mulroy-Dodge anywhere about either. But it was the absence of Tyler Castavette that struck me the hardest, given the bitter attack his father had launched on him down in the lobby.

Something slammed against the door, rattling the heavy wood and forcing the lot of us gathered in the living room section of the suite to lurch backward involuntarily. I was quite certain the screams and cries I heard were coming from Doyle Castavette himself and not whoever he was struggling with.

"Get Eugene," I told Seamus, who backpedaled and then charged out of the suite.

I continued to pound on the door in vain, kept futilely calling Doyle Castavette's name as his unmistakable cries kept raging, the only sound before heavy footsteps pounded the carpeting of the suite and Eugene brushed past me to have a go at the door. Talk about a temp worker earning his keep!

I got well out of his way, so he'd have a clear path smashing it. But the heavy wooden frame, as old as Hill House itself, resisted the first thrust from the massive man's shoulder, and the second. It buckled on the third, and with the fourth finally shattered along the jamb from the latch on up.

The sounds of Eugene's pounding had hidden the fact that all signs of a struggle had ceased inside the bedroom portion of the suite. When the door finally blew inward, it was to reveal Doyle Castavette slumped on the floor with his back resting against the bed, head pitched downward as if to stare at the knife protruding from his chest.

And no sign of his killer anywhere.

It had been a direct strike to the heart that killed Doyle Castavette. Judging by how little blood had leaked from the wound, he had died almost instantly. He had been screaming until he stopped all of a sudden, the explanation as to why now clear.

I surveyed the body but didn't dare touch it or otherwise disturb the scene with Mort Metzger's arrival likely imminent by now. But I couldn't help sweeping my gaze about the wholly disheveled bedroom. The mattress was half on, half off the bed, the bedcovers themselves in tatters. A highboy bureau had tipped over and crashed to the floor in the melee, and both a single table lamp and a floor lamp had shattered and left shards of glass and porcelain scattered across the rug. The big mirror over the desk had cracked, and the desk chair had overturned and was now missing a chunk of one of its legs. The closet door hung awkwardly from its broken hinges, revealing a trio of suitcases: a single oversized one for Doyle Castavette and two

smaller pieces from a floral set that must belong to his companion, Virginia Da Salle.

Doyle Castavette had certainly fought for the life he ultimately lost to his killer, who was nowhere to be found in the
room.

Which was, of course, impossible—even more impossible
than Constance Mulroy's wine ending up poisoned.

"What?" I heard someone blare from the doorway. *"What?"*

I spotted Tyler Castavette standing there.

"Who did this?" Tyler Castavette hissed to himself as much
as anyone else. "Where did they go?"

His eyes, which had been fixed on his murdered father, rotated about the room, and I found myself following his gaze.
He started to enter the room but I blocked his way.

"Constable McGilray," I said, using my most authoritative
tone, with my eyes still fastened on Tyler Castavette, "I'd like
you and Eugene to conduct a thorough search of the premises
we will then secure. We need to uncover what became of Mr.
Castavette's murderer."

Seamus nodded, not hesitant at all and perhaps even wel-
coming the task, given that it was his hotel that had been in-
vaded by a killer. So, leaving the body exactly as we found it, I
closed the door Eugene had shattered at the latch as best I
could behind Seamus and the hulking Eugene, so they might
go about their business unencumbered by curious eyes.

Tyler finally got the message and backed stiffly from the
doorway, into the living room section of the suite. He was
breathing hard and seemed to be shaking, out of shock, I

imagined. I then moved my gaze across those gathered in the living room portion of the suite who'd heard the now-sobbing Virginia Da Salle's desperate pleas and come running. The Sprague sisters sat on either side of her, rotating words of comfort in a constant stream as best they could. So, that was four of our remaining number, and my gaze quickly found Henley Lavarnay, the victim's former wife, who didn't bother with any faux displays of emotion over his passing. Add her weekend companion, Harrison Bak, to the number and we were all of six, I thought, realizing that didn't include Lois Mulroy-Dodge.

"Oh my," I heard her gasp in that very moment, storming into the suite with her hair still wet from the shower.

"It must be her!" a dry-mouthed Virginia Da Salle managed, bursting out of her chair and pointing an accusing finger toward the young woman. "She's the only one who was unaccounted for when Doyle was fighting for his life!"

"Not quite," I realized. "Where are Faye and Ian?"

"Who *are* Faye and Ian?" Tyler Castavette challenged. "Do we even know their last names? Is there anyone among us who'd even heard of either one of them before tonight?"

His mother, Henley Lavarnay, raised her hand tentatively. "I may have once. Allison's college graduation party, I think it was."

"And you're sure this is the same couple?" I asked her.

"Right now," she said, looking past me toward the body of her dead ex-husband, "I'm not sure of anything."

"Why don't we see what's become of them?" I suggested.

"I'll tell you what's become of them," said the belligerent

Tyler. "They hightailed it out of this place when the rest of us rushed in here."

"Then," I suggested, "let's see if they're still in their room."

When a polite round of knocking on the door to the room occupied by Ian and Faye produced no response, I knocked again, more loudly, then pounded the door hard enough to make my fist ache. None of these efforts achieved any result, leaving me no choice but to wait for Seamus to emerge from his search of Doyle Castavette's bedroom with pass key card in hand.

I spotted him emerging from the dead man's suite, with Eugene riding his wake, and I steered him away from the congestion of guests gathered in front of the door to Ian and Faye's room.

"I'm assuming you found nothing," I said to Seamus.

"You're right, Mrs. Fletcher. We checked every hiding place in that room. Behind the curtains, under the bed, in the closet with clothes strung from hangers over suitcases tucked away for the weekend, and finally in the shower." He shook his head. "Nothing, not a trace. I'd almost venture to say that our killer either disappeared into thin air or was invisible in the first place."

"Since we can safely rule out both of those options, the killer must have used another means to exit, and perhaps gain access to, the room."

"Our security software will be able to tell us the sequence of the room's door lock being tripped."

"But we know the killer didn't leave that way, not past all

those gathered witnesses, don't we? Ruling out the door and any possible concealment, what are we left with?"

Seamus shrugged. "The window, I suppose."

"Did you check it?"

"I couldn't even see out of it, my good woman. It's an old-fashioned casement window, and the way it's frozen over and crusted with snow, I can tell you with some certainty that it hasn't been opened since the storm's start." He seemed to regard the guests gathered before Ian and Faye's room at the end of the hall, before continuing in a lowered voice. "We did find something inside Mr. Castavette's closet that will be of significant interest to you, though, Mrs. Fletcher."

I recalled the door hanging awkwardly from its hinges. "I'm listening, Seamus."

I watched him hedge. "It's better you see for yourself, ma'am."

I could feel the eyes of the other guests tightening upon us from down the hall before Ian and Faye's room. "That will have to wait. There's something else that requires your attention right now. I assume you have your pass key on you?"

He was already reaching for the key card in his pocket.

But his pass key card didn't work. Seamus swiped the card again and again, drawing only a repeated red flashing signal from the door's locking system.

"That's truly odd," Seamus managed, backing off.

He'd been going nonstop, but strangely, the exertion of

THE MURDER OF TWELVE

swiping the key card again and again took his breath away more than any other exertion of the evening.

"Should we summon Eugene?" I asked him, not even convinced we could yet trust the big bearded man whom a drunken witness might have easily confused with Bigfoot.

Seamus shook his head. "This is a steel fire door. It would take an entire American football team to shoulder through it. I suppose I—"

Before he could continue, the door clicked from the inside and Ian yanked it open.

"What's the problem?"

"We thought you might be dead," I told them. "Why didn't you answer the door when I first knocked?"

"Because we didn't want to," the ever-petulant Ian said, smirking. "It's our room, our right."

"No," snapped Lois Mulroy-Dodge, from behind me, "it's my aunt's room. All of us are staying in *her* rooms, because she paid for them all. We're her guests."

Ian smirked again. "I guess it's too bad, then, that she's not in any condition to send me to bed without my supper."

Beatrice and Olivia Sprague were shaking their heads in perfect unison.

"You are a very rude—," one of them started.

"Young man," the other finished.

Ian ignored them. I finally spotted the ever-silent Faye riding his shadow, standing just out of sight from the door.

"Constable McGilray and I were just about to begin interviewing the guests about their general whereabouts," I said, making that up on the spot, "and what they might have seen, around the time of each of tonight's tragic events. I believe now that we'll start with you, Ian."

"Whatever you say."

"Just make sure you open the door this time."

"Now, what is it you have to show me?" I said to Seamus, once all the other guests were secured in their rooms.

The plan was for them to wait inside for their turn to be interviewed, the one exception being the actress Virginia Da Salle, the late Doyle Castavette's companion, who had taken her refuge with the Sprague sisters.

"Two things, actually," he said, opening the door to the Castavette suite with his pass key card and tilting his gaze toward me. "Both of them most interesting."

We entered the living room section, leaving Eugene at his post down the hall to make sure no one emerged while we were indisposed prior to beginning our interviews. I noticed immediately that a slightly recessed, rectangular section of the ceiling had been pushed back to reveal a dark space beyond. I remembered that my suite had the very same recessed rectangle—two of them, actually, in each room comprising my suite.

"A crawl space?" I posed to Seamus. "I didn't realize the hotel still had one, thought it had probably been removed during all the renovating over the years."

"We use it as a conduit to string electrical and television cables after they're fished through the walls. Besides workmen and perhaps technicians from time to time, I don't think a soul has been inside the space in years. Here, Mrs. Fletcher, have a look for yourself."

He offered to help me up onto a chair he'd placed immediately before the recessed opening but I managed the task quite easily on my own. He'd had to pull a chair in from the living room area since the desk chair that matched the bedroom desk had broken during the struggle between Doyle Castavette and his killer and now sported only three legs. At five feet eight inches, I found that standing on the chair just allowed me to crest my head through the sliding panel Seamus must have opened to check the crawl space himself. But I couldn't see a thing.

"Take hold of this, Mrs. Fletcher," Seamus said, pressing a flashlight into my hand.

I maneuvered awkwardly to raise that hand through the cramped opening. I switched on the beam, illuminating a long shaft the approximate dimensions of an old-fashioned laundry chute. The crawl space was very much in keeping with his description, save for confines so tight that I couldn't at all picture a cable TV or electric company technician squirrelling around in there. Besides the dust swirling in my flashlight beam, all I saw was a warren of thin and thick cables and wires strung together and either running along the bottom of the crawl space or affixed to the walls with some kind of riveted ties. Although I was balanced precariously on the chair, I maintained the presence of mind to use the flashlight to study the dust-riddled bottom, finished in what looked like tin, for any signs of disturbance. The thin layer of accumulated dust remained untouched, though, at least as far as my beam reached.

"You actually had people working in this?" I said down to Seamus.

"It was quite a few years ago, and we've rerouted a number of our systems with the coming of Wi-Fi. But the answer is yes, for a short time, anyway."

"I can see why," I said, having gained an even closer perspective. "An average-sized man, or woman, would have to hold their breath to squeeze through, and even then . . ."

I let my voice tail off, unsure of what I wanted to say next. I found myself deeply missing the presence of Mort Metzger, even more because he must surely be close by now. I felt like I had as a young child waiting by the window for my father to return from work as the light drained from the daytime sky.

Mort, where are you?

The dust had started getting into my eyes and mouth, and once I'd lowered myself from the crawl space opening in the ceiling, Seamus helped me down from the chair.

"I believe you'll find what I've got to show you next even more interesting, Mrs. Fletcher," he said, leading me across the room.

I resolved to cover the still form of Doyle Castavette with a sheet so as not to be discomfited in the presence of a corpse. I kept my eyes from it and trailed Seamus to the broken closet door he proceeded to open all the way, gesturing upward to reveal a tote bag that didn't match the rest of the collected luggage. It lay by itself on the closet shelf, shoved far enough back to explain how I'd missed spotting it in my original check of the closet after we'd found Doyle Castavette's body. Illuminating indeed.

Because it belonged to Constance Mulroy, a perfect fit for that gap I'd noticed between the medium-sized suitcase and makeup kit in the comatose woman's closet.

Chapter Fifteen

You didn't touch or disturb it, of course?" I said to Seamus.

He shook his head, saying lightly, "I am a constable, after all."

I didn't dare inspect it before donning a pair of plastic evidence gloves. I kept a collection in my suite, although I couldn't readily explain why. I'd sometimes find them still in my pocket, normally unused, after Mort and I had found ourselves involved in something that required their use. I'd discard them in a drawer because I generally couldn't bear tossing away anything new and in perfectly good condition. Call it a consequence of being raised in a large family.

Seamus remained in place, while I retreated to my third-floor suite as quickly as I could and returned with a pair of evidence gloves donned even more quickly. I made short order of easing the tote bag from the shelf and carried it into the suite's living room section to avoid having to keep company with the late Mr. Castavette. There, I set the tote down on the couch and unzipped it.

"Oh my," Seamus gasped, at the sight of the contents.

"I don't want to go back inside there!" Virginia Da Salle protested, stiffening as we reached the open door to Doyle Castavette's suite, where Seamus was waiting. "I never want to go in there again!"

"I fully understand, Ms. Da Salle," I said, still urging her on. "But it'll only be the living room portion, and we managed to keep the broken door to the bedroom closed. And there's something that you really must see. To help in the investigation into Doyle's murder," I added.

She nodded and reluctantly allowed me to lead her inside the suite, her arm as stiff as a board.

The tote bag belonging to Constance Mulroy, opened atop the couch, was stacked to the brim with tightly wrapped bundles of cash. A combination of fifty- and one-hundred-dollar bills, by the look of things.

"What's that?" Virginia Da Salle asked, pointing at the bag.

"We were hoping you could tell us that," Seamus started.

"Especially since it matches the tote missing from the luggage set in Mrs. Mulroy's closet," I added. Seamus and I were becoming like the Sprague sisters, comfortable with completing each other's thoughts.

"How much money is in there?"

"Somewhere around a half million dollars," I ventured, looking toward Seamus, who nodded in assent.

Virginia's expression tightened. "Wait—who . . . How . . . ?" She left both thoughts dangling.

"Exactly the question I was going to ask you, Ms. Da Salle," I said, moving my gaze from her down to the tote bag.

I pointed toward dual handles.

"Notice that mark?" I asked her.

"Looks like a stain," she said, squinting to see it better. "Paint or something."

"Or nail polish, perhaps. Red nail polish, Ms. Da Salle, a fine match for the color you're wearing right now," I said, tilting my gaze in the direction of her hands.

The former actress pulled them aside, as if to hide that fact. I glimpsed Seamus's mouth dropping in surprise at my spotting something that had escaped his attention.

"In fact," I continued, seizing the moment, "looking at your nails now, I'd say it's a *perfect* match. Any idea how that could possibly be, apart from your actually having come into contact with this tote?"

"I assure you that I don't, Mrs. Fletcher."

"Why don't we sit down?"

Virginia's gaze swept toward the closed-off bedroom section of the suite, as if to explain her resistance. "Here?"

"Just for a few minutes."

"You don't think I had anything to do with Doyle's death?"

"Not since you were standing by my side during the struggle.

Constable McGilray and I are interviewing all the members of the wedding party to ascertain their presence at varying times."

"You mean, those of us who are still alive—at least for the time being, with that fiend loose in this horrible place."

I could sense Seamus wincing at that description of his beloved hotel.

"You should be looking into the killer from that plane and that retreat, Mrs. Fletcher," Virginia Da Salle continued. "How he managed to take so many victims in those other locales as well. Have you even spoken to anyone involved in those investigations?"

"I haven't gotten that far in my thinking yet, and in case you've forgotten, we've all been rather otherwise involved since receiving that text message."

"He knew we were all gathered together at the time," the woman said, her voice cracking in fear. "That's why he must have sent the text when he did, to let us know we were all to be his next victims!"

"Ms. Da Salle—"

"Doyle was alive at the time, no idea his name was at the top of the list. Sitting right alongside me," Virginia added, her eyes starting to moisten.

"That doesn't explain the presence of your nail polish on Constance Mulroy's missing tote bag," I said.

"Doesn't it? You just admitted you haven't looked into those other murder sprees, Mrs. Fletcher. How can you be sure similar things didn't happen with those poor people? You know, to cast false suspicions, confuse the issue."

"Well," I told her, "there's one thing here at Hill House that neither that airplane nor that wilderness lodge had."

"What's that?"

"Me. And Constable McGilray, of course," I added.

I'd intended the remark to provide some solace, but the truth was, I found the notion of murder victims being claimed at a wilderness retreat to be especially disconcerting. They would likely have included at least a few hardier sorts, perhaps of the hunting or soldiering mode, on the premises who would have proven formidable adversaries for any killer, especially one who announced their intentions. A struggle with a man like that might have ended in considerably different fashion than the one we'd heard from outside the door to Doyle Castavette's bedroom.

"I know I've seen some of your movies, Ms. Da Salle," I said, changing the subject to something she'd be more comfortable with. "But forgive me for not being able to name the titles or your roles."

She smiled, not sadly so much as reflectively. "That's understandable, Mrs. Fletcher. I've enjoyed a great career as a working actress many recognize but nobody really knows. Never had a starring role, but it's not that I didn't try. I suppose it's not unlike being a writer. There's only space for so many bestsellers like yours, right?"

"I appreciate the kind words, Ms. Da Salle, but there are plenty of authors out there who can match me in every way except longevity."

"Your first book was a bestseller right out of the box."

"*The Corpse Danced at Midnight*," I said, nodding. "I was in the right place at the right time, with a publishing house that desperately needed a popular hit."

She smiled whimsically. "I almost got the biggest role of my career when another actress took sick just before shooting was scheduled to start. I showed up on the set the first day having memorized all of her lines for the day's shoot, as well as my original character's."

"What happened?"

"The production was shut down. The producers realized they could do better claiming the insurance than risking a failure at the box office. Too bad, because it was a wonderful script. I was to play a mystery writer, of all things."

"You're kidding."

Virginia Da Salle shook her head, smiling. "If I'd known you at the time, I could have asked for a few pointers."

"Not that I would have been able to help you much, given that a movie about my life would be the most boring film ever made."

"I don't think you're giving yourself enough credit, Mrs. Fletcher. And that's coming from an actress without a single role anyone really remembers her playing."

I liked this woman much more than I should have, considering how briefly I'd known her and the circumstances that had brought us together. Virginia Da Salle had a quiet humility about her; she was a woman in touch with the limitations forced upon her and she had the ability to persevere in spite of them.

"May I ask you a personal question, Ms. Da Salle?"

"Only if you call me Virginia."

I leaned in a bit closer to her. "How did you meet Doyle Castavette?"

"He invested in a few films I was in. I think it was about the lifestyle, an excuse to be on set and attend nonexistent Hollywood parties everyone believes are real. The truth is, Hollywood is an early-to-bed-early-to-rise town."

I held Virginia's gaze briefly. "Not for Doyle Castavette, I imagine."

She looked down. "This isn't easy for me to say."

I gave her the time she needed. Her face was stoic and reflective when she lifted her gaze again.

"An actress my age goes from small roles to no roles. Mr. Castavette seemed to be aware of my financial situation. I imagine it may have been what led him to approach me, Mrs. Fletcher."

"Jessica, and I find that horrible."

"Because he took advantage of me? Don't blame him for that, Jessica. I was doing the very same thing to him. A wealthy older man who'd fallen out of love with his wife, if he'd ever loved her in the first place. I doubt it, because Doyle didn't seem the kind of man who could love anyone. But that was okay, because we both accepted each other for what we were. And I appreciated the fact he didn't try to woo me with false promises of a starring role in the next film he was financing. You'd be amazed at how often that still happens out there."

"Not really. But I suppose I should feel grateful that doesn't happen to writers. You know, Richard Burton once said that if he had to come back to life he'd want to do it as a novelist, because you're only famous if you tell people who you are."

"Everyone knows who you are, Jessica."

"Many know my books, even my name—at least J. B. Fletcher—but they don't know me, and the only time anyone ever approaches me is during the summer right here in Cabot Cove to ask for directions to this place or that while I'm out on my bicycle."

"I envy you that—not the lack of recognition so much as the value you're able to place on your privacy. In my world—well, former world—your success can often be judged by how many people recognize you on the street. For a while there, I was doing pretty well."

"Would you mind another personal question, Virginia?" I said, leaning back again.

"Not at all."

"Did Mr. Castavette ever discuss with you the financial problems he was experiencing?"

She looked genuinely surprised. "I wasn't aware he was experiencing anything of the sort. If you're right, he hid it from me very well, and never skimped when we were together."

"Then he never mentioned the money he'd been swindled out of after investing in the late Heath Mulroy's investment fund?"

"No, not a word, Jessica. Like everyone else, I could sense some friction between Doyle and Constance Mulroy, but I passed it off as nothing more than prewedding future–in–law jitters. I did a romantic comedy once where that was basically the log line."

"Because, Virginia, it occurs to me that his financial issues, together with the cause of them, make for a great motive for stealing a significant sum from the family that cost him his fortune. Of course, that brings up the issue of why Constance Mulroy would be carrying around a tote bag full of cash."

"You think maybe she gave it to him, like a payoff of some kind?"

I held her stare, not letting myself blink. "That wouldn't explain the presence of your nail polish on the handle," I said, pointing out the small smudge yet again.

"I can't explain it either, Mrs. Fletcher," she responded, going back to referring to me in a more formal manner.

I wanted to believe her—I really did. "Do you have that nail polish with you, Virginia?"

"Yes, right here in my bag," she offered.

She was already searching through its contents, which rattled around as she sifted through them.

"That's odd," she said, coming up empty. "It doesn't seem to be here. But I'm sure it was earlier in the day—I'm sure. I might have left it in the bathroom." Her eyes fixed on the closed door separating the living room from the bedroom. "Would you mind checking? I can't bring myself to go in there."

I nodded and moved through the door into the bedroom, then closed the door so as not to give her any view of the murder scene and was very glad I had covered the deceased Mr. Castavette with a sheet. I found the small bottle of nail polish on a modest shelf between the bathroom wall mirror and the sink, where Virginia Da Salle must have left it. Looking up, I noticed the closet door still hung open and moved to close it. Something else grabbed my eye as I started to do just that. I was about to pass it off as a trick of my imagination when I noticed the large suitcase in the closet was unzipped. But I distinctly remembered it being fully closed when I did a check of the room with Seamus McGilray after we'd discovered Doyle Castavette's body.

"Might this be it?" I asked Virginia, emerging from the bedroom with a tiny bottle of nail polish in exactly the right shade of red, tabling for now the apparent anomaly of the suitcase being opened.

She rose to take it from my grasp. "Yes, yes, it is. Royal Magenta, it's actually called. They have a hundred names for these colors that are basically red."

"Kind of like my book covers. You know what Samuel Goldwyn once said when asked what he wanted in his next movie? 'Give me the same thing, only different.'"

We shared a smile, hers slipping from her face ahead of mine.

"Do you believe me? Do you believe me, Jessica?"

I nodded. "I do, Virginia, yes."

She looked from the small bottle of nail polish to the smudge of it on Constance Mulroy's tote bag full of cash. "I just wonder how that got there."

"Since you're clearly innocent of Mr. Castavette's murder, I don't think we need to worry about that now."

It was time to take our conversation in a different direction. "One more thing, Virginia. After the wedding party left

Mrs. Mulroy's room, and her son Mark made his way to the gym, where did you go?"

Her expression tightened. "You just said I wasn't a suspect."

"You're not. But Constable McGilray and I are doing our best to ascertain everyone's whereabouts when someone tried to murder Mrs. Mulroy and succeeded in murdering her son."

"Back to our suite, of course, where I remained until we were called to the lobby and learned of that young man's death—murder."

"Was Doyle Castavette with you?"

"The whole time, I believe. If he was out of my sight, it wasn't for much more than a few minutes."

"And can you account for anyone else's presence between the time you left Constance Mulroy's room and the time Constable McGilray summoned everyone to the lobby?"

"Let me see. . . . Well, I thought I heard footsteps at one point, right outside our door. But when I opened it no one was there."

"What about the younger Mr. Castavette?"

"What about him?" Virginia said defensively.

"You didn't see him again until the two of you were seated next to each other down in the lobby?"

"No. Why would I?"

"Listen to me, Virginia," I said, hardening my tone a bit. "Two people have been murdered tonight and a third is lying in a coma. Since it's my firm belief that the same person is responsible for all three, I'm trying to figure out who among the original twelve of you remaining had the opportunity to do so."

She swallowed hard, didn't seem to enjoy meeting my gaze. "No, I didn't see Tyler Castavette anywhere until we all got to the lobby. So I suppose he could have killed Mark Mulroy, if that's what you're asking. But his father? Not based on when he appeared in the suite, which was just seconds after that big man broke the door down."

I didn't bother challenging her assertion, having arrived at that same conclusion myself.

"Given that, I do have one final question for you. You say you haven't returned to the bedroom since Mr. Castavette's death, yes?"

She nodded. "And I don't intend to either, not so long as his . . ." Her voice cracked, broke off. "You know what I mean."

"You're sure?"

"That I haven't been in the bedroom since his death? Absolutely. What makes you ask?"

My memory was suddenly fuzzy on whether Doyle Castavette's large suitcase had been opened or closed on my initial inspection of the room.

"No reason," I told Virginia Da Salle.

"You were quite the good sport back there, Mrs. Fletcher," Seamus said to me after we'd delivered Virginia Da Salle back into the care of the Sprague sisters down the hall. "I could see your mind working when she asked you how the nail polish got there."

"She didn't ask, Seamus—she was just wondering."

"All the same, you could have answered her, but you chose not to."

"Was it that obvious?"

"It was to me, Mrs. Fletcher, but then, I have read all of your books, so I know the signs."

I nodded, seeing no reason to hold anything back from him. "I think Doyle Castavette planted the nail polish on the tote bag, so he could blame Virginia for the theft if his crime came to light. Call it a contingency plan."

"How awful."

"But not surprising, given what we witnessed from Castavette tonight."

He frowned. "I suppose. Does it say anything about Mr. Castavette's killer that he, or she, left the money behind?"

"That he, or she, either didn't know about it or didn't care."

We stood in the hall alone, well apart from Eugene, who remained at his post.

"A private investigator was found murdered in Cabot Cove this morning," I confided in Constable Seamus McGilray. "Yesterday morning now," I added, since it was well past midnight, closing in on one a.m. "I learned this evening that he had been hired by Constance Mulroy."

"That doesn't explain why she'd bring so much cash along with her."

"Unless she had planned to hand it over to someone."

I could tell my assertion sent Seamus's mind whirling. "For

a payoff of some kind, you think? Some form of blackmail or extortion?"

I nodded. "I'm leaning in that direction, yes. It would certainly be consistent with Doyle Castavette's character."

"In which case, Mrs. Fletcher, Constance Mulroy would be the most likely suspect in his murder, but we can safely rule her out."

"Right now, Seamus, I'm not ruling anyone out."

Chapter Sixteen

I had learned plenty about the late Doyle Castavette from Virginia Da Salle and decided to interview his ex-wife, Henley Lavarnay, next. Before doing so, though, I called Seth Hazlitt.

"At last, Jess! Why haven't you been returning my calls?"

"I haven't gotten any. My phone hasn't even rung."

"Blasted cell service! I tell you, these things aren't worth the metal they're made of. I'm of a mind to turn mine back in."

"If I didn't have one, you wouldn't be able to contact me at all."

"Which I wasn't able to do anyway. Just tell me you're okay."

"I'm okay."

"And that there've been no further murders."

"That would be a lie."

"Oh no . . . Who was it this time, Jess, on top of that young man in the weight room?"

"Did you get the pictures I sent you of the scene?"

"That's what I was calling you about. From what I can tell, your initial diagnosis was correct. The young man died of asphyxiation, not a broken neck. Now tell me about this most recent victim."

"The father of the bride, killed by a knife to the chest."

"No mystery as to the cause of death there."

"Have you heard from Mort?" I asked him, wondering if Mort, too, had been unable to reach me by phone.

"Not since he was setting out for Hill House by snowmobile, but that was quite a while ago. He should have arrived by now."

"It'll be an awful ride in these conditions, Seth. It's been two hours, during which the storm's only gotten worse. Maybe he turned around and went back to the station."

"He would have called you if he'd done that, Jess."

"Maybe I didn't get his call just like I didn't get yours," I said, determining to check my phone log and voice mail to be sure.

I heard Seth sigh on the other end of the line. "I knew this night was going to be bad, but it's gotten even worse."

I decided to interview Henley Lavarnay in the company of her date for the occasion, Harrison Bak. It's been my experience that sometimes a joint interview produces far more usable information, in part because the participants are more likely to let their guards down. It also allows me to judge those participants' reactions to each other's answers and comments, and

sometimes those reactions prove more fruitful than the answers themselves.

"Harrison," I said to the man currently seated in the room's
desk chair, his hands looped through the handles of his crutches
on either side of the chair as if to balance him, "you have the
distinction of being the one suspect I can cross off the list, since
we were seated next to each other at dinner and you never had
the opportunity to poison Constance Mulroy's wine."

He held his crutches up. "These are good for that much,
anyway. You'd like to know how I came to use them."

"I was curious, under the circumstances."

"A spinal cord injury suffered in a car accident closing in
on twenty years ago."

"I'm sorry."

"Why?" Harrison Bak asked, coming up just short of a
smile. "Since you've ruled me out as a suspect, it's the first time
they've ever come in handy."

Bak had positioned himself alongside the armchair in
which Henley Lavarnay was seated. I had taken the matching
ottoman, and Seamus was leaning forward just to my right on
the edge of one of two beds.

"How did the two of you meet?" I asked them both.

Henley laid a hand over Harrison Bak's. "He represented
me in my divorce from my ex-husband—*late* ex-husband now."

He grinned. "Took him for a pretty penny, didn't we? And
before the whole mess with Heath Mulroy surfaced to boot."

"A criminal attorney of your stature handling a divorce
proceeding?" I posed to Bak.

He shared a smile with his client before responding. "I

made an exception in this case, though I relied heavily on my firm's family law specialists. And it was a true pleasure putting the hurt on Doyle Castavette."

"Harrison had represented my ex-husband on several matters," Henley said, by way of explanation.

"Criminal matters, I suppose?"

"Since he's no longer with us, I can tell you there were DWIs, among other matters handled discreetly for both Doyle and his son. Doyle liked his 'people'—that's what he called us—to be available for him at all hours of the day or night. He expected us to jump when he said so, and I suppose for five hundred dollars an hour, he had that right."

"I gather the two of you had a falling out," I advanced.

Harrison Bak nodded. "I wasn't going to suborn perjury," he said, and left it there.

"May I ask you a legal question?"

"Of course."

"If the late Mr. Castavette had come into any funds due him as a result of the money he lost to Mr. Mulroy's scam, a settlement or the like, would Ms. Lavarnay be entitled to half of it?"

"Almost certainly."

I nodded, wondering if Doyle Castavette had asked Constance Mulroy to pay him in cash in order to hide the transaction—a payoff, essentially—from his ex-wife. Might that have somehow played into the scenario unfolding before us?

"You should keep your eyes on my son, Tyler, Mrs. Fletcher," Henley Lavarnay said, quite out of nowhere.

"You have reason to suspect him of something?"

"I have reason to suspect him of *everything*. He used to

steal cash from my handbag as a child, and he's only gotten worse from there. We like to believe our children can do no wrong, because otherwise they'd reflect badly on us. But Tyler was his father's son. He's barely said a word to me since the divorce."

I was tempted to tell her of how he'd accessed my room with a master key card, but I decided against it. She had, after all, stuck up for her son down in the lobby, though I suppose that was likely more about siding against her former husband than defending Tyler.

"Do you think Tyler killed his father, Ms. Lavarnay?"

She hedged. "He was standing in the doorway when we found Doyle's body, so it doesn't seem possible, does it?"

I didn't respond.

"Just like we were all in our rooms when young Mr. Mulroy was murdered in the gym," Harrison Bak put forth. "As a defense lawyer, Mrs. Fletcher, I might go so far as to venture that all the suspects here had alibis for at least one and potentially both murders, as well as the attempt on Mrs. Mulroy's life. I could be wrong, but I don't think your efforts are going to point to anyone in particular."

"Nothing new, at this stage of an investigation," I told him.

I decided to interview Lois Mulroy-Dodge next, figuring she was the guest most likely to have the answers I was seeking, now that I'd learned that Loomis Winslow had been retained by Constance Mulroy, clearly to ferret out some level of the financial malfeasance that had laid ruin to the family. My assumption was that Winslow was on the trail of whatever money Heath Mulroy had managed to squirrel away, but only Connie could tell me that for sure, and she was in no condition to do so.

Beyond that, my challenge was to determine whether her husband's financial dealings were connected with the attempt on her life and the murder of her son Mark, not to mention the very real possibility that Loomis Winslow's killer was also responsible for the disappearance of Daniel Mulroy and his fiancée, Allison Castavette. I had the sense that the killer wouldn't stop until all twelve members of the wedding party were dead.

Thirteen, including me.

Lucky thirteen.

The young woman opened the door after our initial knock, a slight pause indicating she had checked the peephole first.

"Hello again, Mrs. Fletcher," she greeted. Then, to Seamus, she added, "Constable."

"May we have a word, ma'am?" Seamus said, growing more and more comfortable in his role.

I nodded toward him, impressed.

"Is there news? Has something else happened?"

"No," I replied this time. "Just an interview to help the constable and me determine the whereabouts of all the guests at the time of each of the murders and the attempted murder."

"Weren't we all together in the Castavette suite when Doyle was murdered?"

"I recall you storming in late, after the deed was already done, and the couple's friends Faye and Ian weren't there at all. The constable and I are trying to determine who was in a position to poison your aunt, as well as murder your cousin and Doyle Castavette."

"That would seem to be a very short list."

"Appearances can be deceiving," I noted.

"In that case, come right in," Lois Mulroy-Dodge said, moving away from the door so we could enter.

She was staying in one of Hill House's smaller single rooms, featuring a king-sized bed and modest space to maneuver around it. It had only a single desk and armchair for additional furniture. Lois sat down on the edge of the bed, while Seamus and I opted to simply remain standing. Her window was crusted with a thick layer of snow that hid the outside world from us as well as drawn blinds would have. I'm not claustrophobic by nature, but the notion of being essentially entombed in here by the ever-growing mountains of snow—now stretching past three feet—beyond had begun to wear on me. I actually felt in my head a light pressure that could have been the result of tumbling barometric pressure from the storm or, just as easily, a symptom of my growing unease over being trapped. And then there was Mort Metzger, who could be stranded somewhere between here and the fire station where he'd retrieved the snowmobile, and no one, including me, would even know it.

"May I ask you a blunt question first, Ms. Dodge?"

She nodded, not looking exactly thrilled by the prospect of that.

"What was the nature of your relationship with your late cousin, Mark Mulroy?"

"Close."

"Could you be more specific?"

"We were practically raised together. I was like the third sibling with him and Daniel."

"And you and Mark stayed close, by all accounts."

She nodded. "More like brother and sister, as I mentioned before."

"Which also left you close with your aunt, Constance Mulroy."

"Like mother and daughter. I don't know what I would have done without her after losing my mom."

"This family has been struck by an unusual amount of tragedy, hasn't it?" I asked Lois Mulroy-Dodge. "Your parents, your husband, Connie's husband before and after he was revealed to be a fraud . . ."

She nodded slowly, the motion looking painful for her. "Heath Mulroy destroyed a lot of lives, Mrs. Fletcher, his own family included."

"Before he took his own life."

I could see her hedging. "Well . . ."

I nodded, coaxing her on.

"Can I confess something I've never told anyone else before?"

"Of course."

"I don't believe he killed himself. I think he staged his own death so he could disappear."

I wonder if Lois Mulroy-Dodge noticed the rise her supposition produced in me. "What makes you think that?"

"My uncle was a survivor, Mrs. Fletcher. He always believed there was a way out, even when there wasn't. I heard him say things to that effect on multiple occasions."

The young woman was getting at a potential rationale for why Constance Mulroy had hired Loomis Winslow: to find the missing millions before her "late" husband could claim them, her intention being to return to the victims of Heath Mulroy's fraud whatever she found.

"I don't have any proof, of course," Lois resumed. "But . . ."

"Go on," Seamus McGilray urged, before I had a chance to.

Lois responded with her gaze fastened on me. "It was Mark, the way he was acting after the suicide, after the funeral. I knew something was wrong, kind of off."

"But you never asked Mark about it."

She shook her head, eyes pitched downward almost like she felt guilty about that.

I decided to get back to the task at hand. "Does anything unusual stick out in your memory about the minutes before Constance Mulroy's collapse?"

"Going back how long?"

"To the time everyone was seated."

"You don't consider me a suspect, do you?"

"I consider everyone a suspect," I told her, "and there are indications there may be someone else in our midst who hasn't shown himself yet."

"That's frightening."

"Murder always is, Ms. Dodge. We were speaking of what you may have noticed after everyone was seated at the table."

She considered my question before responding. "I remember a server filling our wineglasses, and then refilling them. I remember because he poured the rest of a bottle into an empty glass after my aunt covered her glass when he was about to top it off."

"This would have been shortly before the toast she rose to give then," I said, excited by the first hard piece of the timeline of Connie's attempted murder.

"Probably. Maybe. I really don't remember exactly."

"So that was your aunt's first glass of wine."

Her eyes widened. "I just remembered something else!"

I urged her on with a nod.

"When her glass was first filled, my aunt noticed a crack in the stem and gave it to the server. He returned with a fresh glass that had already been filled."

"Where from?"

"That I can't tell you. I assumed the bar area."

"How much time passed before your aunt's wine was replaced?"

"Let me see. . . . I'd taken a few sips from my own glass, and I'm a slow drinker. Five minutes, maybe?"

So the wineglass the server filled at the bar might have sat awaiting his return for between five and ten minutes. Ample opportunity for whoever had topped off the glass with poison to manage the deed, especially if he or she chose a time when the bartender was otherwise engaged. This was more than a minor breakthrough, since I now had a much clearer notion as to when Constance Mulroy's drink had been poisoned. And it was a much clearer notion as to how the killer had escaped our detection after stabbing Doyle Castavette to death moments before our entry into the bedroom.

"You can't consider me a suspect, Mrs. Fletcher," Lois Mulroy-Dodge insisted. "You know I was with you when my cousin Mark was killed."

"I know you knocked on your aunt's door on the pretext of seeing him. But none of us know right now when, exactly, he was killed. The timing doesn't absolve you."

"But . . ."

"What absolves you, to a degree, for now is your witnessing the broken wineglass, something that can easily be checked even if it was tossed in the trash. I can't believe a murderer would draw attention to their own method that way."

The young woman breathed a hefty sigh of relief. "Thank you, Mrs. Fletcher."

"Don't thank me yet. Remember, I only said 'for now.'"

"Who's next, Mrs. Fletcher?" Seamus McGilray asked me, after we'd adjourned to the hallway.

"I think it's time we had a talk with Ian and Faye. The rest of the wedding party barely knows who they are, and even that might be generous. Let's find out why."

Before I could head down the hall with Seamus, my phone rang with a call from Harry McGraw.

"What do you want first, the weird news or the strange news?" Harry asked me, after I answered.

"Take your pick."

"Doesn't matter anyway. It's all weird and strange. These birth records were actually a snap to locate, Jess. You didn't tell me this involved Heath Mulroy, known in these parts as 'the Mini Madoff.'"

"I thought I had—at least I gave you his wife's name, the one who hired Loomis Winslow."

"You're talking to the racehorse of private investigators, my dear. I only focus on what's immediately in front of me, so I missed the connection."

"I didn't think anything escaped the world's greatest detective."

"It doesn't," Harry told me. "But you're stuck with me, since Sherlock Holmes wasn't available. Anyway, it wasn't hard to track down the family history, including the day his children were born. I'm looking at digitized versions of three birth certificates on what passes for a computer right now. How did we ever get along without these things?"

"Seems to me we did just fine, Harry," I said, intrigued by something he'd just noted. "You said three birth certificates, not two?"

"The births took place at St. Catherine's, a small hospital acquired around the turn of the century from the Catholic Church by Mass General Hospital, and Massachusetts law requires a birth certificate to be issued, even in the case of a stillborn. In this case, the parents even named him: Owen Francis Mulroy, to go with his surviving brothers, Daniel Patrick and Mark Andrew."

"That's the one," I said, nodding to myself, while down the hall Seamus knocked on Ian and Faye's door. "Anything strike you as strange about the birth certificates themselves or any of the other material you came across?"

"Just the fact that the accompanying death certificate for Owen Francis wasn't issued until the following day. But since the births took place at night, I'm thinking that's a clerical issue."

"Still an anomaly, though."

"I guess, depending on how suspicious your suspicious nature wants to be. Mother and the now-twins remained in the hospital for four days prior to discharge. Nothing else of note to report."

"Okay," I said after giving his words a chance to settle, "now tell me the truth."

"About what?"

"About whatever's bothering you. I can tell there's something. And you did mention weird *and* strange."

"Well, here's something you can definitely file under *weird*. I just brought a digitized copy of the original hospital records up on my screen, the discharge portion specifically."

"And what do you see there that's so weird, Harry?"

"Constance Mulroy was checked out of the hospital on April twenty-third at one thirty p.m."

"So?"

"So there's no record of the surviving twins being discharged from the nursery. If I didn't know better, I'd say the woman left the hospital empty-handed and her two infants never left there at all."

Which, of course, made no sense, the mystery continuing to deepen with the mounting snow outside. The most obvious explanation for Harry's discovery was a simple clerical error, made perhaps when the hospital records from so many years ago were all digitized by Mass General, which hadn't even owned St. Catherine's at the time Constance Mulroy gave birth to two living babies and a single stillborn one. If it hadn't been for the circumstances, I would have bought that and been done with it.

But it felt to me like something else, another factor, was to blame here. The problem was that I didn't know what, and I resolved to ask Seth Hazlitt when time allowed. He'd delivered more than his share of babies over the years, although he was always complaining, falsely, about how much he despised the company of children.

"I'm going to keep checking," Harry resumed, "see if there's something in the records I've missed somehow."

"You never miss anything, Harry."

"You mean besides my ex-wives? Oh," he added, seeming to think of something else, "I checked out that other thing for you, too."

"What other thing?"

"Now who's missing things?"

"It's been a long night," I said.

"You know, those other mass murders, on the plane and at that wilderness retreat or hunting lodge."

Harry was right; I had indeed forgotten I'd even asked him to look into those.

"And?" I posed.

"You're not going to like this, my dear."

"Par for the course tonight, Harry."

"The FBI does indeed suspect the same killer was behind both."

I wasn't surprised by that, and I knew Harry McGraw wouldn't be either. That meant there was something else.

"And?" I prompted.

"Surprised you didn't notice this yourself."

"Notice what, Harry?"

"The plane was four years ago; the lodge was two years ago. Both occurred the same week. *This* week, Jess. Happy anniversary."

Our call ended and, still shaking off the shock from that revelation, I joined Seamus in front of Ian and Faye's room. "You didn't have to wait for me."

"I didn't. I've knocked several times."

"Again?" I said, shaking my head. "I wonder if I could have them arrested for being so detestable."

"A moot point until Sheriff Metzger arrives," Seamus noted, taking his trusty pass key card from his pocket and running it through the slot.

This time the door clicked open without a need to summon Eugene from the head of the hall.

A mildly sweet odor pushed into my nostrils as I followed Seamus inside and froze at the sight of Ian and Faye resting side by side on the double bed, faceup, their bodies touching and their eyes locked open.

Dead.

Chapter Seventeen

Open the window!" I cried to Seamus, fearing the room's air would still be thick with the most likely cause of the couple's death, carbon monoxide. "Break it if you have to!"

Before I'd gotten a single word out Seamus was already in motion, realizing the same thing that I had. Clearly not wanting to break anything in his beloved establishment, he opened the window as wide as it would go, and the sill was covered immediately with snow from a wind gust that blew it into the dead couple's room. In spite of that, he fought forward and forced his head and shoulders through the window, daring the storm.

The snow was already collecting all around Seamus when he yanked himself all the way back inside, dragging a torrent of frigid air and a fresh blanket of snow with him.

"The heat vents are blocked!" he said through the layer of

snow that had crusted over his face, leaving only his ample mustache exposed.

"By snow?"

"Rags, it looks like, maybe cut-up bathroom towels. I can't reach them, so I can't be sure."

I was checking both Ian and Faye for a pulse to confirm their deaths, but the pink pallor of their complexions told me all I needed to know.

"Carbon monoxide poisoning," Seamus was saying, brushing the snow from his clothes.

"But what about that smell?" I asked, uncomfortable with the anomaly I couldn't explain.

"Five now," Seamus muttered, instead of answering my question. "Five victims of the twelve."

"Four," I corrected. "Constance Mulroy's still alive. And carbon monoxide doesn't have a smell."

He sniffed the air, discerning the smell I'd noticed before. "What the bloody . . ."

I was starting to feel light-headed. "Seamus, quickly!" I called.

He fell into step behind me, the effects of the lingering gas taking longer with him because he'd been breathing outside air for a time. Once back in the hallway, he slammed the door behind us. The hulking Eugene heard the commotion and started to rush toward us, but an upraised palm from Seamus sent him back to his post.

I was already calling Seth Hazlitt.

"Please tell me Mort made it there. I haven't been able to reach him, and I've tried a hundred times."

"Not yet, Seth."

"Then what are . . . Not another murder!"

"Two. A couple, the best man and maid of honor."

"Not anymore."

"They died in their room. We think it may have been carbon monoxide," I reported, not able to shake the fact that Loomis Winslow had been killed the very same way, except while he'd been duct-taped to the driver's seat of his car.

"We?"

"Seamus McGilray and I," I told Seth.

"The hotel manager? What does he know about any of this?"

"He was a constable back in Ireland—"

"Well, that surely explains it."

"—specializing in traffic."

"Perfect résumé for diagnosing a murder, Jess."

"I noticed a smell, Seth, kind of sweet, like something baking in the oven."

"Methylene chloride," he said after a pause.

"Never heard of it."

"It's a solvent commonly found in paint and varnish removers, can break down into carbon monoxide when inhaled. Exposure to methylene chloride can cause carbon monoxide poisoning. Very dangerous when used in poorly ventilated areas, and deadly if, say, it was poured into the blower of a room heater."

"Would there be any lingering sign of it?"

"You're not still in the room, are you?" Seth asked with panic edging into his voice.

"No."

"Well, it's good to see this night hasn't totally stripped you of your senses, Jess. And the answer's no. No lingering sign besides that smell you detected, since methylene chloride, also known as dichloromethane, evaporates swiftly."

"Making it the perfect murder weapon," I said.

Seth hesitated. I heard something rattle on his end of the line. "Did you check the outside vents?"

"They're clogged."

"With snow?"

"Towels or rags."

"No doubt soaked with the chemical that took the lives of these latest victims." Another pause. "This killer of yours knows exactly what they're doing, Jess."

"The ones I go up against always seem to. I have another question for you, Seth, on a totally unrelated subject."

"I could use that right now," he told me.

"Something's come up, thanks to information uncovered by Harry McGraw."

"Good old Harry . . ."

"Anyway, I asked him to look into the birth records of the Mulroy children after learning one of the original triplets was a stillborn. Harry was able to turn up all three birth certificates—"

"Standard, even for a stillborn."

"—but according to hospital records, the surviving twins were never formally discharged."

Silence followed, as Seth considered the anomaly.

"How many years ago would this have been?"

"Twenty-nine, I believe—approximately, anyway."

"Could have been as simple as this particular hospital's administration at the time not requiring any formal record of the babies leaving the hospital."

"Makes sense."

I heard Seth go, "Hmm . . ."

"What is it?"

"Well, Jess, there is an alternative explanation."

"Isn't there always?" I asked him.

"Not necessarily nefarious, in this case. You say only two of the three infants survived birth?"

"I don't have any details beyond that."

"What was the hospital?"

"St. Catherine's outside Boston, before it was gobbled up by Mass General."

"I'm well acquainted with their obstetrics department and administrative policies, even back then. Wouldn't happen to know the name of the doctor who handled the delivery, would you?"

"No."

"Let me do some digging, see what I can come up with."

I could hear the edge in his voice. "What are you after, Seth?"

"Not sure. That's why I need to do some digging. But there may indeed be an explanation for the lack of formal discharge documents for the infants."

"Care to give me a hint?"

"Not until I've got more of a notion of how to find what I'm after with the whole region shut down by this blasted storm. But hospitals stay open twenty-four hours no matter what, Jess, and I'm itching for something to keep me busy until Mort gets there. You've done me a great a favor."

"Hope you're able to return it," I told him.

I ended the call and joined Seamus McGilray down the hall. Having confirmed the remaining guests were all present, accounted for, and safe, he was conferring with Eugene about something.

The shock of finding two more bodies, bringing the total number to four, would have been greater had I known Ian and Faye better or held them in higher regard. I had begun to look at them as the most likely suspects here among the wedding party, and I wondered if the killer's targeting them next had to do with that as much as anything else. That would indicate that the killer was toying with me, toying with us all. I was the one wild card here, the one factor he or she couldn't possibly have expected or planned for. Yet the succession of interviews was leading me to consider more and more the possibility that we were indeed trapped in the clutches of the same serial mass murderer who'd struck at least two times before. If that were the case, all this was just a game to him, taking place exactly two years since the last time he'd played it, according to Harry McGraw.

I heard the muffled echo of the grandfather clock in the lobby striking two o'clock, meaning two hours had passed since we'd convened there following the discovery of Mark Mulroy's body. But I'd lost track of time, had begun to judge its passage by the mounting snow out the window and nothing more.

"Who's next on our list?"

I figured we'd interview the Sprague sisters last. That left Tyler Castavette as our next subject. I would've really liked to hear what Ian and Faye had to say. They were such an odd couple, even outside of the fact that only Lois Mulroy-Dodge was familiar with them—and only vaguely.

"Tyler Castavette," I chose, referring to the young man I'd first met when he broke into my suite.

"I was hoping you'd say that, ma'am," Seamus said, grinning.

Tyler had propped his door open with the swinging metal security lock I always engage before I go to sleep—not here at Hill House, for some reason, but whenever I'm on the road, on a book tour or something of that sort.

I knocked and led the way in without waiting to be invited.

Tyler Castavette was standing by the window, looking out into the storm as if transfixed by it, his reflection captured in the glass displaying a face flat in amazement.

"I've never seen anything like this before in my life." He still hadn't turned around, but I gathered he'd spotted my and Seamus's reflections in the glass. "It just keeps piling up."

His television, like all others right now, was tuned to the Weather Channel, where a banner that read FIVE FEET PREDICTED FOR PARTS OF MAINE dominated the bottom of the screen. I wasn't sure what was more historic in that moment: the storm itself or having loose among us a killer who might well be a serial mass murderer.

Or, perhaps, one of the survivors.

Tyler Castavette turned slowly, reluctant to take his eyes off the storm as if afraid he might miss something. He looked somehow smaller when measured against the scope of the storm beyond, and more timid without others around him to either impress or intimidate. I had to blink away the notion that I was looking at his now-late father as a young man.

"I have nothing to say to you, Mrs. Fletcher," he said, not as staunchly as he'd meant to. "I have nothing to say to either of you. I suppose that makes me a prime suspect, doesn't it?"

"Not at all," I said, trying to sound as conciliatory under the circumstances as I could manage with two more bodies having been added to the tally just minutes before. "In fact, it's my experience that guilty parties are normally the most cooperative, not the least. Call it a costume they don for the occasion."

"And you're dealing with a shrinking list of suspects, aren't you?"

"You mean *we're* dealing, don't you? We're all in this together."

Tyler's gaze jerked from me to Seamus before darting back. "Not the two of you, though. You're not part of the wedding party."

"I don't believe that will stop the killer who struck on that plane and at that wilderness lodge from claiming us as trophies as well."

"You believe he does it for sport?"

"Or *she*, Tyler, and the answer's yes, since I can't find another explanation. And the list of potential suspects among us was just shortened by another two."

Tyler Castavette's expression remained blank. "Those two weirdos, Faye and Ian?"

"How'd you guess?"

"Wishful thinking. Maybe I'm a jerk for being glad that if it had to be somebody, it was them."

Tyler's expression tightened as he said that, faint lines springing up over the brow of his otherwise youthful face. He was a handsome young man who had managed to retain his boyish good looks. I had the sense he wore his hair the same way he had in middle school, never mind high school. A blessing and a curse since, between his good looks, charm, and money, he'd maintained an existence that was extremely superficial in nature. Tyler Castavette was used to having things come his way, virtually fall into his lap. I could probably count on fewer than my ten fingers the number of times he'd been told no in his life.

I found myself wondering if he had any idea about the tote bag full of cash in his father's room, a likely payoff from Constance Mulroy. And I supposed the placid reflection that had fallen over him must've been rooted in the shock over his father's murder. Their lack of a relationship aside, the death of his father wasn't something he would get over quickly, especially since this most recent trio of murders confirmed that any of us could be the killer's next victim.

"I would like to cover one item with you," I said to Tyler, "concerning your father's murder."

He swallowed hard. "What about it?"

"You charged into the room moments after the struggle had ceased, after Eugene had battered down the door."

"Eugene?"

"The large kitchen worker."

"Oh, him," Tyler said matter-of-factly.

"In any case, in my recollection you seemed a bit winded."

"I rushed there from the other end of the hall to see what all the commotion was about, fearing the worst." He hesitated, tried for a laugh but failed. "So—wait a minute—you think I killed my father, climbed out the window, made my way back into the hotel through the storm, changed clothes, and then joined the rest of you back in his suite? I'd expected plenty better from you, Mrs. Fletcher."

"Actually, I have an alternative theory. You're young and strong and clearly know your way around a gym."

"Are we talking about Mark Mulroy's murder or my father's?"

"Your father's. See, one of the theories I'm pursuing is that the killer has been using the narrow crawl space that runs between floors of the hotel to make their way from one room to another. But the only means to climb back up into it from your father's bedroom was a desk chair that broke in the struggle. That means whoever killed him must've hoisted themselves up into the crawl space, a task that would require just the kind of upper-body strength you possess."

Tyler Castavette's gaze tightened. "On whose authority, exactly, are you accusing me of murdering my father?"

"I wasn't accusing you. I was merely pointing something out."

"Right, because the truth is, you have no authority and I'm under no obligation to talk to you."

"Are you under any obligation to stay alive, Tyler? Because my questions are meant to rule things out as much as in."

We locked stares, each of us waiting to see who would make the next move.

"Show us your hands, boy," said Seamus, breaking the standoff between us. "If you pulled yourself into that crawl space, there'll be cuts or bruises on your palms and fingers."

At first I didn't think Tyler was going to comply, out of either indignation or something far more nefarious. Then he held his hands up, palms out, and turned them around for both Seamus and me to see.

"Satisfied? Because I've got nothing else to say to you." Tyler Castavette's face was starting to darken. "If you ask me for the time of day, don't expect me to check my watch."

"And quite a nice one it is," I remarked. "I noticed your father wasn't wearing one when we found him stabbed to death. Might you have come by it somehow? Because you don't impress me as someone who could afford a watch of that quality on his own."

"Are we done now?"

"Just one more thing, if I may. Did either Mark or Daniel Mulroy ever mention their brother to you?"

"Brother?"

"The third triplet, who was stillborn."

"A few times, but . . ."

"But what?" I pushed gently.

"That was when they'd been drinking. They even mentioned his name—Owen—a few times. Sober, I don't think they ever said a word about the third triplet's death at all. It's like there was something about that night in the hospital they wanted to avoid at all costs."

*   *   *

"What an unpleasant young fellow," Seamus said after we'd adjourned to the hall.

I heard Tyler close the door and throw the locks behind us. "Let's go to the lobby, Seamus."

"Has something come up, Mrs. Fletcher, something the good doctor told you before speaking with that wretched chap?"

"Nothing like that," I said. "I just want to check something."

I wasn't surprised by what greeted us in the lobby, because I'd been fully expecting it. Somehow, though, that didn't lessen the impact, which still felt like a punch to the gut.

"Well, I'll be gobsmacked," Seamus muttered, following my gaze.

The roman numerals marking three, four, and five o'clock on the grandfather clock had been crossed out.

Chapter Eighteen

I don't like this, Mrs. Fletcher," Seamus remarked stiffly, unable to lift his eyes from the clock face. "I don't like this one bit."

"We'll catch whoever it is before this goes any further," I promised.

"We'd better," he said, sounding angry. "That clock dates back to the eighteenth century, property of the original owner of this establishment. The blasphemy of it all!"

"The blasphemer is also a murderer, Seamus."

He finally turned from the clock toward me. "There is that, too, Mrs. Fletcher," he said, with a calm that belied the gravity of our circumstances.

Worrying about what had become of Mort had begun to consume me. I had this horrible vision of him freezing to death ten feet from the entrance to Hill House because he couldn't see the door. It was closing in on three a.m., meaning three hours had passed since Mort had set out for Hill House aboard a snowmobile. Even in these wretched conditions, it shouldn't take that long for him to cover a distance of slightly more than three miles. And the fact that he'd never piloted a snowmobile before left me even more worried over what had become of him.

Besides that, the storm seemed determined to bury us all, and I had this desire to confront it on its own terms. See it in its true form, instead of through a frost-encrusted window.

There is something placid and beautiful about falling snow, to go with the sense of security one has while watching the inches pile up safe at home. Once the inches become feet, though, that placidity tends to change. And with the total approaching four feet, the scene had long since stopped qualifying as placid or beautiful. This was downright terrifying and foreboding, much more like something out of a horror novel than a murder mystery.

But a murder mystery was what I found myself embroiled in now, one that continued to deepen and grow deadlier as the evening wore on and the snow continued to pile up. It all made for a strong contrast with the vast bulk of my real-life experience with murder, in which my participation had started after the fact instead of during it. I could, in other words, sleep soundly in my bed, comforted by the notion that I was not necessarily in danger myself and that the murderer's work was likely finished. Tonight, I found myself a participant rather than a spectator, a witness to murder instead of a mere observer of its aftermath. I suppose if I had time to ponder that further, I'd be nothing short of terrified by the prospect of what awaited me and the remaining members of the wedding party while we remained hostage to this storm and the number of crossed-off numerals on the grandfather clock threatened to mount.

I suppose I'd hoped getting away from the second floor might yield some eye-opening insight into the mystery. Maybe, like an expectant child again, I believed if I stared out the window long enough it would make a loved one appear—in this case Mort Metzger. There was nothing to see beyond the lobby windows, though, except white cast almost blindingly bright by the persistent spill of Hill House's outdoor floodlights. The trees had disappeared; the landscape beyond Hill House had disappeared; the whole world had disappeared. There was only this building and those who remained alive inside it. That defined my life, my very existence, at least for the time being.

The families of the bride and groom seemed to have enough skeletons in their respective closets to stock an entire cemetery, never mind a wedding. All members of the wedding party, both living and now deceased, seemed to have their share of secrets and sins, with the possible exception of the Sprague sisters. And all of us now found ourselves subject to the whims of an especially sadistic killer, potentially the same killer who'd struck two other isolated settings two and four years ago this very week. I hadn't had the opportunity to do a deeper Internet dive into those occasions, and I knew only the bare minimum: that then, as now, the murders had been committed in a remarkably short period of time, not exceeding a day in either instance.

Or night, as the case might be.

Since my options for ferreting out a monster who had perfected such a formula for murder were few, I resolved to keep my focus on the possibility that someone in our midst had devised this devilish scheme for reasons yet unknown.

"Seamus," I said to the manager of Hill House, between the lobby's snow-encrusted windows, "I need you to play Sheriff Metzger for me."

"And how might I do that?"

"Just act as a sounding board for me."

"I'm hardly an expert investigator."

"That's okay—neither is Mort." I tried to joke, but my remark fell flat. "Let's start with Loomis Winslow."

"The private detective you mentioned."

"The very same. According to Harry McGraw, he was apparently hired by Constance Mulroy. Since Mr. Winslow's specialty is—er, was—financial forensics, we can assume the case involved large sums of money, especially in view of the cash found in Mrs. Mulroy's tote bag."

"The one we found in Mr. Castavette's closet, with that smudge from the actress Virginia Da Salle's nail polish."

"Which she denies ever touching," I picked up. "How the tote bag was moved from Constance Mulroy's closet and into Doyle Castavette's remains one of the biggest mysteries facing us."

Seamus sighed. "These people are exhausting, ma'am. I'm knackered by all the whining and recrimination."

I nodded in agreement. "Everyone seems to have something to hide, and we're neglecting perhaps the most important facet of any investigation."

"What's that?"

"Its origin. First, we have the murder of Loomis Winslow, and second, we have the disappearance, the likely flight of the bride and groom from their rented Lexus, those two incidents being connected by the gravel from the Cabot Manufacturing Company parking lot."

"There would have been no motorcars when the factory first opened. That would be correct, wouldn't it?" Seamus posed.

"Of course. The parking lot was created years and years later, on land the company purchased for the first of their expansions. The gravel had to be trucked in and was likely replaced or supplemented on any number of occasions, explaining its distinctive nature. What were you getting at?"

"Nothing in particular," he said, not all that convincingly. "It just seems like too obvious a clue, as if we were meant to believe that Winslow's killer and whoever the young couple fled from into the frigid cold were the same person."

"Are you sure traffic was your only responsibility when you were a constable? Because you definitely have a flair for this kind of work."

"Coming from an expert like you, Mrs. Fletcher, that means a lot."

"Expert at making fake crimes up or solving real ones?"

A slight smile danced across his lips. "Does it matter?"

"Well, in this case my imagination is at a loss to determine a firm suspect here, Seamus. And we must consider the chance that all our ruminations will be rendered moot if Hill House becomes like that airplane or wilderness lodge: no survivors found when the outside world finally reaches us."

Seamus stiffened. "That's not going to happen, Mrs. Fletcher, not on my watch."

My cell phone's ringing jarred us both, and I yanked it from my pocket in the hope that it was Mort Metzger at long last.

"Hello, Harry," I greeted, after *HARRY MCGRAW* lit up at the top of the screen.

"Put Mort on."

"I wish I could, but he's not here."

"Where is he?"

"I was just wondering the same thing. . . ."

"He left hours ago."

"At least three now."

"I haven't been able to get through to the station. My calls keep getting routed to an emergency number that nobody answers. Has all of Cabot Cove fallen victim to this killer you're chasing?"

"I have no idea, Harry, since we're cut off from the rest of the town. And what was it you wanted to speak to Mort about?"

"Guess I'll have to settle for you, under the circumstances. I was able to dump Loomis Winslow's phone records—again, don't bother asking me how. Private detectives are like magicians in that we never give away our tricks."

"What did the trick reveal in this case?"

"I've been checking all the numbers in search of some connection that will explain who's behind all this. Along the way, I've found calls to and from a number with lots of zeros at the end."

"Government?" I asked him.

"Department of Justice. Whatever this private detective found, he must have forwarded it to the Boston office of the FBI."

"Still there, Jess?" Harry asked, after I'd lapsed into silence.

"Just trying to process that on top of everything else here that doesn't add up. Any way of telling whether his client Mrs. Mulroy was aware of that?"

"I can only tell you that there are no calls to a number I've identified as hers any time around when he spoke with the DOJ."

"What about other calls?"

"Many of them, a few pretty long in duration."

"What about voice mails? Did you check those, too?"

"You talk like I flunked out of detective school."

"I believe you told me once that you did, Harry."

"That was the police academy."

"They're not the same thing?"

"You know what you have to do to get your PI's license?"

"Apply online?"

"Besides that. In New York, you go down to the Business Affairs office at City Hall and get a business license. That's all you need to open for business. They just want to make sure you file your taxes and everything. Did I tell you I'm five years behind and the IRS has hit men after me? When they arrest me, I'm going to plead insanity from working with deadbeat clients like you."

"What if they ask to see copies of your invoices?"

"I'll tell them they're in the same place as my tax returns. Anything else?"

"You called me."

"I know. Anything else?"

I thought back to what Seth Hazlitt had said about no re-cords existing for infants Mark and Daniel Mulroy ever being discharged from St. Catherine's Hospital, and I explained the anomaly to Harry.

"Make any sense to you?"

"You said there were originally triplets, until one was still-born. Maybe the most fortunate of the three, as things turned out."

"Is it relevant that one of them was dead?"

"Shouldn't be. And I can't think of any reason why record of the surviving twins' discharge might have been conve-niently lost."

"Neither can Seth. So far, anyway."

"See, Jess, even not-so-great minds think alike."

"Mrs. Fletcher," Seamus interrupted. "Did you hear that?"

"What?"

And then I *did* hear it. A light thumping coming from somewhere, the sound akin to that of the beating heart in Poe's "The Tell-Tale Heart."

"I'll call you back, Harry."

He started to say something, but I hung up. Seamus and I were looking at each other when the next series of thumps came.

"The front door!" he realized, and burst toward it.

I caught up with Seamus just as he was thrusting open the front door to reveal a snow-covered figure standing almost waist deep in the pile that had accumulated before the hotel entrance.

The figure fell forward, dragging a hefty blanket of that snow over the threshold with him while shaking enough of it from himself to reveal a nearly frozen Mort Metzger practically buried in the cushion of white that had pushed into the lobby with him as he collapsed to the floor.

I pictured Mort's snowmobile having broken down or crashed as much as an hour or so before, pictured him trying to trudge the rest of the way on foot through the teeth of a killer blizzard at its peak. How far had he come? A mile? More? Whatever the case, he was shaking horribly, clearly in some stage of hypothermia.

"Blankets!" I cried out to Seamus.

He dashed off for the back office, where a fresh supply of bedcovers and linens was always available for any guest requiring an extra blanket, pillow, or even sheets at any hour too late for the modest housekeeping staff to respond. He did this while I moved to get the door closed.

The collection of snow before it rendered my efforts futile, even before the powerful wind made its presence known. As I tried again to get the heavy front door closed, it felt like someone far stronger than I was pushing against it from the other side. Finally, I gave up and found the strength to drag Mort out of the snow pile, away from the door and the wind pushing through it.

I managed to get him into a nesting of potted plants, the leaves of which had been speckled white by the intrusion of the storm into the lobby. I shifted Mort onto his back and was relieved to find he was breathing, rapidly but strongly, and gently tried to rouse him.

"Mort? Mort, can you hear me? It's Jessica—Mrs. F.," I added, as if that might get more of a rise out of him.

He didn't stir.

"Wake up, Mort. Come on—I know you're in there," I resumed, still shaking him mildly at the shoulder. "Wake up."

He was still unconscious and shivering when Seamus emerged from the back office with an armful of blankets. Together we covered Mort up in the first few, and he left me to finish the task on my own while he moved to try to get the big entry door closed. That task was complicated by the additional curtains of snow that had blown in while the door was open.

I got Mort wrapped in all five of the thick woolen blankets made for king-sized beds, so that only his face was exposed. His shaking began to ebb and his breathing became less shallow. My will recharged by the slight improvement, I pushed myself over to his feet and raised the blanket wrapped there enough to strip off his lace-up boots and socks. Not surprisingly, both sets were soaked through to the gills and would certainly have negated much of our effort to warm him had I not removed them. I then proceeded to wrap the blankets more tightly around his exposed feet, as the body can shed a great measure of its heat through cold feet and Mort could afford to lose none now.

Next, I moved my hands under the sections of soft woolen

fabric to tighten it around his head, another prime conduit for heat loss. I could feel the melting snow already warming under my touch, the soak of it dampening my fingers from tip to base, and I took this as another good sign.

"Mort?" I repeated. "Mort, can you hear me?"

I needed to call Seth Hazlitt, needed to be coached on exactly what to do from this point. I eased my left hand from beneath the blankets, drawing my phone out with it, and pressed Seth's number.

Nothing.

I pressed *SETH* again when the call didn't go through.

Still nothing.

Then I saw the dreaded *NO SERVICE* icon in the upper-left-hand corner of my iPhone, along with something else.

Blood, the fingers of my left hand covered with a thin coat of it. I jerked my right hand from beneath the blanket wrapped tightly around Mort's head to find the same thing there and remembered the feeling of what I had taken for melting snow when it hadn't been that at all.

Because Mort hadn't merely gotten waylaid atop his snowmobile somewhere in the area. He'd been attacked.

Chapter Nineteen

I realized the cold bursts of air carrying sheets of snow had ceased and I looked up to see Seamus returning to my side after somehow managing to get the front door closed.

"Are you hurt, Mrs. Fletcher? What happened?"

"Not me. It's Mort."

Seamus's eyes bored into me. "You try the good doctor Hazlitt?"

I flashed my phone. "Cell service is down."

He nodded, processing the information. "We'll need to get the sheriff upstairs, under covers, with the heat turned up as much as the blowers will allow."

I nodded. "My suite, where we need to gather everyone to ride out the rest of the night."

He looked at me grimly. I said no more, because I didn't have to, because Seamus had come to the same conclusion I had: Unless our murderer had somehow made his or her way out of Hill House to attack Mort on his approach, that killer wasn't among the surviving members of the wedding party.

He or she was someone else entirely.

"I'll stay with Sheriff Metzger while you and Eugene get everyone into my suite," I continued.

I wanted to ask him about Eugene, his credentials and references, anything that might assuage my fears that he was the man Hank Weathers had mistaken for Bigfoot. And how could we be certain he'd remained at his post this whole time through the long hours of this night? Might he have overheard us discussing the sheriff's imminent arrival? Might he have ventured outside long enough to ambush Mort and leave him outside to freeze to death in an apparent accident?

Seamus narrowed his gaze on me, clearly reluctant to leave me on my own.

"I'll be fine," I assured him, brushing some stubborn stray snow from my hair. "And the wheelchair—we'll need the wheelchair as well."

"It must still be in Mrs. Mulroy's room. I'll bring it down here straightaway, once the guests are collected in your suite, Mrs. Fletcher."

I found myself amazed by Seamus's composure in the face of the worst snowstorm in Maine history on top of being confronted by a mass murderer, perhaps even a *serial* mass murderer. I've seldom known even professional law enforcement types capable of remaining so calm and collected under such dire circumstances, and I began to wonder seriously whether his constable duties back home in Ireland might have indeed extended beyond traffic detail.

"We're going to get through this, Seamus."

He forced an uneasy smile. "I have no doubt of that, ma'am, no doubt at all," he said, not sounding very convincing.

I remained seated on the lobby carpet, sodden with puddles from the melting snow. Mort's head was still cradled in my lap so I could apply pressure to the gash that was the source of his blood loss in order to stanch it as best I could. His shaking had subsided even more, down to barely a quiver now, and I was confident we'd managed to get his body temperature up despite the loss of cell service preventing me from reaching Seth for medical advice. I imagine he would have described the treatment for hypothermia as pretty much what instinct dictated and what Seamus and I had already done.

"Mort," I said, trying to coax him awake through force of will as much as my voice. "Wake up, Mort. I need you. I need you to wake up and help me figure this all out before anyone else is murdered."

I heard a chime and the brief whisk of the elevator door sliding open. Except for that, the only sound was that of the howling wind continuing to hammer away at the windows.

I turned to find Seamus McGilray wheeling the same chair we'd used to ferry Constance Mulroy up to her room after she'd suffered a seizure in the Sea Captains Room. And it took the concerted efforts of both of us to get Mort raised into its seat, and the now-damp blankets tucked tight around him anew.

Seamus made the pushing efforts from there.

"Any objections from the guests about being resettled?"

"They were too scared to object."

"So am I, Seamus," I confessed.

"Oh, and I instructed Eugene to carry Mrs. Mulroy into your suite, then take his post outside the door while the staff member who's been tending to the woman resumes her duties."

"Who is she?" I asked suspiciously, still unable to chase away the potential resemblance in a drunken man's eyes of Eugene to Bigfoot. "Another temp?"

"No, Janey from the front desk," he said, referring to the clerk who'd been berated by Doyle Castavette the previous afternoon.

"I can't remember how long she's been working here."

"Since around the time you moved in, Mrs. Fletcher."

"You checked her references?"

Seamus nodded. "Sterling."

"Interviews?"

"Sterling as well. Janey Ryland answered every question in textbook fashion."

"I was talking about interviews with others who knew her and had perhaps worked with her, maybe someone from her school."

Seamus hedged, then shook his head. "It didn't seem necessary, though in hindsight . . ."

"I think in hindsight," I started, intending to relieve him of any burden of guilt, "all of us would have done plenty of things different. The wedding party, for example, would have set their celebration in a warmer climate. When was Florida last hammered by a blizzard?"

"When was the last hurricane or tropical storm to hammer Maine, Mrs. Fletcher?"

"Good point."

"I should also mention that Janey Ryland has been an exemplary employee through all the fall and winter months."

"I still need to talk to her," I told him. "We probably should have already. If Janey Ryland was the killer on board that plane and at that wilderness lodge, it could be that she'd waited in both cases for the right opportunity to come along, with the planning and preparation already laid."

Seamus looked at me questioningly. "But you don't believe it's the same killer we're facing here tonight, do you?"

I ran my gaze along the windows yet again, nothing to see beyond those floodlights fighting to cut through the muck of the storm. "I didn't. I'm not so sure anymore."

Seamus sighed. "We can't be sure of anything really, can we, Mrs. Fletcher?"

"We can be sure of one thing, Seamus: that whoever the killer is, he or she isn't finished yet."

The blanket slipped off Mort's head while Seamus wheeled him across the lobby, revealing a patch of matted hair around the wound he'd suffered. At least I'd succeeded in getting the bleeding stopped, and I checked my phone again in the forlorn hope cell service might have been magically restored. But this was no night for miracles.

I stayed close to Mort to keep him from sliding out of the chair while Seamus wheeled him toward the elevator. The wrapping of blankets had held over his waist, hiding the presence of his nine-millimeter pistol. Once we got him safely settled on the couch, with Constance Mulroy settled in my bedroom, I resolved to remove it from Mort's holster and give it to Seamus for safekeeping. He was the only one I was absolutely certain I could trust here.

As the elevator wound upward to the third floor, I felt a thick wave of fatigue wash over me and suddenly felt unsteady on my feet, the way drivers describe feeling themselves dozing off behind the wheel. I had a coffee maker in my suite and intended to make good use of it as soon as I was inside. It was the one-cup variety and I had stockpiled enough of those K-Cups to keep all of those still alive caffeinated through what remained of the night.

It was just past three thirty a.m., leaving another several hours before sunrise—what we might be able to see of it, anyway. And how did I know that daylight would bring any solace to our situation? We'd still be alone and isolated, no one able to get to us any sooner in the light than in the dark. Perhaps the murderer was toying with us even now, intending to complete his twisted game when we lapsed into the false security of the promised dawn.

On the third floor I emerged from the elevator, after Sea-

mus and the wheelchair bearing Mort, to find Eugene standing at his post before the entrance to my suite.

"Anything to report?" Seamus asked him, handing me his
pass key card to save me the bother of fishing my own key card
from my pocket.

"One thing I think you'll find interesting," Eugene said as
the green light flashed.

When Eugene eased the door open he was angled in such a
way that something on the side of his head, near his ear,
grabbed my attention.

"Jessica, thank the stars," I heard, before I could question
him on what I'd noticed; I recognized the voice immediately.

Constance Mulroy was seated in an armchair positioned
just beyond the living room's coffee table, fully awake now.

"Connie!" I beamed.

She looked groggy, her eyes narrowed and dull, but she was
free of the coma I feared she'd slipped into forever.

"Thank the stars!" she repeated, her voice raspy and dry.
"It's him—I'm sure of it! You've got to stop him, Jessica—you
must stop him!"

"Stop who?" I asked, heading toward her.

"My husband, Heath Mulroy. He's the one behind all this!"

The young woman Janey Ryland, who normally worked the
now-vacated front desk, stood vigil by Constance Mulroy's

side, likely the person who'd informed Connie of what was going on once she awoke.

"You don't believe he's dead," I heard myself say, as if it were someone else speaking the words.

"Only in the eyes of the world. It was a ruse, a fabrication, so he could avoid prison."

I glanced toward Lois Mulroy-Dodge, who'd voiced the very same theory to me. Her expression was empty, a blank canvas waiting to be filled in.

"I can't be sure of that," Connie conceded, "but I am sure he was plotting something. I'm sure his investment scheme must have included a contingency escape plan." She hesitated, tried to swallow and seemed to fail. "And I know he had help."

"From who?"

"My son Daniel," she said, a combination of embarrassment and misery ringing in her voice.

"He wasn't duped by his father, Jessica," Constance Mulroy continued. "He was a willing participant, a coconspirator in the eyes of the law."

So Heath Mulroy had supposedly plunged to his death off the Brooklyn Bridge and now his son, and coconspirator, might well have disappeared into the woods on the eve of a killer blizzard. That brought my thinking back to the murder of Loomis Winslow and finding on the backseat floor mat gravel that made for a perfect match with gravel from the parking lot of the Cabot Manufacturing Company. Something was bothering me again about that particular image, something I'd seen but hadn't quite registered and couldn't locate in my memory.

"Daniel was the heir apparent," Connie continued, "always the apple of his father's eye far more than Mark. I didn't want to believe he was complicit, wanted to believe he'd been duped by the scheme like everyone. But I was naive, wasn't I? When I told you I feared my life was in danger . . ."

She let the rest of the thought dangle, leaving me to pick it up. "Because you suspected your husband was still alive, because you were cooperating with the authorities against his interests and wanted to see whatever money he may have squirreled away returned to the investors that he'd swindled."

Connie nodded. "I felt I was being watched for some time. I know it was him, Jessica. I know it was Heath, waiting for the opportunity to escape for good with the money he must have stockpiled."

"That's why you hired Loomis Winslow, isn't it? To find whatever's left of the money your husband stole from his clients."

Her face flashed surprise at my knowledge of that. "He told me he was onto something, that he needed to check a few more things out. He was supposed to call me this afternoon, but he never did."

"Because he was murdered this morning, just a few miles from here, where it appeared he was meeting someone."

"How awful!" Connie's voice turned desperate, pleading. "It was Heath, don't you see? It must've been! He killed Winslow and now he's coming for me. Now he's—" Her face paled, the slow realization of terror spreading over it. "And Mark—he must have killed Mark, too! It's him, Jessica! He tried to poison me and then he murdered his own son!"

"Mark wasn't involved in your husband's business, was he?" I asked, as the others in the room looked on in rapt fascination.

"He tried," Connie offered as an explanation. "It didn't work out." She left it there.

"An inconsistency surfaced when I looked into the twins' birth records," I told her.

"An incon—," she started to repeat, but stopped.

"There was no record of the infants ever being discharged. I was wondering if you might have some idea why."

She shook her head. "I have no idea, none at all, Jessica. If I did . . ."

Her voice tailed off again, as if she was having trouble completing her thoughts. No surprise, under the circumstances, having just awakened from a brief coma.

"Tell me about Owen, Connie."

"Owen?" she repeated, eyes widening at my mention of the name.

"The triplet who was stillborn."

"I know who he was. You don't need to remind me."

"So the report was true," I advanced, not sure where I was going with this.

"Of course. Why wouldn't it be? It was the saddest moment of my life, Jessica—until tonight."

At that, Constance Mulroy broke down hysterically. I was beginning to fear she was going to lapse back into her coma, before Lois Mulroy-Dodge, the niece she had practically raised as her own daughter, rushed to her and swallowed Connie in a hug, the two of them sobbing horribly.

I looked to the Sprague sisters, to Virginia Da Salle, Henley Lavarnay, and Harrison Bak, who was leaning on his crutches, before I settled on Tyler Castavette, whom I still found no reason to trust. But Tyler's reaction was pained as well, along with something else he wore on his expression like a scarlet letter:

Fear.

He was just as scared as the rest of us and it showed. His cousin Mark was dead. His father, too, along with Faye and Ian. Four dead and another nearly so, leaving eight members of the wedding party.

While Lois Mulroy-Dodge continued to comfort her aunt, Seamus and I wheeled Mort into the bedroom portion of the suite. I asked Seamus to go about the task of removing Mort's wet clothes and getting him settled beneath my bedcovers; despite the circumstances, I couldn't bring myself to violate his privacy by seeing him stripped down to his underwear, though I suppose it would make for quite a tale to tell at Mara's later.

If we both survived the rest of the night, and the storm, that is.

I stood in the doorway between the bedroom and living room, surveying the potential victims, who were all still potential suspects as well. I was afraid to rule out even the Sprague sisters any longer, my thinking so jumbled and my mind struggling to recall what had struck me about the Lexus's backseat.

The attack on Mort lent a new wrinkle to our state. The gash on his head I intended to dress with the first-aid kit Sea-

mus had brought along from the lobby could have been inflicted only outside the hotel. It certainly had the contours of
a wound made by some kind of blunt instrument, but I supposed it could have also been inflicted in an accident that had
separated him from his snowmobile. The former scenario
meant someone I was looking at right now would have had to
venture outside to do the deed, and then return without showing any signs of the storm on their clothes or person, much less
a trail of melted snow. I supposed they could have used another entrance, but that wouldn't have explained the lack of
any indication of puddling or discoloration due to wetness on
the lobby rug. The basement where the gym and hotel conference center were located, meanwhile, had a single emergency
exit that would have set off a blaring alarm if opened.

Or so I thought.

Anything was possible at this point. Nothing could be
ruled out.

Once Mort was settled under the covers, I used the considerable contents of the first-aid kit to wash and dress the gash
on the back of his head. It was deep enough to require stitches,
so I kept the pressure tight and added layers of adhesive tape
after clearing Mort's sodden hair from the area.

"He could do with another blanket, Mrs. Fletcher," Seamus
noted, after feeling Mort's forehead and detecting a slight chill.

"I have extras in the living room closet," I told him, already
moving in that direction.

All eyes were upon me as I made my way across the room
to the closet I used mostly for books and such, with no shelves
in my suite. You'd be amazed at how much I'd accumulated

during such a lengthy hotel stay necessitated by the ongoing reconstruction of my home.

The people whose eyes followed me wanted reassurance that they'd be alive beyond the dawn, something I could in no way provide them. I turned away from the remainder of the wedding party to retrieve those extra blankets for Mort, drawing open the closet door as I had a thousand times.

Only this time, a body tumbled out straight into me.

Chapter Twenty

The body knocked me to the floor and I narrowly missed striking my head on a leg of the dining table. I shoved it off me in a panic. I heard screaming and wondered it if was my own, though not the words that followed.

"That's Heath!" cried out Constance Mulroy. "That's my *husband!*"

It was Tyler Castavette, of all people, who helped lift me back to my feet, even as Seamus McGilray charged in from the bedroom.

"Oh no . . . Oh no, oh no, oh no," Constance Mulroy kept repeating on a constant loop.

The shock of seeing dead for real the body of a husband she believed had faked his own death, coupled with just having learned of her son Mark's death, was too awful to even consider. The body was stiff and cold, as if it had been pulled from a freezer or a car trunk in these frigid conditions. It was impossible to tell how long Heath Mulroy had been dead or determine the manner of his murder without the kind of thorough examination Seth Hazlitt would perform if he were here. Or the simplified version he would talk me through if cell service hadn't been down in the area. I tried my room phone, but no dial tone greeted me.

Still shaken myself, I moved across the room and crouched before Connie. "You're sure that's your husband, Heath Mulroy?"

She managed a single nod.

Seamus skirted the man's stiff corpse to fetch the blankets required to keep Mort warm. He also located some extra sheets, which he laid down alongside the body. I couldn't imagine leaving Heath Mulroy in place, even covered by sheets, but I couldn't focus on choosing a suitable alternative at present.

"How long has it been since you've seen your husband, Connie?" I posed gently.

"I don't remember exactly. He supposedly jumped to his death three months ago now. It would have been the morning of that night."

"I have another question for you, Connie," I said, holding her knees with my hands, "a difficult one. Could you answer it for me?"

"If I know the answer," she offered.

"You came to Hill House with a great deal of cash stuffed in your tote bag. That's true, isn't it?"

She nodded, and looked toward Virginia Da Salle. "You

carried it up to my room for me after I checked in, Ms. Da Salle—remember?"

Virginia Da Salle's gaze met mine, the mystery of how her nail polish had ended up on a handle of the tote bag solved. "Yes, I do. You really had your hands full. I remember now. . . ."

"And I appreciated the gesture."

"The money was for Doyle Castavette, wasn't it?" I asked Constance Mulroy.

She nodded again.

"You gave it to him, didn't you?"

No nod this time. "Mark delivered it to Doyle's suite on my behalf."

I couldn't resist glancing toward Tyler to gauge his reaction to learning his father had a tote bag with a half million dollars stuffed inside. His mouth had indeed dropped, no doubt as he was pondering how he might have made off with it.

"Was it a payoff, a bribe?"

Another nod.

"But your husband was already thought to be dead. It must've been your sons you were protecting."

"Only Daniel," Constance Mulroy corrected. "He managed to escape prosecution, but Doyle had proof of his complicity. He'd lost a great deal of money in my husband's supposed fund and I made up for that as much as I could to buy his silence and keep Daniel out of jail."

"Not Mark?"

She sighed deeply and shivered, forced to recall his murder. "He was only peripherally involved with my husband's business, like I just told you. Tried his hand at a bunch of things, but none of them clicked. But he figured out what was going on and told his father he'd report him to the authorities if my husband didn't turn himself in."

"Mark was the whistle-blower," I said.

"Only internally. When my husband learned the authorities were preparing to arrest him, he concocted the ruse of his suicide."

"Mark told you about what he'd uncovered, didn't he?"

"Not exactly. It was me who told Mark. He went to the authorities because I instructed him to."

The pieces were falling into place and the puzzle taking shape, centered around the Mulroy family's financial deceptions and general duplicity. I was starting to see the other victims, with the exception of Doyle Castavette, as collateral damage. That might not rule out that serial mass murderer who'd struck two other similarly isolated venues, but it certainly suggested a far more personal motivation behind the potential murder of the twelve guests originally gathered here.

As that thought sifted through my mind, I was left considering what it indicated about the murderer's identity, which got me thinking about Heath Mulroy's corpse, specifically how it had found its way into my suite. Given that the wedding party was clustered on the second floor, the third had likely gone untraveled through the bulk of the night. There would have been ample opportunity for Heath Mulroy's real murderer, and the killer of four others here tonight, to get the body up here. But how had he or she managed to access my suite?

I looked toward Tyler Castavette again. "Tyler, do you have that key card with you? I believe you know the one I'm referring to."

He nodded, grateful I still hadn't mentioned that the previous afternoon he'd accessed my door, which was later opened by whoever had hidden Heath Mulroy's body in the closet. He felt through his pockets and wallet, his expression growing tense when he came up empty.

"It's gone, Mrs. Fletcher," he reported finally. "I swear I don't know what happened to it."

I had expected as much, although I was still far from ruling Tyler out as a suspect. Except that he wasn't a Mulroy and the Mulroys were where all this kept coming back to. A family steeped in betrayal, graft, and malfeasance. Was all this about revenge, then, or something else?

"You've gone uncharacteristically quiet, Mrs. Fletcher," noted Harrison Bak, seated now to take the pressure off his legs. "It would seem all roads here lead to Castle Mulroy, that this financial scandal is at the root of the threat against all our lives."

"Then why the whole ruse trying to make us believe what's happening here is just like how that killer struck in those two other places?" Henley Lavarnay challenged.

"The murderer, I believe, was creating his own cover story, following the scenario exactly as it had been performed in those other cases. By the time help finally got here, they'd find all of us dead and come to the same conclusion we did: that we'd fallen into the clutches of a fiend who'd done it before and will do it again."

Tyler seized the floor. "But he—"

"Or she," I interrupted.

"—couldn't possibly have planned for a blizzard, never mind a storm of this magnitude, right?"

"I suspect the killer altered his plans to take advantage of the storm, but he—or she—would have targeted you all anyway over this wedding weekend. The storm became a random stroke of luck for our killer."

"Someone—," Beatrice Sprague started.

"In this room," her sister, Olivia, finished.

"How absolutely—"

"Horrible, and we can only hope that—"

"You, Mrs. Fletcher, flush out the killer—"

"Before he can strike again," Olivia finished again.

"Or she," Beatrice corrected. "Maybe it was—"

"You. I never did fully—"

"Trust you. Not in—"

"These seventy years."

With that the Sprague sisters made it a point to put more distance between their chairs—in perfect unison, of course.

Seamus returned from tucking the fresh blankets around Mort in the bedroom portion of my suite and set about covering Heath Mulroy's corpse with bedsheets until we determined what to do with it. Heath was a good-sized man, and it would have taken at least moderate strength to maneuver him about. That certainly seemed to eliminate the Spragues, Virginia Da Salle, and Henley Lavarnay, as well as Lois Mulroy-Dodge in all probability, and certainly Harrison Bak, given that he couldn't manage his own weight without use of his crutches. Beyond them, there were also the hotel staff, Janey Ryland and Eugene, to consider; or, I supposed, some number of those seated before me might have been working together.

While covering Heath Mulroy's body, Seamus noticed something near him on the floor and scooped it up.

He glared at Tyler. "Might this be your missing key card?"

I answered for him. "No, his is a different shade altogether—isn't it, Tyler? Identical to the Hill House brand."

"I suppose," the young man said, face squeezed taut in an expression that was hateful and uncertain at the same time.

I accepted the key card from Seamus and held it before me. "It's not a Hill House key card at all, is it, Seamus?"

"No, Mrs. Fletcher. Ours are printed in black and white and feature the hotel graphic."

I took the key card from Seamus and tucked it into my pocket for safekeeping while the Spragues chimed in, though I wasn't paying enough attention to them to tell exactly who was finishing whose statements.

"I never liked Heath anyway. Always found him—"

"Too arrogant—"

"With his nose always up in the air. Remember the time—"

"We drove to the country and—"

"He pushed his seat back—"

"All the way so I couldn't—"

"Move my legs."

"No, they were my legs. I was the one—"

"Sitting behind him. Cramped and—"

"Uncomfortable," the Sprague sisters finished together, never settling on which one of them had been seated behind Heath Mulroy that day.

Something scratched at my mind, something that brought me back to the Lexus SUV that had been abandoned miles from here. I remembered what hadn't quite registered initially about the vehicle's backseat.

"Lois," I said, facing her again, "what do you know about your cousin who died at birth?"

"Owen," Connie muttered, before her niece had a chance to speak his name.

"Why would I know anything about him?" Lois Mulroy-Dodge challenged. "He died."

"Mark never shared anything with you?"

"I don't know what he could have shared, because there was nothing. Owen was stillborn."

"Jessica," Constance Mulroy interjected, "what are you suggesting? After all these years, what does it matter?"

"I believe it matters plenty. Why did you keep the third crib in the nursery?"

She looked befuddled that I knew that. "I'm sure I don't know. If I ever did, the memory's gone."

"I think you do know, or at least suspect the truth."

"What truth are you talking about? What on earth are you saying?"

I looked at Constance Mulroy as if she were the only person

in the room. "I don't think your son Owen, the third triplet, was stillborn at all. I think he's still alive today."

"And I believe he may finally be getting his revenge," I continued, as a heavy wave of shock descended upon the room. "He tried to kill his mother and succeeded with his brother and father."

I went into no further detail than that, avoiding the conclusions that were still crystalizing in my mind. I felt it all coming together, but I still didn't have a tight grasp of what had transpired in the hospital delivery room that night almost thirty years ago and explained why there was no record of the surviving twins ever being discharged.

I turned again toward Lois Mulroy-Dodge. "I'm going to ask you again, what do you know of this?"

Her gaze had already been rooted on me. "Mark didn't like talking about it. He didn't learn about what happened that night until years later."

Constance Mulroy's mouth dropped.

"And what happened that night?" I persisted.

Lois Mulroy-Dodge sought at all costs to avoid looking toward her aunt. "Owen wasn't stillborn, but . . ."

Her voice tailed off, and I coaxed the young woman on with my gaze.

". . . there were problems. Owen Mulroy was the last of the three my aunt gave birth to. And according to Mark, who only learned about this years later, he was deformed, disfigured—

not someone worthy to bear the Mulroy name in his father's mind."

"No," I heard Connie mutter, her face having paled to an almost milk white tone. "No . . ."

"My aunt was sedated at the time, so she never was to learn what happened next. Heath Mulroy swore all the doctors and nurses to secrecy, with ample payoffs to follow later. He arranged to have Owen listed as a stillborn and placed in the nursery as an orphaned John Doe."

"Explains why there's no record of any of the brothers being discharged from the hospital," I noted, wondering whether this was the hunch Seth Hazlitt said he'd need to check out before sharing it with me. "To cover up the fact that he'd fabricated Owen's death, Heath Mulroy arranged for the discharges of all babies born that day to disappear from the system. Maybe he had to do it that way because their birth names were all included on a single document that would have otherwise revealed that Owen was actually alive."

Alive . . .

It was all coming together now, everything. I thought back to what I'd discovered upon searching Doyle Castavette's bedroom. I thought back to the breaking-glass distraction Mark had set just before his mother was poisoned.

"Owen would never have been a candidate for adoption, because of his deformity," Lois picked up, as if reading my mind. "According to Mark, he bounced around from facility to facility, never remaining in any one for very long. Behavioral issues," she added, by way of explanation.

"He was prone to violence, wasn't he?"

She nodded. "Extremely. What he lacked in size, he made up for in attitude and rage. Never backed down, never allowed himself to be made fun of. The stories Mark told me of what he did to the people who made that mistake . . ."

"Lacked in size," I repeated.

"Owen was a dwarf," Lois Mulroy-Dodge told me.

Chapter Twenty-one

And in that moment everything fell together, starting with the crime scene out at the Cabot Manufacturing Company where Loomis Winslow had been murdered. I now understood exactly what Hank Weathers had meant about witnessing a giant he called Bigfoot murder the private detective. I pictured him peeking out from that thick post he'd taken cover behind, spotting Owen Mulroy perched on the ladder Seth Hazlitt had bumped into, and mistaking him for someone seven, even eight feet tall. Owen must have lured Winslow to that very spot and jumped down to take him by surprise, by which time Hank Weathers was cowering in fear. I understood now why there hadn't been a second set of footprints, dragging the body having erased any trace of them.

Owen Mulroy was the triplet who'd never gotten to occupy that third crib in the nursery, which explained why it had remained forever empty. . . . But all that would've been different if he hadn't been born a dwarf. Renounced by his own father, who convinced his wife, Constance, that he had been stillborn, not so much to save her pain as to save himself the embarrassment of having a disabled child, whom a man like Heath Mulroy would have seen as beneath his station in life and not worth the bother. Indeed, the real villain in this tragedy was the late Heath Mulroy, since he'd renounced the youngest of his three triplets entirely and left him to the whims of the social services system, before destroying the lives of those who'd trusted him with their life savings.

"'Why, I, in this weak piping time of peace, have no delight to pass away the time,'" I found myself reciting, "'unless to spy my shadow in the sun and descant on mine own deformity.'"

"What's that?" Tyler Castavette wondered aloud.

"Shakespeare," Seamus answered, before I had a chance to. "Richard the Third, and a splendid rendition at that."

"And now Owen is taking revenge on his entire family, and all the rest of us because of our connections to the family. But he hasn't done it alone. Ultimately, he reconnected with his brothers, didn't he?" I asked Lois Mulroy-Dodge.

She nodded. "Mark never told me the precise circumstances, which of them approached which, though I always believed it was Owen who sought his brothers out, likely for money."

More pieces of the puzzle were falling into place, all the empty spaces of tonight's murders and attempted murder filling in. Yet I found myself pondering what might have led Owen to target his two brothers. Why chase Daniel and his fiancée into the deep woods rimming the freeway, where they might well have frozen to death by now? Why murder Mark in the Hill House gymnasium after he had lied about Daniel being holed up at the Roadrunner Motel?

It must have been Mark who'd helped Owen place the body of their murdered father in my closet, my assumption being that the stray key card we'd found minutes before on the floor must have accessed some hotel room where Heath Mulroy had been hiding out after his fake suicide. By all accounts, his sons must have set him up, intent on using for themselves the illicit funds he'd stashed away someplace. All but the cash their mother had come up with to pay off the late Doyle Castavette to keep Daniel from going to jail. That clearly explained why Doyle had been killed early on in the night. I hadn't yet figured out the need to kill Ian and Faye, but I suspected their murders might be no more than a distraction to draw me away from the truth, while further establishing the ruse that the wedding party had been targeted by a killer who'd done this before, this very week both two and four years ago.

So why not again? Why not here?

"Anything else, Mrs. Fletcher?" I heard Lois Mulroy-Dodge ask me.

I didn't answer her, not wanting to disrupt the conclusions that were starting to dawn on me. I thought of the gravel at the scene of the Winslow murder, a perfect match for what I'd spotted on the rear floor mat of the abandoned Lexus. In the likely scenario, Owen Mulroy had killed Winslow before dispatching his brother Daniel and Daniel's fiancée, Allison Castavette. The latter act made perfect sense with what had transpired here at Hill House tonight. But why would Owen care about Loomis Winslow? How would he even have known of the private detective's involvement?

And then everything hit me like a hammer blow, the whole scenario—the timeline, motive, and everything else—falling together.

A moment before the lights in my suite went out, plunging us all into darkness.

The only illumination came from the dull glow off my laptop screen. I'd forgotten I'd left it on and I had no memory of the last time I'd checked it. And that dull haze that extended little beyond my desk was enough to illuminate the realizations that had just dawned on me.

I nearly tripped over the body of Heath Mulroy on my way to the closet to fetch a flashlight. I assumed it must have been Owen who'd killed him. Something had lured him to Maine, where the son he'd abandoned at birth finally got his long-sought revenge.

I snatched the flashlight off the closet shelf, tensing a bit in the fear that there might be something else waiting for me upon the shelf, another surprise. I switched the beam on and swept it about, my room otherwise lit only sporadically by Hill House's outdoor floodlights struggling to pierce the snow and darkness beyond. Shining the light across the room made me think of how I hadn't quite gleaned what a different kind of light had revealed for me almost from the beginning about this near murder of twelve. Not one clue so much as a series of them, all pointing in a direction I hadn't followed:

To Owen Mulroy.

"Let's all try to stay calm," I said to the group gathered before me. "I have an ample supply of candles, so we'll have plenty of light in no time."

"We've got another problem, Mrs. Fletcher," Seamus said after poking his head into the hallway. "First, the emergency lighting hasn't kicked on, meaning the hotel's backup generator hasn't activated automatically as it should have."

"Well, that's not good. What about the second thing?"

"Eugene is gone from his post."

I peeked out through the same crack in the door Seamus had peered through and I confirmed the big man was indeed nowhere in sight. Where might he have gone without alerting us? There were no signs of a struggle, and surely someone the size of Owen Mulroy, no matter how monstrous he was, wouldn't be able to contend with an opponent of Eugene's bulk.

"What do you think happened to Eugene, Constable?" I said, closing and locking the door behind me.

I couldn't make out all of Seamus's face in the flickering, naked light, making him appear more shadow than substance. "I'm sure I have no idea, ma'am."

"I think I do," said Virginia Da Salle. "I believe him to be our killer, in spite of all this talk of a missing triplet. I believe he's the killer from those other two locales and everything he's done has left us pointing fingers at each other. That bear of a man checks all the boxes, and all this madness about a third triplet abandoned by his parents at birth sounds like nothing more than a clever sideshow. A distraction."

"Posed by a writer," Henley Lavarnay added, the ex-wife of one of our victims seeming to be in lockstep with the woman that victim had been dating. "Surely, you can't expect us to value your imagination above our own good sense."

"I'm not here to argue the point," I told her, and everyone in the room for that matter. "Finding the killer pales in comparison to staying alive until help can arrive. And we should be safe so long as we remain here, together."

In making that statement I didn't pay enough attention to the fear I felt that had never accompanied any of the other investigations I've found myself pursuing. In fact, I scared myself far more in the writing of especially tense scenes conjured for my books. Reality was usually not a prime consideration for the villains I could build in my mind.

Not so the case here tonight, though, thanks to the realization that Owen Mulroy was likely still somewhere among us, close by, which struck me with the force of a baseball bat. I thought of the crawl space Seamus had directed me to in Doyle Castavette's bedroom, how I'd noted that no one of average size could have ever negotiated it.

Which, of course, didn't include Owen Mulroy. That explained how he'd managed to move among the rooms to commit his dastardly deeds without ever being noticed. I could now explain virtually all the anomalies that had been plaguing me through the day and the night, though I didn't voice my revelations to the assembled group because they clearly had other concerns in mind, and rightfully so.

"What's the plan?" Henley Lavarnay, Doyle's ex-wife, asked me.

"I thought this *was* the plan," her date for the weekend, Harrison Bak, interjected. "You heard what Mrs. Fletcher just said: Stay alive until help arrives."

"A mystery writer," someone said derisively, under their breath.

"We've got another problem, Mrs. Fletcher," Seamus chimed in. "That is, if we don't all want to freeze to death. It's not just the power we've lost, but also the heat. And we're looking at a steep drop in temperature before dawn."

Dawn . . . I'd forgotten what sunlight even looked like. And while I didn't expect it to do much in terms of speeding up the help we were depending upon, the world brightening beyond was the best recipe to assuage a person's fears, no matter how extreme or trivial.

"How do we get the emergency generator on, Seamus?"

"That's the rub, isn't it? See, the unit's outside. There's a breaker on the propane-fueled generator's housing, and a breaker in the basement responsible for constantly replenishing its power supply."

"A two-person job, in other words," I concluded.

"I'd be happy to handle the exterior duties," Seamus offered, "except for the fact that throwing the interior breaker requires a whole sequence of steps while the outside generator breaker is a simple switch."

"I should be able to manage that," I offered.

Tyler Castavette rose from his chair. "Let me. It's my father that's dead at this killer's hand. Let me go," he said, addressing both me and Seamus.

I gave Tyler an approving nod. "A noble gesture, but one I

can't accept. You may be able to throw a switch as easily as I can, but the generator is buried in snow now. No easy task to locate it if you don't have at least a general idea of where to find it." I looked toward Seamus. "I'll handle the duties outside while Constable McGilray does the same in the basement. And we'll have the light, and heat, restored in no time."

Back to Tyler now.

"You can make yourself just as useful by keeping these folks safe while we're gone."

"In that case," said Tyler, "how about I offer some tried-and-true advice from something I once read, Mrs. Fletcher: Don't get dead."

Chapter Twenty-two

Which was easier said than done, of course, I thought as I bundled myself up in extra layers, topped with my parka, the outer shell of which was still moist from my initial foray into the storm in the company of the currently unconscious Sheriff Mort Metzger.

How I wish I were working alongside him, as was our custom. I might not miss his calling me "Mrs. F.," but with Mort by my side I've always felt more like an opening act than the headliner. As if reading my mind, Seamus eased Mort's nine-millimeter from beneath his jacket and extended it toward me.

"Familiar with the use of one of these, Mrs. Fletcher?"

"Operation, yes, from shooting at ranges just to learn what I need to for my books. That doesn't mean I can hit a target. You keep it, Constable," I said before he could interrupt me. "Whether the power and heat come back on or not, your first responsibility is the safety of your guests."

THE MURDER OF TWELVE

He nodded grudgingly. "We'll need to get you a walkie-talkie so we can coordinate our efforts. You'll also need a shovel to dig out enough of the snow around the generator to locate the breaker switch. It's contained in a steel box you need to lift up and hold while you flip the breaker."

I looked out the window, into that blinding world of swirling white that gave up nothing of the night.

"I think I can handle that," I told Seamus.

"How concerned should we be about Eugene's disappearance?" he asked me, as we took the stairs down to the lobby.

I had a small penlight in my bag and it was now serving as our sole source of illumination. We'd left the larger, lantern-style flashlight with the others in my suite, along with lit candles placed at various intervals, before we'd headed out. Once in his office, Seamus would be able to retrieve additional flashlights, along with the shovel I'd need to take with me to the propane generator located around the back of the property. But I actually preferred my small, powerful Maglite for its focused beam and simple heft.

"On the one hand, there were no signs of a struggle. We heard nothing, and he gave no warning to us that something concerned him."

"That doesn't answer my question, Mrs. Fletcher."

"Then let me ask you one, Seamus. How much did you look into his background?"

"Speaking frankly, because he was only a temp and a kitchen worker not likely to come into contact with any guests, not at all—at least not beyond what the temp agency sent over."

"This the same Boston agency that fills spots for Cabot Cove Catering?"

"Yes. Why?"

"Because they're very good at what they do and have never let our own local catering company down. Could be that Eugene is off hiding somewhere. Could be that this wasn't what he signed up for and he decided to let us handle the heavy lifting ourselves."

"In other words, Mrs. Fletcher, he was scared off."

"As good a way of putting it as any, I suppose," I said, not informing Seamus of what I'd noticed about Eugene when he'd opened the door to my suite for Mort's wheelchair.

As we entered the lobby, both sets of eyes went to the grandfather clock and we noticed the same thing: the roman numeral six was now crossed out as well.

For Heath Mulroy.

According to the grandfather clock, it was closing in on four thirty a.m. when I finally opened the front door and felt a stiff wind buckle me in my tracks. I had sampled the storm's fury upon opening the door to drag Mort Metzger in, but entering it in full was like nothing I had ever experienced before. The notion of needing a rope line to traverse even five feet outside had never made much sense to me until I was battered by a combination of wind and snow that struck the parts of my face I couldn't cover with a scarf like shattered windshield glass thrown inward by a crash.

I had read once that it was actually possible to die of asphyx-iation in such conditions, something else that had made no sense to me until now. It literally hurt my chest to breathe in this snow-laced air that made it feel as if I'd swallowed mouthfuls of icicles. I suppose that wasn't far from the truth, given the coagulation of the blowing snow into pellets that my lungs sucked down.

I hadn't been outside for more than thirty seconds when I became utterly disoriented, able to see nothing before me and hearing only the relentless howl of the wind as it swirled around me. I felt like Dorothy in *The Wizard of Oz*, about to be swept up and away by a vortex of energy I was utterly pow-erless to resist. Trying to trudge in any direction was like bat-tling a riptide even though in shallow currents close to the shore. There might be pockets of smooth motion, but other-wise you could go only where the motion took you.

I'd mused to people that I'd been living at Hill House for so long, I could find my way about its grounds blindfolded. Now that boast was being put to the test, though I realized a blindfold would have been far less handicapping than these raging snows and winds. Indeed, at least with only a blindfold I'd be able to feel my way about, whereas at this point my gloved hands could find within easy reach no purchase on anything to guide me. I couldn't tell which of the snow was falling and which of it was blowing. And in my determined effort to follow a well-charted, simple course to the generator I'd glimpsed on hundreds of occasions, I grew confused and couldn't even have told you where Hill House itself was.

I fought against the grip of panic beginning to tighten around me everywhere I could feel, but mostly in my chest and

# Jessica Fletcher & Jon Land

stomach. It felt like a vise slowly closing, to be loosened only by some indication I was at least headed in the right direction— an impossible notion at this point, given that I'd already lost my bearings. The walkie-talkie crackled in a side pocket of my parka, Seamus McGilray's voice reaching me only as a muffled sound. And I didn't dare extract it for the further distraction and disorientation that mere effort might cause.

Instead, I collected my bearings and looked for some landmark that might reassure me and guide my way. And I found such a landmark in the shiny silver weather vane that sat atop the hotel roof. I heard the creak it made when spinning through a few gaps in the storm's wind gusts and I focused my gaze upward in at least its general direction.

Sure enough, I caught a reassuring glimpse of it, making my position no more than twenty feet to the right of Hill House's entrance, on the side of the building where the generator was located in the far corner. That meant if I steered myself in that direction, I'd arrive where I needed to be after covering the hundred yards between the front of the building and the generator's location. The problem, of course, was that in these conditions distance was no easier to judge than direction. And I couldn't feel my way there with the building as my guide because far too much snow had accumulated against it.

The total snow accumulation had likely passed the four-foot mark by now, and that was without taking the wind into account. On the one hand, its northerly direction pushed the snow hard past me to buttress the building's exterior, where it continued to mount in horrific proportions. On the other

hand, that left a more modest path of snow—maybe eighteen inches to two feet in depth—to negotiate. Not easy to trudge through in any respect, but passable at least.

I found I did better when I eased the shovel before me with both gloves clinging tight to the handle and used the tool in much the same way as Harrison Bak used his crutches. I realized my thoughts were running away from me, the creeping panic from the storm's onslaught beginning to edge into my brain. I resolved to focus on the task at hand, which was no more than to locate the generator and flip the switch. I began thinking only of the next foot before me, the next step, the next place to plant my shovel and draw up to it before I would repeat the same process again. And I fell into a strange rhythm, by which the slight progress I was making in the right direction cushioned me from the terror raised by the storm and the threat of losing all orientation and freezing to death fifteen feet from Hill House.

The process continued and I stopped counting steps or measuring distance. I could make out the shape of the hotel structure on my right and would thus know when it came to an end in the general location of the generator I needed to switch on. Only the fact that I kept myself in reasonably fine shape through biking my way around town in the good months, and through using the Hill House gym treadmill or elliptical in the not-so-good ones, allowed me to keep my breath, though barely.

As I continued to push ahead with the shovel through the snow that climbed past my waist, I marveled at Mort Metzger's having made his way to Hill House from wherever he'd lost his snowmobile. Thinking of the gym, though, brought me back more resolutely to the matter at hand, since my mind filled with a vision of the murdered Mark Mulroy, along with the fact that eight more victims would likely be there for the taking if my efforts out here didn't succeed.

My uneasy rhythm through the windswept mounds continued, the handle of the shovel now barely protruding from the snow I repeatedly sank it into. The effort reminded me of winters when I was a little girl, and visions of storms like this burying me up to my neck. I was experiencing the very real thing now, and it didn't make me feel like a little girl again in the slightest. Indeed, there was now the question of whether the storm would kill me before Owen Mulroy ever got the chance.

I finally spotted an utterly black void and took that to mean I was nearing the back end of the Hill House footprint, right around where I'd spotted the emergency generator a thousand times. It was right in line with the shed where I'd been storing my bicycle since taking up residence here, but that storage shed was utterly hidden by the storm's relentless fury and mostly buried by the snow at this point anyway.

I held fast to the shovel with one hand and extracted the penlight from my pocket with the other. The beam struggled to make a dent in the snow-riddled darkness, hardly penetrating it at all. Only when a gust of wind temporarily cleared the air before me did it reveal a mound I took to be the generator I sought. The plan was for me to call Seamus on the walkie-talkie now to make sure we activated the backup power system in the proper sequence.

Angling for what I believed to be the generator, I felt an incredible rush of excitement for managing to triumph over the deadly conditions that could swallow a person whole who strayed too far. The penlight finally illuminated clumps of snow collected atop the generator's casing. I drew closer, tamping down that strange sense of elation, which vanished in the next moment anyway.

Because what I could see of the generator had been smashed beyond recognition, destroyed by the determined efforts of someone wielding a sledgehammer like the one stored among the other tools in the same storage shed that contained my bike. I planted the shovel in the ground and leaned against it, sweeping the penlight about as I freed the walkie-talkie from my pocket and squeezed it inside my parka's hood, which was fastened tightly around my head.

"Seamus, do you read me?"

Static greeted me for a reply.

"Seamus, come in. Seamus, please come in."

Nothing but more static.

"Are you there, Seamus? Seamus, are you—"

Through the screams of the wind I heard the crunch of snow, felt the presence creeping up on me an instant before something swept my legs out from under me. I went down hard but landed soft in the cushion of the freshly fallen snow that receded to accept my weight. And there, standing before me, little bigger than the snow pile itself, was the murderer.

Owen Mulroy.

Chapter Twenty-three

He laughed hideously, the wide grin stretched across his pearl white face, which made a fitting match for the snow. One eye drooped. The arm on that same side hung limp, and his opposite leg seemed canted inward. I realized he was standing atop the remains of the generator, which explained why all of him was in view, and I imagined he'd used the same sledgehammer—now deposited at his feet—with which he'd destroyed the generator to slash through the snow pile and rob me of my balance.

"Owen Mulroy," was all I could think of saying.

"Jessica Fletcher. A pleasure to make your acquaintance," he said, bowing slightly and still grinning as if he were enjoying every moment of this. "Though you've proved a royal pain this long night, haven't you?" He took a deep breath and coughed out a thin mist into the air. "'Is there a murderer here? No. Yes, I am. Then fly! What, from myself? Great reason why: lest I revenge.'"

"Richard the Third," I said, recognizing the quotation. "You must have heard me quote another section."

"I've heard much from you tonight. As I said, you've proved a royal pain, haven't you?"

There was an almost Elizabethan cadence to his words, born of a tortured soul condemned to spend the bulk of his life an outcast; alone, isolated, and unwanted by the world. Hence, I thought, the revenge.

"This is about the missing money, isn't it? The family fortune made by your criminal father at the expense of others."

"Didn't serve him well tonight, did it? Got him back for his indiscretions, didn't I?" Owen said, his voice carving through the wind that howled between us.

I tried to push myself up from the snow to mount some form of response, but I couldn't manage it from the angle at which I'd fallen.

"For his indiscretions," I posed to Owen Mulroy, "or abandoning you as his son at birth?"

"A man is the sum of his deeds, Mrs. Fletcher."

"Or the sum of his murders, Owen."

"The night's not done with them yet."

I saw a dull glint captured in the meager spray from one of the outdoor floodlights and realized Owen was holding a small-caliber, but nonetheless deadly, pistol.

"And you're to be the next victim, Mrs. Fletcher."

*   *   *

"Of course," I said, stalling for as much time as I could, "because if everyone's found dead, suspicions will fall on the serial mass murderer from that plane and hunting lodge."

"The perfect alibi, you might call it."

"But you didn't act alone, did you? You had your brother Mark's help, until you murdered him, too."

I'd hoped my remark might get a rise from him, but it didn't.

"He'd outlived his usefulness," Owen said in a voice colder than the air.

"I should have known earlier," I said, finally pushing myself up to a seated position and trying to find his eyes through the snow tumbling from the sky. "As soon as I saw that open suitcase in Doyle Castavette's room. That's where you hid after you killed him, isn't it? After the chair broke in the struggle you had no way to climb back into the crawl space."

"I expected you to find me in that moment. The great Jessica Fletcher, proving herself to be a most able adversary."

"You didn't know I was living here, did you? You didn't know until tonight."

I thought the shrunken figure looming over me shrugged, but I couldn't be sure. "How could I?"

"How could you know about this storm in advance?"

"Simple," Owen Mulroy said, a fresh grin stretched across his anvil-shaped face. "It was predicted in the *Farmers' Almanac*." He extended the gun farther down at me. "Now get on your feet."

THE MURDER OF TWELVE

Poking the tiny pistol in my back, he forced me into the woods that rimmed the back of Hill House, where the thick umbrella of tree cover had notably mitigated the snowfall, leaving the ground beneath comparatively passable. I might surprise him if I twisted suddenly enough, might even manage to separate Owen from the weapon. But there was still enough snow cover here to deny me firm purchase on the ground, and such an effort would as likely lead to a fatal slip as not. I needed to buy time until a low-hanging branch or some other weapon of convenience made itself known.

But there was nothing available. It was as if we'd strayed into a patch of woods flattened by the storm. The snows had thickened again, stealing my sight beyond just a few feet and rendering any move to thwart my attacker impossible, as the snow would certainly deny fast-enough movement.

Where was I? My disorientation was palpable, like something out of a nightmare from which I couldn't rouse myself.

"You were hiding under the dinner table, weren't you?" I said to Owen Mulroy. "That's how you were able to poison your mother's wine when everyone was distracted by Mark's glass breaking at the bar."

"Another clue you missed, Mrs. Fletcher. Perhaps you're slipping."

"Or perhaps I've met my match."

"Keep walking," he said, the gloating evident in his voice. "You're going to appreciate what I have planned for you. People might even advance the proposition that you went mad and created your own mystery. Until your body turns up, of course."

And then I realized where I was. Owen Mulroy had led me out to the center of Booker's Pond, a small body of water that had swelled through the especially wet fall months but struggled to freeze, as always when winter set in. I recalled all the DANGER! NO SKATING signs posted around it and felt the snow-covered ice bowing beneath my weight.

Owen gave me a hearty shove, uttering that hideous, throaty laugh once more. I turned awkwardly to find him backpedaling toward the shore, small-caliber pistol still trained on me.

"They say freezing is a good way to die, if there's any such thing to be had."

"You killed Loomis Winslow because he was closing in on the money your father had hidden away, the money you intended to claim for yourself."

"Clever girl, aren't you?"

"But not clever enough to figure out how you learned about his involvement. Not clever enough either to figure out why you killed your brother Daniel and his fiancée."

He continued backing up, then stopped, still within easy shooting range. "Not all mysteries are meant to be solved, Mrs. Fletcher."

"Did you lure them somehow to the old Cabot Manufacturing Company? Take them captive in the Lexus SUV they'd rented at the jetport?"

"Figured that out too, I see. Perhaps I didn't give you enough credit."

"I don't deserve it. The front passenger seat was pushed all the way back, no room for a regular-sized person behind to tuck his legs," I told him, explaining what I'd finally realized had been bothering me. "I should have made the connection then and there."

"That's quite enough, Mrs. Fletcher."

With that, I watched the tiny, shriveled form of Owen Mulroy angle the barrel of his pistol downward and fire a series of shots into the ice at my feet, coughing snow up into the air from the depressions left by the bullets. Almost immediately, I felt the ice weaken beneath me, starting to crack and give, the murderer before me intent on sending me to a frigid grave.

"Goodbye, Mrs. Fletcher. I wish we'd gotten to know each other better. You seem like a hoot."

The ice continued to crack, audibly now, the sound like that of paper crunching. Then, suddenly, I heard the pounding of footsteps back a ways along the path we'd taken, then grinding to a sliding halt just short of the pond's edge.

"FBI!" a voice bellowed through the night and the storm. "Hands in the air! Do it now!"

I felt the ice about to give in the same moment I spotted a familiar figure standing a hundred feet away, a pistol aimed straight for the small shape of Owen Mulroy.

"Drop the gun, and hands in the air!" a familiar, hulking figure ordered.

Eugene.

But Owen lunged for me instead, drawing too close for Agent Eugene, or whatever his name was, to chance a shot in such awful conditions. Owen tried to angle himself behind me, but he slipped at the last moment, providing an opportunity for me to manage a leap onto a still-whole portion of ice. It held under my weight, though a terrible crunching sound from where I'd just been standing pierced my ears. I was looking straight at Owen Mulroy when he plunged downward, disappearing into the black hole that had appeared when the ice finally gave way.

I saw his one good hand flailing desperately for something to latch onto, but every bit of jagged ice he clutched broke off in his grasp. I dived forward and slid across the ice, scattering the snow pile like one of the plows in Ethan Cragg's failed armada, and I groped for Owen's gloved hand with mine.

My grip fastened briefly on his wrist, but I couldn't find clean purchase through the sodden woolen material. Then something was yanking me away by the feet from the cracking ice, the shape of Owen Mulroy's gloved hand disappearing from sight before it disappeared altogether into the icy waters below.

"Took you long enough," I said to Eugene, once we'd finally reached the safety of the shore, no trace of Owen Mulroy anywhere to be seen.

"When did you figure out I was FBI, Mrs. Fletcher?"

I pointed a gloved finger toward his left ear, at what I'd spotted there before being distracted by Constance Mulroy's calling my name from inside my suite somewhere around an hour ago. "The pale impression around your ear is in the shape of one of those law-enforcement earbuds you people use. You must've been wearing it while standing in the sun someplace, because the rest of the skin around it is tan. I noticed when you opened the door to my suite for me."

"I could have just been listening to music on the beach, couldn't I?"

"Not when the impression's only on one side, Agent . . ."

"Finnegan," the man I'd known as Eugene said through the howling winds.

I should have been utterly freezing right now, but a combination of adrenaline and exertion was keeping me warm for the time being.

"It was a private investigator named Loomis Winslow who alerted the Department of Justice to what he'd uncovered about the Mulroy family's financial shenanigans, wasn't it?"

My question clearly threw Agent Finnegan for a loop. "How'd you know that?"

"Did you know Winslow was murdered this morning?" I asked him, instead of answering his question.

It was clear he didn't. "Winslow?"

I nodded. "Right here in Cabot Cove."

"An investigation was already underway before he fanned the flames," Agent Finnegan told me. "As one of the lead agents, I came up here to keep an eye on the family, the mother and two sons, thought the wedding might be an opportune time for them to let their guard down, maybe make a mistake. Was it Owen who killed Winslow?"

"Yes, but he wasn't alone," I said, thinking of the abandoned Lexus SUV and realizing something I probably should have earlier.

*   *   *

We found Seamus McGilray in Hill House's mechanical room, unconscious with a nasty lump on the back of his head. He was dazed but otherwise fine, and we—well, Agent Finnegan, mostly—dragged him up the stairs to my suite.

"Mrs. F.?" I heard as soon as I entered, visible from the bedroom where Mort Metzger lay beneath the covers.

I rushed to his bedside. "Mort!" I said happily, taking one of his hands in both of mine.

"Easy there, Mrs. F." He smiled. "Don't want Adele to get the wrong idea about our relationship. Bad enough I woke up in your bed."

"I won't tell if you won't."

He rubbed the spot that I'd bandaged on his head, still clearly disoriented and starting to assemble into a picture what he was seeing before him.

"Why do I get the feeling I missed something?" he asked me.

Chapter Twenty-four

Mort also missed what came next, as he was in no condition to do anything but rest for a few days anyway, according to Seth Hazlitt.

Seth took enough time off to drive me to Boston and the Encore Boston Harbor, the new casino that had recently opened on the city's waterfront. I met Agent Finnegan in the lobby and accompanied his team to a blackjack table in the middle of the lavish casino floor.

"Hit me."

I can't say how I picked out that voice, but I turned to find a face I recognized for its likeness to another man's: Mark Mulroy's, because I was looking straight at his fraternal twin brother, Daniel, the groom-to-be I'd originally believed had fled into the woods from that abandoned Lexus and almost surely met his death—because that's what whoever found the rented vehicle was supposed to think, thus absolving Daniel of suspicion. His disappearance would be quickly judged a murder, freeing him and Allison Castavette to live off his father's pilfered fortune in this country or that.

Daniel Mulroy met my gaze without a spark of recognition flashing in his eyes. But Agent Finnegan and his team of five FBI agents were something else again. Daniel's gaze trailed them all the way to the table, where he was handcuffed and placed under arrest by one agent while the others formed a ring around him to ward off onlookers. He stood there arrogantly, not ready yet to accept defeat.

"How'd you find me?" he asked finally, surprisingly composed.

Finnegan looked toward me for a response, and I waited for Daniel Mulroy's gaze to follow his before answering his question.

"The key card we found in my suite underneath your father's body, the one we couldn't identify. I let myself believe the obvious: that it had been your brother Mark who'd tucked your father's body away in my closet. But he was already dead, wasn't he, killed not by your brother Owen but by you?"

Daniel Mulroy's mouth dropped at that. I thought I saw him swallow hard, or at least try to.

"Because the bench press was perched too high for your brother to hold it down with enough pressure to suffocate Mark. I realized that as soon as I learned of your brother's deformity. That's when all this fell into place. It was the three of you all along, the Mulroy triplets together for the first time. That is, until you murdered Mark."

"He was weak, would have eventually talked if we'd given him the chance. He didn't have the stomach for it."

"'We,'" I repeated, "you and Owen. Did he find you or did you find him?"

"I found him, years ago, the only person who hated my father more than I did. Reason enough for us to join forces."

"Your brother exposing the financial misdeeds—that was part of the plan, wasn't it? Force your father on the lam with a hidden fortune you'd then be in a position to steal."

"It was ours. You can't steal what belongs to you. That man never gave us anything, least of all Owen. You want to know the truth? Killing my father was a pleasure. I only wish I could have done it twice."

"Murder done right normally works the first time," I told him.

Daniel's eyes narrowed on me as he stopped, Finnegan letting him hold his ground for the time being.

"You planned all this," I couldn't help but continue, "your wedding included, to coincide with the anniversary of those mass murders on the plane and at the wilderness retreat, Hill House serving as a similarly isolated setting that would have turned the investigation in just the direction you wanted it to go. Even absent the blizzard, you could have used Cabot Cove in winter to your best advantage."

"Who are you, exactly?" he asked me.

"Jessica Fletcher."

"*Who?*"

"Doesn't matter. What matters was the key card that must have slipped from your pocket when you were tucking your father away. We matched it to the Bayside Motel, where you and Allison must have gone in the backup vehicle one of you must've been driving while the other set up the whole ruse with the abandoned Lexus. You could've had your pick of any empty room in Hill House to wait the storm out, thanks to Tyler Castavette's master key card, which your brother Mark must have taken before you murdered him. Oh, did I forget to mention that Allison Castavette was arrested upstairs in your room ahead of our coming for you? After setting up the whole ruse with the Lexus, did she drop you and Owen close to Hill House before the storm reached its peak? In any event, you used the weather to your best advantage, accelerating the timetable with the full knowledge that no one was coming to our rescue."

Daniel Mulroy didn't bother denying any of it. He stood there amid the other gamblers mingling about and was transfixed by the neat summary of what I'd managed to compile in the forty-eight hours since his brother Owen had plunged to his icy death.

"Anyway," I continued, "a security camera caught that second car you must have rented leaving the Bayside Motel parking lot. We matched the license plate to one captured on a security camera for this place's parking garage."

Daniel stared at me. "And here you are."

"Yes, here we are. But where's your father's money, Daniel? You might find your path forward a bit easier if you were to turn it over."

He was silent, finally at a loss for words.

"Loomis Winslow had to die because he'd found wherever

your father had stashed his money," I resumed. "I'm guessing you learned he was coming to Hill House to meet with your mother, so you lured him to the Cabot Manufacturing Company with a text message from your mother's phone, the one she thought she'd misplaced because Mark must have stolen it. You lured him there so Owen could kill him. And your mother feared for her own life after Winslow failed to show for their meeting at Hill House. When I got back, she was still waiting for him in the lobby, not for you and your fiancée, like she told me," I finished, not bothering to add that she hadn't been waiting for my return to Hill House either.

Daniel Mulroy's expression was utterly blank. "Who did you say you were, again?" he asked, as Agent Finnegan started to lead him through the casino, the other agents forming a protective shield around them.

"A mystery writer."

"Sorry I've never read any of your books."

"You'll have plenty of time to catch up on your reading now, Daniel."

A week later, his first day back to work, Mort Metzger was finally well enough to meet Seth and me for breakfast at Mara's Luncheonette. It turned out he hadn't been attacked by Owen Mulroy after all, the gash on his head having come from a spill he'd taken when his snowmobile overturned. I couldn't wait to chide him for not wearing a helmet. Based on where the snowmobile was found, Mort must have walked nearly a half-mile through the storm, a miraculous feat in itself.

Meanwhile, it had taken much of that week for the big town plows and Ethan Cragg's armada of private contractors to get the roads completely clear and for Cabot Cove to be up and running again. The final snowfall measurement, according to none other than Jim Cantore, was somewhere between fifty-eight and sixty-two inches, monumental and unprecedented by anyone's standards.

"Well, Mrs. F.," Mort greeted, taking his eyes from the wall-mounted television still tuned to the Weather Channel, "records were meant to be broken."

"We'll never see another storm like it in our lifetime—that's for sure."

"I was talking about the record for murder," Mort corrected.

"That, too, I suppose."

"I've been looking into the life of this Owen Mulroy, Mrs. F. You sure can pick them. As a boy, he was suspected of burning down the only foster home that would ever have him and spent as much time in jail as group homes after that. He even spent some time playing a circus clown, if you can believe that."

"I'm guessing that didn't come to a good end either, Mort."

"Depends what you call breaking the finger of a little girl who tried to squeeze his red nose. The only thing I haven't been able to figure out is when he and his brothers got together to hatch this plan."

"Go back to Heath Mulroy's arrest and subsequent 'suicide.' Since Mark's turning him in was part of the plan, it must have all started right around then."

Seth Hazlitt looked up from his pancakes, which were

swimming in maple syrup. "Leads me to wonder how things might have been different if those people had raised that poor boy as their own."

"'And thus I clothe my naked villainy with old odd ends stolen out of holy writ, and seem a saint, when most I play the devil,'" I said, quoting Shakespeare again.

"You'd make a fine Richard the Third, Jess."

"I actually played Queen Elizabeth in a version of the play once."

"This whole thing has the feel of a Shakespearean tragedy, doesn't it?" said Seth.

"You had a hunch you said you needed to check out before you could say more," I recalled. "You already had a notion that the hospital discharge records had been tampered with to hide the fact that Owen Mulroy wasn't stillborn after all."

"And I turned out to be right, didn't I?" Seth beamed. "Guess I proved myself to be a pretty good detective, while you proved yourself a pretty good doctor, Jess, *ayuh*," he added, gesturing toward Mort, who'd been my patient.

"I'll tell you what I can't get out of my mind," Mort said, sifting a spoon through the coffee our server had set down without waiting for him to ask for it. "How the three of them pulled all this off, even with a storm they couldn't possibly have built into their plan."

"The storm gave them the opportunity to make it seem like the guests had perished at the hands of the same mass murderer from that airplane and wilderness lodge," I told him. "The perfect alibi, you might say. Misdirection to get the authorities looking in the wrong direction."

Seth looked up from his pancakes. "And what about the elaborate setup for the bride and groom appearing to have fled into the woods, Jess?"

"Their bodies would never have been recovered and they would've been listed as missing and presumed dead. With everyone else dead, nobody would be any the wiser, leading investigators to settle on the most obvious conclusion."

"Here's my conclusion," Mort said as our server set a bagel and cream cheese down before him, again without his having ordered. "Never mind solving the crime; you saved eight lives that night. Makes you a candidate for Cabot Cove Citizen of the Year."

"I never put much stock in such things. More a popularity contest than anything else."

"Then how'd I win last year?" Seth asked me.

"You're as popular as it gets. Anyway, maybe I'll nominate Hank Weathers," I told him.

Mort frowned at that.

"He identified Loomis Winslow's killer," I reminded them. "We should have listened to him."

"He identified Bigfoot."

"I should've given more thought to that ladder, why it was there. Maybe I'm slipping a bit."

"Maybe you just need my help more than you'd like to admit." Mort's eyebrows twitched as he smeared cream cheese on his bagel, his eyes darting to an old campaign flyer for Sam Booth, our "Do-Nothing Mayor," still taped to a bulletin board near the cash register. "Speaking of politics, maybe you should think about running for mayor, Mrs. F. I'm sure you could come up with a better slogan than 'Vote for me and I'll do nothing.'"

"How about 'A chicken in every pot'?" I posed, aping Herbert Hoover.

"I was thinking more like 'A body in every cupboard,'" Seth suggested.

"That works, too."

"More accurate, at least," Mort said, "now that you've broken your own record."

"Seems like the year for that, doesn't it?" I noted. "By the way, did the weather people ever name the storm?"

Mort and Seth looked at each other.

"You never heard?" Seth asked me.

"I've been kind of busy."

"Weather people called it Jessica," Mort told me. "Winter Storm Jessica."

"Really?"

He shrugged. "Hey, blame the alphabet, Mrs. F."

"Uh-oh," Seth muttered, his gaze angled out Mara's plate glass front window.

Outside it had started to snow, the first flakes since the great storm had ended.

"Here we go again," said Mort.